9/19

GOL

P9-DFX-841

ALSO BY GOLDIE GOLDBLOOM

The Paperbark Shoe

ON DIVISION

ON DIVISION

GOLDIE GOLDBLOOM

~~~~~~~

FARRAR, STRAUS AND GIROUX

NEW YORK

Farrar, Straus and Giroux
120 Broadway, New York 10271

On Division is based on a short story that was originally published, in a
very different form, in *Word Riot* and *You Lose These*.

Library of Congress Cataloging-in-Publication Data
Names: Goldbloom, Goldie, author.
Title: On division / Goldie Goldbloom.
Description: First edition. | New York : Farrar, Straus and
  Giroux, 2019.
Identifiers: LCCN 2018060811 | ISBN 9780374175313 (hardcover)
Subjects: LCSH: Life change events—Fiction. | Hasidim—Fiction. |
  Brooklyn (New York, N.Y.)—Fiction. | Jewish fiction.
Classification: LCC PS3607.O4516 O5 2019 | DDC 813/.6—dc23
LC record available at https://lccn.loc.gov/2018060811

Designed by Jonathan D. Lippincott

Our books may be purchased in bulk for promotional, educational, or
business use. Please contact your local bookseller or the Macmillan
Corporate and Premium Sales Department at 1-800-221-7945, extension
5442, or by e-mail at MacmillanSpecialMarkets@macmillan.com.

www.fsgbooks.com
www.twitter.com/fsgbooks • www.facebook.com/fsgbooks

1   3   5   7   9   10   8   6   4   2

Written with the assistance of an Individual Artist Grant from the City of
Chicago Department of Cultural Affairs and Special Events, and with the
assistance of residencies at Ragdale and Yaddo.

To my son Yuda, who came afterward and,
with his music, made this book happen

And God said to Abraham, "Your wife Sarai—you shall not call her name Sarai, for Sarah is her name.

"And I will bless her, and I will give you a son from her, and I will bless her, and she will become [a mother of] nations; kings of nations will be from her."

And Abraham fell on his face and rejoiced, and he said to himself, "Will [a child] be born to one who is a hundred years old, and will Sarah, who is ninety years old, give birth?"

וַיֹּ֤אמֶר אֱלֹהִים֙ אֶל־אַבְרָהָ֔ם שָׂרַ֣י אִשְׁתְּךָ֔ לֹא־תִקְרָ֥א אֶת־שְׁמָ֖הּ שָׂרָ֑י כִּ֥י שָׂרָ֖ה שְׁמָֽהּ:

וּבֵרַכְתִּ֣י אֹתָ֗הּ וְגַ֨ם נָתַ֤תִּי מִמֶּ֙נָּה֙ לְךָ֣ בֵּ֔ן וּבֵֽרַכְתִּ֙יהָ֙ וְהָֽיְתָ֣ה לְגוֹיִ֔ם מַלְכֵ֥י עַמִּ֖ים מִמֶּ֥נָּה יִהְיֽוּ:

וַיִּפֹּ֧ל אַבְרָהָ֛ם עַל־פָּנָ֖יו וַיִּצְחָ֑ק וַיֹּ֣אמֶר בְּלִבּ֗וֹ הַלְּבֶ֤ן מֵאָֽה־שָׁנָה֙ יִוָּלֵ֔ד וְאִם־שָׂרָ֔ה הֲבַת־תִּשְׁעִ֥ים שָׁנָ֖ה תֵּלֵֽד:

The Yiddish used throughout this novel is in keeping with the pronunciation used by Hungarian and Romanian Jews, who replace the *u* sound with *i*. "Shul" (synagogue) becomes "shil," "kugel" (potato pudding) becomes "kigel," "rabbeinu" (our rabbi) becomes "rabbeini."

THE ECKSTEINS OF WILLIAMSBURG, 1890–2007

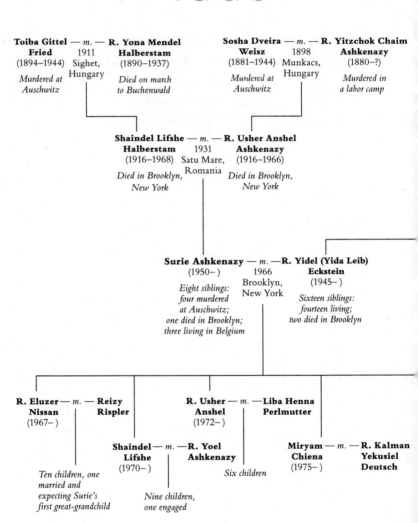

Toiba Gittel — *m.* — **R. Yona Mendel**
Fried   1911   **Halberstam**
(1894–1944)   Sight,   (1890–1937)
     Hungary
Murdered at   *Died on march*
Auschwitz   *to Buchenwald*

Sosha Dveira — *m.* — **R. Yitzchok Chaim**
Weisz   1898   **Ashkenazy**
(1881–1944)   Munkacs,   (1880–?)
     Hungary
Murdered at   *Murdered in*
Auschwitz   *a labor camp*

Shaindel Lifshe — *m.* — **R. Usher Anshel**
Halberstam   1931   **Ashkenazy**
(1916–1968)   Satu Mare,   (1916–1966)
     Romania
Died in Brooklyn,   *Died in Brooklyn,*
New York   *New York*

Surie Ashkenazy — *m.* —**R. Yidel (Yida Leib)**
(1950–)   1966   **Eckstein**
    Eight siblings: Brooklyn,   (1945–)
    four murdered   New York
    at Auschwitz;   *Sixteen siblings:*
  one died in Brooklyn;   *fourteen living;*
  three living in Belgium   *two died in Brooklyn*

R. Eluzer — *m.* — **Reizy**
Nissan   **Rispler**
(1967–)

Ten children, one
married and
expecting Surie's
first great-grandchild

Shaindel — *m.* —**R. Yoel**
Lifshe   **Ashkenazy**
(1970–)

Nine children,
one engaged

R. Usher — *m.* —**Liba Henna**
Anshel   **Perlmutter**
(1972–)

Six children

Miryam — *m.* — **R. Kalman**
Chiena   **Yekusiel**
(1975–)   **Deutsch**

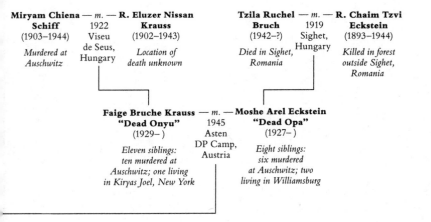

Miryam Chiena — *m.* — R. Eluzer Nissan
Schiff   1922   **Krauss**
(1903–1944)   Viseu   (1902–1943)
Murdered at   de Seus,   *Location of*
Auschwitz   Hungary   *death unknown*

Tzila Ruchel — *m.* — R. Chaim Tzvi
Bruch   1919   **Eckstein**
(1942–?)   Sighet,   (1893–1944)
Died in Sighet,   Hungary   *Killed in forest*
Romania   *outside Sighet,*
            Romania

Faige Bruche Krauss — *m.* — **Moshe Arel Eckstein**
"Dead Onyu"   1945   **"Dead Opa"**
(1929–)   Asten   (1927–)
Eleven siblings: DP Camp,   *Eight siblings:*
ten murdered at   Austria   *six murdered*
Auschwitz; one living   *at Auschwitz; two*
in Kiryas Joel, New York   *living in Williamsburg*

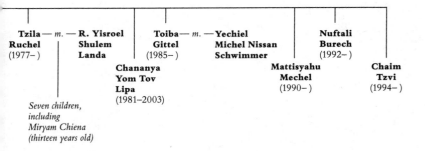

Tzila — *m.* — **R. Yisroel**   **Toiba** — *m.* — **Yechiel**   **Nuftali**
Ruchel   **Shulem**   **Gittel**   **Michel Nissan**   **Burech**
(1977–)   **Landa**   (1985–)   **Schwimmer**   (1992–)
       Chananya   **Mattisyahu**   **Chaim**
       Yom Tov   **Mechel**   **Tzvi**
       Lipa   (1990–)   (1994–)
Seven children,   (1981–2003)
including
Miryam Chiena
(thirteen years old)

ON DIVISION

The midwife said to the Chassidic woman, "Your due date will be the thirteenth of July. Isn't that exciting?"

Surie hesitated. "No," she said. "I was looking forward to having a little time to myself at last."

"Don't you already have grandchildren? You must be busy anyway. What's one more child to a family like yours?"

Surie only answered gently that a single child is a whole world.

ONE

After the appointment, Surie sat at the bikur cholim bus stop, staring at the stream of people walking into and out of the Manhattan hospital, trying not to cry. It was late Friday afternoon, the day after the fiasco of her daughter's wedding. The lab-coated professionals, the trim secretaries with their folders, the mothers in leggings and transparent tops, their ponytails sweeping their backs, all were racing toward their weekends. There was even a young Chassidic man who looked just like her son, Lipa, standing on the other side of the road, staring straight at her. So much for privacy! The hospital rose up behind him, a tower of glass and steel, smelling of germicide even from a distance.

"This is *All Things Considered.*" A taxi stopped next to her, blocking her view of the young man and blaring an American radio channel. She didn't ever listen to the radio. The announcers spoke in English and were much too fast to follow. Though for some reason, her husband, Yidel, kept a broken radio from the fifties in the basement and occasionally opened it up to tinker with the tubes.

Yidel loved puns and riddles and the old jokes that came off the wrappers of the candy the children liked to eat. He loved to sing in the shower at night before he went to bed, even though Chassidic men try not to make sounds in the bathroom. It was a transgression, but a little one. He loved to build fires in their backyard and feed rotten tree branches into the flames. He loved to take control of situations, figure out solutions, do the right thing. It could be a bit annoying, but on the whole, it wasn't the worst thing ever. He loved to sit with his whole family piled up around him on his bed and tell stories in the semidark. He'd loved all of his sons. All of them. Even though she was a deflated fifty-seven years old, he hadn't stopped loving her either. But could he continue after the news? Or would something close in him like a mousetrap?

She put her hand in her purse to find her prayer book. For the past four years, her mouth had needed to say the words of the psalms the way other mouths need to chew gum. But there was no book. There was nothing in her bag except for a pair of green-framed glasses, a pamphlet about pregnancy, an appointment card for the hospital because apparently home birth wasn't an option this time, a bottle of prenatal vitamins, and a free disposable diaper. Every time before this she'd been filled with bubbles of delight, a baby-scented seltzer of happiness. She'd wanted every one of her children with something close to craziness beginning from the moment she found out she was pregnant. But this was different. She was too old. It had been an invitation to the evil eye, to schedule a doctor's appointment for the day after a wedding!

Last night Yidel, annoyingly upbeat Yidel, had been

oblivious to all of the wedding's disappointments. "It's so good to see the whole family dressed up and in one place," he'd said in the back of the taxi bringing them home from the wedding hall. "Such a good-looking bunch! Such nachas!"

"The groom's mother," Surie said, scandalized, "was wearing an uncovered wig. Why didn't we know she was that kind of woman? That they were that kind of a family?" It was after three in the morning. Her innocent daughter was off somewhere with a boy who trimmed his side curls, a boy who wore long pants to his own wedding instead of dignified three-quarter length, black socks instead of white stockings. His cheap shtreimel—dyed squirrel tails, probably!—sat on the back of his head as if he'd never wear it again, dripping modernity. In the kabbolas ponim room, everyone had seen this spectacle walking toward her beautiful child and turned their noses. All Surie's friends snuck glances at her, to see how the former queen of their circle felt about such a low-class match for her daughter. Even her best friend slipped out ten minutes into the dancing, mumbling something Surie hadn't caught. Never mind. She knew the real reason.

During the usually solemn covering of the bride's face, the boy grinned at her daughter without a shred of modesty. He hadn't just timidly held his wife's hand after the chuppah. He'd snatched it up with a gleeful smirk. Her daughter's face had been crimson and so had Surie's. And her friends'. Who knew what was going on in their hotel room? She wanted to close her eyes and not open them again for a long, long time.

Yidel patted the sleeve of her beaded black gown. "Our

daughter is twenty-two," he said. "She was already long on the shelf. We should be thankful. And they are nice people. Really. The boy has a good job selling electronics."

"You knew?"

"It's not like we are a perfect family anymore, Surie. People talk."

"What?" she asked, hot, flustered, her powdered face turning red for the twentieth time that evening. "What do they talk about?" But she knew, of course. Behind their hands, the community gossiped about Lipa, her sixth child, who had died four years earlier. And as a result, her little pearl, her seventh child, had to settle for a husband and a new family well beneath her or risk remaining unmarried.

Earlier on that awful Friday after the wedding—would she ever forgive herself for the timing?—the midwife had given her a handful of materials and said, "Take a vitamin every morning and every night. You need folate."

"What is folate?" she'd asked, translating the midwife's sentences slowly into Yiddish in her head. Which was still full of the wedding. "What is a neural tube?"

"Neural tube defect," Surie muttered in English, before reopening her purse and placing the bottle on the concrete. The vitamins weren't kosher. She'd have to buy her own at a pharmacy outside the community. They'd stare at her scarf, her clothes, giggle about her accent, but at least they wouldn't spread gossip.

The midwife, Val, had delivered all ten of Surie's previous babies. But Val, for all her skill, was childless; she couldn't know how it felt. She couldn't know what it was like to be tied to a small and demanding physical body for *years*. To feel the burden of keeping something alive. All those hard years raising them up and for what? A marriage to such a lowlife? Such shame and embarrassment?

And then, a strange look had come into the midwife's eyes. A glancing light, like sun across the dark river, an illumination but a temporary one. What had Val expected from Surie? Tears of joy? Smiles? Surie was *ancient*. From the moment she had noticed the early symptoms, she had known, in her heart of hearts, what they meant. Despite her shame, she'd almost resigned herself until Val said it was twins. Twins! Since the breast cancer, the muscles of her arms were so stiff that she could barely get her cardigan on in the morning. How would she lift two babies? As Surie sobbed, the midwife looked away and said something about glucose stress tests and multiparous women. The words were unfamiliar. There were no words for neural tubes and stress tests and private places in Yiddish. There was no Yiddish word for *please*, so she said it in English.

"Please," she begged no one. "Please."

The midwife leaned forward, wanting to put out a steadying hand, but feeling some coldness, some rejection, before she even reached out, she rattled off words about Surie's exasperating body: Condom. Withdrawal. Rhythm. IUD. The Pill. You are responsible for your own fertility. Val had made her own peace long ago with this occult knowledge. She'd grown up in a religious Catholic home but left her faith behind forty years earlier when she started working as a midwife. Faith was no excuse for ignorance. For her, this was a core belief.

Surie was no stranger to her own fertility. She still checked her menstrual chart every morning, even though she hadn't bled in over ten years. She'd been delighted when the chemotherapy had sent her straight into menopause. Only after many cancer-free years had she thought she was in the clear and stopped taking the tamoxifen. Maybe her body, rejoicing at being free of the drug, had bounced right back to whatever was the opposite of menopause? Maybe that's how the pregnancy had happened? But Val said tamoxifen wasn't a form of birth control. It seemed obvious to Surie that the midwife was mistaken.

Val was older than Surie. Loose wattles wobbled under her chin, though she was rail thin. She talked until white flecks appeared at the corners of her mouth and then she removed the spittle with her blue-gloved fingertips. Surie couldn't remember this woman speaking at all when she'd delivered the other babies. She'd had the impression that the midwife was a little afraid of her back then. But now she rattled on and on. Remember how you bled the last time? You're at risk of hemorrhaging. I'm talking to you. Can you pay attention, please? Blow your nose. This is not the time to fall apart. Do you know what hemorrhaging means? Bleeding. To death. The midwife's gabbing must have been sanctioned by someone somewhere.

"Your husband is going to have *such* a surprise when you tell him!"

Surie usually told Yidel everything. But strangely, two months in and for some reason, she still hadn't opened her mouth to announce that they were going to be parents again. How had she allowed the time to pass? She hadn't realized she was pregnant for the first few weeks. Then, once she had, the pregnancy seemed like a bad dream, something that just wasn't possible. Later, there'd been the flickering at the edge of her vision, faces that couldn't exist, the scent of freshly turned dirt, mint and apples. The madness of old age, she'd thought. It was a miracle she'd made an appointment at all. And at the wedding, she'd danced as if she were an ordinary grandmother, not a pregnant woman. Although, of course, she hadn't known she was expecting twins.

"If necessary, take time off from work. Do you work? Don't drink any wine." Too late. She'd gulped several glasses to quench her horror at the wedding. Val could probably smell the alcohol on her breath. "It's been known to cause fetal alcohol syndrome."

Val said this as if Surie had, at some time, been familiar with fetal alcohol syndrome. As if she *should* have heard about it. Well, she probably had, but she didn't remember. She wasn't a bad woman, Val. Each time Surie didn't remember something, the midwife went away and came back with another pamphlet to stuff into her hands. Each time, Val patted her on the shoulder as if to say it would all be all right. Expecting twin babies at Surie's creaking age couldn't ever be all right.

"Coffee brings on preterm labor, a major risk for geriatric mothers," she added.

Geriatric. That word . . . did it mean old people? Did Val think Surie should be in a nursing home instead of a birthing center?

"If you don't want to carry these babies at your age, you don't have to." Val lowered her voice, drew closer. "Most older mothers miscarry. If you want, I could talk to the doctor about a therapeutic abortion."

Surie wanted to vomit. Her mouth was full of saliva.

Her throat burned. She shook her head. Such hideous and forbidden words. God forbid! Chas vecholila! *Abortion.*

A long silver knife in the midwife's hand, an unearthly screaming, blood everywhere. Hushed whispers behind closed doors, her three sons who still lived at home pointing their fingers, an iciness encasing the few friendships that had survived Lipa. A stone wall disconnecting her from Godly light. What hushed comments had she heard about abortions? It was all bad, that was for sure. Only other people killed babies. Only goyim thought fetuses weren't really alive.

———

The next morning, Saturday, she washed all of the dishes from the fancy Friday night meal her married children had prepared for the new bride. It made Surie's skin crawl to see how her daughter smiled at the obscene groom, as if she liked him, as if she would have chosen him herself, as if he were just like her holy brothers. How could her daughter think that Surie would choose such a man for her if she had better options? Her beautiful, innocent granddaughters took turns lying on the couch, massaging one another, complaining that they weren't getting the full five minutes, groaning from the pressure of a hand between their scapulars, completely unaware of the tragedy that had befallen the family, that would soon befall each of them! Their matches would also be affected.

Surie's mouth wanted coffee and a big slice of cake. Could she? Her stomach rolled over every time she saw a chocolate bar, but mysteriously, she craved chocolate cake. Only a day later and already she couldn't remember any of the midwife's advice. Maybe, besides being pregnant, she had early-onset Alzheimer's? Val spoke too fast. A Yiddish translator might have helped, but Surie would have been ashamed to cry in front of someone from her own community. And not just that . . . she could picture the translator totting up the years—thirteen!—since Surie's last birth and shooting her a glance of surprise and disbelief. Der Oibershter knows what he does. Der Oibershter will give you strength. No evil eye, darling! Your babies will keep you young! It's bashert. But silently, the woman would be thinking it was time for Surie's kids to be raising babies, not Surie. She'd be wondering who she could tell this crazy news to first.

To give birth was to announce publicly that she and Yidel still found each other desirable long past the usual age of childbearing. None of her peers had been pregnant in a decade. The girls she'd grown up with, her friends, never discussed their private lives. It was easy to assume that they never even looked at their husbands, to imagine they had returned to the virginal state of their youth. These girls who she still imagined in school uniforms and braids were now grandmothers, one even a great-grandmother. They would ponder the logistics of her pregnancy. Most mothers in the community had shut up shop as they passed their early forties, and that seemed right, appropriate, modest. No one wanted to bring home a baby—two babies!—with Down syndrome or some other disaster of getting older. Here she was, fifty-seven, grandmother to thirty-two grandchildren, still going strong. The women of the community would say mazal tov, but privately, they'd blush for her, the sex-crazed hussy. And this strange news on top of Lipa's death and Gitty's match . . . her poor granddaughters! They'd never be able to escape the family's new status, no matter how perfectly they or their mothers behaved.

Surie leaned against the sink, cringing. Several noodles floated in the cold soapy water. It was revolting. The morning sickness rose in her throat again. It was much worse with the twins than it had been with the singletons. Because of her size, because her belly swelled out in front of her and overflowed at the sides, and because her flesh was hard, not soft, she could barely reach the taps behind the sink. Stretching, she flicked off the stream, turned, and went out on the fire escape, to the cool breeze from the river.

She was careful with her feet because she was off-balance with the extra weight. She stood on a section of rusty metal grid. The railing was loose. It wouldn't do to fall three stories down to the street and splatter on the road like an overripe watermelon. Paper wasps had made colonies under the eaves, and though it was already early December, already cold, they fell clumsily out of their nests, stunned, one by one. They spread their wings but did not move. The empty lots behind and to one side of the apartment building were full of wilting Queen Anne's lace and blackened golden rod. When the wind blew, the aspen leaves clapping together sounded like rain.

Yidel was just above her, on the flat part of the roof, walking among the hides stretched on frames and placed in the sun to dry. He couldn't touch them on Shabbos morning, but he liked to look at the skins when he came back from the synagogue. He was a sofer, a scribe. He called out to her.

"Good Shabbos, little wife!"

The pregnancy, which had shown from the very first moments (she'd thought it was more change-of-life fat!), rose up from between her hips in a dense ball and pressed against her thighs as she crouched, her back against the wind. She was enormous. It was insulting, really, that her family thought all of this flesh was her own. Yidel called again, urging her to climb the last flight of rickety steps and join him on the roof.

"I'm too fat," she yelled. A Chassidic man, passing below on the street, looked up, shaded his eyes to see better, and then hurried on.

"You'll need to come into the clinic every week so we can keep an eye on you. Don't look so horrified. It's not a death sentence. You know I'm not scary," the midwife had said. "Aren't I pleasant to talk to? Together, we'll learn a lot about these babies." Val had awkwardly patted Surie on the shoulder as if she were a small child. Surie wanted to bite her.

Such a stereotype! A sandal-wearing graduate of the Peace Corps, makeup-free, gangling, large-nosed Val. A confirmed spinster if only because she was, underneath everything, intensely shy. She was the only person in her cohort who'd been willing to work in the slums of Williamsburg with women who couldn't speak English and had a baby every year. Val—lonely, idealistic, eager to love everyone and make their lives better—had wanted all the mothers to laugh at her funny T-shirts and her dyed bright orange hair, but the Chassidic women didn't know where to rest their eyes.

"You're not fat!" Yidel bent over the parapet, smiling down at her, beckoning. In the marriage raffle, she had won first prize. Before the pregnancy, she'd tipped the scale at 263 pounds. "Even if you were, double my money's worth! Come up."

He would not be so delighted with her if he knew he was in for two more tuitions, two more weddings, at a time when he had been preparing to retire. They'd been hoping the whispers about their family might die down. Double the financial drain, double the shame. Not double his money's worth.

For almost twenty years, he'd trained their two eldest sons, Usher and Eluzer, to be the same kind of meticulous calligrapher that he himself had always been. Klei kodesh, holy vessels those boys were, both ordained rabbis and scribes. He'd steadily transferred all his clients to them. These days, Yidel was a specialist. He never wrote mezuzahs, megillos, marriage contracts, divorce decrees. He only wrote new Torah scrolls, all of them special orders from the Rebbe. A single scroll took an entire year of writing from nine till noon, Monday to Friday, with a hand-cut feather. Each afternoon he sanded the stretched skins of fetal calves until they were smooth and glassy, cut them to size, ruled lines into the parchment, sewed the sheets together with dried tendons. He carved the wooden rollers, cut his quills, mixed his own jet-black ink. Their basement was always full of frames holding dried hides. It smelled of rotting meat and lime, wet oak and burned hair. The odor was the first thing guests noticed about their home. Surie could smell it three floors up, on the fire escape, in a strong wind. But in the past four years, Yidel had only written two scrolls. Now weeks went by without him bringing home fresh hides. The hides on the roof were the last he'd ever stretch. He'd told her, with glee in his voice, that he was going to retire on his birthday. Six days before her due date.

"Rebbetzin Eckstein!" he called again, and he put his hand on the railing, his foot on the first step down toward her. Very few people called her Rebbetzin, though she was married to a rabbi. It was his little joke.

"Don't come down!" she said, shaking her head and backing away. "I have work to do." She needed time to think, time to figure out how to tell him.

Surie was no longer sure of that flash of light she'd seen in the midwife's eyes. At the time, she'd hoped it had been admiration. The old-fashioned Jews who lived in Williamsburg, the midwife's bread and butter, belonged to a people that had never been part of the secular world. They lived the way they had always lived. They cured skins in their basements and laid them in the sun to dry as they had done in Europe. They read books about laws and ethics and history from two thousand years ago. They dressed in styles from the forties and fifties and revered elders who had never read a word of English. The men sat and studied the word of God their entire lives, and instead of becoming wide and stodgy, they grew lean and speedy, and their eyes burned with the bright light of sharp intelligence. The women raised beautiful families, glorious families with hundreds of grandchildren, thousands of great-grandchildren. Surely the midwife, when she told Surie the news, had viewed the twins as a miracle and Surie as a holy woman? Surely that flash in Val's eyes had been respect? She wouldn't be able to hold herself together if that light had been pity.

———

She went inside and drained the sink, took off her damp apron, and pulled on her Shabbos ponzhelo. She transferred the green-rimmed glasses from the pocket of the apron to the new garment. The hem of her housecoat smelled of vomit from the previous evening, but it couldn't be cleaned until after nightfall. Surie closed her nose to the smells coming from the Crock-Pot and the blech. Chulent. Kigel. Fatty soup. In the evening, she'd have to dress up again and go out for a huge sheva brochos for her daughter. She'd wear a tight smile like a girdle on her face. The big clock in the living room chimed twelve times. She poured a cup of coffee, but her stomach turned and she slid into the bathroom and closed the door.

"Are you all right?" Yidel waited outside the bathroom door, as he had almost all the days he had been married to her. He was sixty-two, older than her by five years. A respected rabbi, he wore long white socks and a silk coat, a bekishe, that came down past his knee-length pants; his gray beard reached the third button of his shirt; his fur shtreimel, real sable, lay curled on a chair like a cat. Under his arm was the folded yellow tallis she'd given him on the day they were married, forty-one years earlier.

His work with the holy scrolls had engraved itself on his body. His shoulders were rounded, his hips ached, he had arthritis in his ink-stained fingers. He had varicosities and a belly from so many hours of sitting. But his work had marked him in positive ways too. Yidel could concentrate on a single thing for hours. He never lost his temper. His face was as calm and innocent as an angel's. Over time, he'd become famous. People across the world knew instantly when they saw a parchment he had written. Eckstein's, they said. Beautiful.

Surie flushed the toilet and spat into the water. Most of the vomit spun down the drain. She cleaned her teeth and her tongue with a dab of toothpaste on her finger and then flushed again.

"Give me that izei?" she said. "The brown one?" He knew what thingamabob she meant from years of experience, and her favorite towel was slipped into the gap created by the partially opened bathroom door.

"What do you want to make kiddush on?" she asked after wiping her face. She covered her mouth with her hand, afraid that he might be able to smell the twins on her breath. "When will the boys get home?"

"What's that?" Yidel said. He fumbled with his hearing aid, remembered it was Shabbos, jerked his hand away. "What's that?" he asked again, cupping his good ear. His hearing was ruined from the screaming of the rotary sander he used to polish the skins.

"I defrosted a bundt and two bilkelach," she said softly as she passed.

When she'd rapidly gained weight, she'd had herself checked for all those fat-lady things, reflux, diabetes, a thyroid imbalance. Her regular doctor—not suspecting—told her to cut back on sweets and eat more protein. She'd finally figured out she was pregnant a couple of weeks earlier, at the end of the sixth week, when she realized that fat couldn't squeeze her bladder or make her nauseous. The early weeks of the pregnancy had passed in a blur. She'd been too busy with the engagement and the wedding to tell Yidel. And now it wasn't just one baby she'd be confessing, but two. Maybe she *was* hoping for a miscarriage? For shame!

"Surie," he said, and he caught her hand and held it without any pressure. There was a very pale light like clouded crystal behind his pupils. Was that what love looked like? Was this fog the thing that caused old people to go blind? Catinkelach? Something like that? Maybe he wanted to lie down with her? Or was he upset that she hadn't gone upstairs? So many years of this wordless communication had passed between them that he thought he could read her silences. He usually could. She, however, still struggled to understand this unspoken language of theirs.

She'd always been proud of his craftsmanship, proud that she was married to the man who wrote the Torah scrolls for the Rebbe. She would no sooner interrupt his morning hours writing than go outside without her stockings. The first year they were married, they had developed a sign language so that she might ask him if he needed something and so that he might respond without speaking and interfering with his holy work. A slightly raised eyebrow, a hand gesture, a smile, a nod. Yidel noticed everything down to the smallest movement of her lip. She'd often laughed and said that he could read her mind. Now this silence was a deeply ingrained habit.

They both assumed that anything important would float from one to the other. With words, they were a little out of practice. She waited for him to notice the hard bowl of her stomach, to turn to her one morning and casually ask for her due date. When this didn't happen, she was lost. She worried that there was something wrong between them, that Yidel no longer loved her in quite the same observant way. And so she waited, hoping he would see.

He'd guessed she was pregnant all of the previous times, bought her pregnancy tests before she knew to ask. They'd hugged each other, laughed, started suggesting names. They both loved being parents. He always remembered the mystical words he'd been thinking when each child was conceived, and he'd written each phrase in a tiny book he'd given her on their twenty-fifth wedding anniversary. For a man, he was intuitive. But not now. What was wrong with them? Why didn't he guess? Why didn't she say?

She gently pulled away from him and took a few steps down the hallway.

"The boys will be home any minute," she said, looking pointedly at his hand. She could somehow feel what he wanted through the light touch of his skin on hers, the way the dark place at the center of his eyes widened. "It's not right."

"Surie," Yidel said, but when she turned away from him, he just sighed and shrugged.

How could she tell him she was pregnant when he had so happily refinished the old baby furniture for Tzila Ruchel's sixth child? Four years earlier, right after they'd returned from their trip to California, he'd hauled out their battered crib and the changing table and the high chair and painted them with rural scenes from Romania. How could she take that away from him, his relish at being a zaidy after all the dry and terrible years of being a disciplinarian, something not in his nature? He'd know she'd known and kept it from him. He'd always adored her, announced to their children that their mother was a saint, a love, his favorite, the best of all women. What would he think of her?

"I am a lucky man," he said, walking after her. He took her hand again, pulled her toward him, and raised her fingers clumsily toward his mouth. He made the same gesture to his mother on Friday nights. Surie had an idea that he was supposed to kiss her fingers, that it was the proper conclusion of the gesture, but he simply held her hand aloft for a moment and let it go. They went into the kitchen together, and she laid out the challah rolls and the cake and poured him a glass of wine, and when her three youngest sons came home, she sat and watched them all eat, her lips pressed together, barely breathing for fear she would vomit.

———

The next morning, she dressed in her good black cardigan and houndstooth blouse. She smoothed her bangs to one side of her scarf. The nylon hair was stiff and coarse and refused to be swept. Yidel had given her a gold choker at their engagement and she wore it whenever she left the house, even though it was the ugliest thing she'd ever seen. Every Sunday morning, when the big clock—her mother's clock—chimed ten, they went out into the crowded Williamsburg streets. Yidel went in front, both of them towing a shopping cart with one hand and holding an umbrella over their heads with the other. It was like him, to go shopping with her, something he had begun the first week after they were married. "Wait," he'd said then, when she'd put on her coat to go out for the groceries. Even though no other husband she knew helped his wife in that way, the brave young man he'd been, twenty-one years old, had put on his coat and carried the grocery cart down the stairs. He'd waited outside on the sidewalk until he saw her paying the merchant for her purchases. They had an endless string of stories about shopping together, episodes they laughed over at night when they were already tucked into their beds and the lights were off and the children were asleep.

"Remember the lady who bought the lawn flamingo and wanted to name it after you?"

"Remember when you won the lucky thousandth customer and you could get everything in your cart free, and you only had a bar of soap?"

"Remember when that man brought his parrot to help him pick out cheese?"

———

Surie wound the clock every Sunday morning, the heavy lead weights rising up inside the mahogany case, and then she set the time. Her mother's clock was over two hundred years old and had been left in Surie's parents' home by the previous tenant, who probably couldn't figure out how to move the massive thing—taller than a person, mounted with golden onions, and a silver face engraved with the name of some New York clockmaker. When her mother died, Surie had walked around the apartment, touching the photographs, the knickknacks, the hairbrush, the scarred cutting board. Eventually, she'd picked up the

Shabbos candlesticks. Hesitating at the door, she'd asked Yidel to bring the clock. All through her childhood, she'd lain in her bed, loving the reliability of the ticking, the high-pitched chime, the gleam of the mahogany, the strangeness of something so old when everyone she knew came to the United States with nothing.

That Sunday, she stood in front of the clock as it struck ten. She was eighteen, holding her mother's candlesticks. She was fifty-seven. How was it possible to be both at the same time? Surie followed Yidel downstairs and pushed aside two white chickens with her foot before darting through the opening behind her husband. The Ecksteins raised their own chickens. They didn't eat red meat. The poultry lived in the backyard in a large coop Dead Opa, Yidel's father, had built in 1951. He'd had chickens in the displaced persons camp in Austria too. The birds picked worms and rusty screws out of the dry, pale gray dust. The Ecksteins owned twenty-five chickens at a time, thirty before Rosh Hashanah, but never a rooster. On Sukkos, when Tzila Ruchel, Surie's oldest daughter, had a sukkah that stretched across the entire front of their house and the doors opened and shut constantly, the chickens wandered out into the road and caused collisions.

They were silly animals. They bounced into the air like rubber balls. They clucked and purked and squawked. Surie had not thought, when she married, that she would be raising chickens. None of her friends in the neighborhood had a yard full of white feathers and manure. Sometimes Yidel called faraway hatcheries and ordered dual-purpose chicks, birds that laid eggs in every corner of the henhouse but were also good for soups and stews when their laying tapered off. As her own fertility should have.

———

When she was growing up, her family hadn't kept chickens. They hadn't tanned skins in the basement, or pressed grapes to make wine, or squeezed olives for oil. They'd been perfectly normal until her mother was diagnosed with breast cancer at fifty. Surie was the youngest of eight children, the only unmarried one left at home. Her father, panicking, had rushed to marry her off so her mother could take her under the chuppah. The irony was that her father had died of a heart attack shortly after the wedding, but her mother had lived for another two years.

Surie was sixteen when she'd been introduced to Yidel in the matchmaker's dining room. They'd spoken for half an hour. Once. Yes or no? she'd been asked. She couldn't remember his name. Yuda Leib? They hadn't discussed raising poultry. He'd had a gentle smile and a laugh that filled the room. Later, she realized he smelled faintly of chickens and skins, but back then, in the matchmaker's house, the smell coming off his clothes had seemed exotic and unfamiliar and exciting. His beard had been a gingery orange.

"Like King David," he'd said, touching it when he saw her noticing. Despite being older than her, he was still just a boy, his beard barely an inch long. He'd been blushing the entire time, excited and ashamed of his excitement, eager and shy. The same Yidel, really. "Mazal tov!" her father had shouted when she'd mumbled yes. Her married siblings and her mother and father had rushed in to celebrate, as if they'd been waiting just outside the door, listening. Her mother had cried and cried, wishing that her four older children who were murdered in the Holocaust could be there, but Surie hadn't wanted to be sucked into that old sadness. She was making a new life, a new home, beyond the shadow of Europe.

The Rebbetzin's first question after the engagement had been, "When was your last period?" Was she supposed to keep track? Apparently she was. Luckily, she remembered. The wedding was set two months later, perfectly timed for peak fertility.

The morning after the wedding, a newly married friend came over to show her how to tie a scarf over her shaven head. Surie looked at herself in the mirror. Every married person knew what had happened to her the previous night. The women would wince with her when she sat. The men would pat Yidel on the back, smirk at his smiles. But on the outside, besides the scarf, she looked the same. It had been hard to believe that there weren't words stamped on her forehead, announcing what she had done in that dark room. And more: She was not sure if she was supposed to have enjoyed herself, but she had, and she kept on grinning at Yidel and then covering her teeth with her knuckles. And even more: She hadn't known it, but she was already pregnant.

———

She was pregnant now too, pregnant at sixteen and pregnant at fifty-seven, two ages that one might hope to be pregnancy-free. The rain came down and made wide puddles on the sidewalk. The water came inside her shoes.

Yidel and Surie made their Sunday walk up Division and onto Lee. They stopped to pick up pickles and herring at Flaum's. There was a fish shop two doors up from their house, but they'd shopped at Flaum's for forty years. Yidel dropped some coins into the withered hand of the man who was parked outside in his wheelchair and who constantly muttered. "Tshebiner yeshiva," the man said. "Tshebiner yeshiva."

On Rodney Street, the butcher. Back on Lee, Wagers the grocer. Fish scales floated, glittering, on the freshets running down the side of the street. Rain spilled off the roofs and onto stacked bags of garbage and flattened boxes. Sparrows picked amongst the rubbish. At the bakery, Yidel added five fancy cookies to the decorated cake they'd ordered as a present for the host of that night's sheva brochos. "For Tzila Ruchel's girls," he said. Their thirty-year-old daughter lived on the floor below them. "And one for my best girl," he said, tossing in a sixth cookie and smiling at her. The carts grew heavier and heavier and leaned to one side, their wheels squawking. Yidel took the heaviest parcels out of Surie's cart and put them into his. Just before lunch they returned to their apartment building. Her mother's clock struck midday.

"Go on up," Yidel told her. He would pull both carts up the stairs, but he wasn't getting any younger either. Sometimes she worried he'd have a heart attack or a stroke. What would happen if she suddenly blurted out that she was expecting twins?

"I'll heat the soup," she said.

TWO

On the second afternoon after the ultrasound, a full forty-eight vanished hours after she found out she was carrying twins, Surie stood again at her sink, washing the small glass cups that held the Shabbos candles with ammonia and a rag. She had tears in her eyes, but she always had tears in her eyes when she used ammonia.

"I've decided to go with the bikur cholim bus each week with Schwartz néni," she told Yidel. "On Friday afternoons. I have free time." It was a Monday. She was giving him plenty of notice.

It wasn't exactly lying, to say that she was going to the hospital to visit the sick. She'd bring chocolate cake. She'd stop and say some psalms at the patients' beds. And then she'd make her way to the obstetrics clinic. If it was a lie, it was by omission.

Yidel didn't say anything. He sat at the table reading the Yiddish newspaper.

"I'm bored," she explained. Moisture pooled under her arms, at the base of her spine. It collected under the bulge of her belly. "Empty days do strange things to a person."

Why was she lying? She'd never lied to Yidel before. She put the rag in the glass and twisted it.

"The other wives say they get antsy when they go through the change."

Yidel blushed and rustled his paper, then folded it and stood up. "So, you are normal. A normal wife. Good. Thank God." Yidel had always been the most loving of fathers, infinitely patient. Though he'd be surprised at the situation, he would be proud of the twins. His age hadn't slowed him down; he still ran up and down the stairs, schlepping multiple grandchildren on his back, shouting out old Hungarian counting rhymes. Every day, he would roll the twins to shil and his friends would have to tell him to shut up, they'd already heard all his stories about the babies, and no, they didn't want to see his new photos either. At two in the morning, when she would be too exhausted to lift the babies out of their cribs to feed them, he'd help her. Afterward, when she was lying in her tousled bed, smelling of sour milk and unwashed linen, she would hear him murmuring lullabies, an infant over each arm, rocking them in the front room so as not to disturb her. Was his enthusiasm for anything baby-related the thing that held her mouth closed, his inability to see the long-term consequences? The happiness she knew he'd feel when she wasn't yet capable of feeling anything close to joy?

Her granddaughters, home from school because of the wedding, came bounding up the stairs, each a lovely thing, a shining golden peach, and she dried her hands and pulled them toward her. "My darlings, my little lambs, come, let Bubbie give you a nice hot cocoa to drink. And I think Zaidy has something for you too."

The girls went to a cheder that was one block closer to the river down Division. All day long she could hear the Ikvei bells ringing, the voices of hundreds of girls singing, their chattering as they lined up to get on the buses after school. Her granddaughters only had to cross Wythe to get home. But she didn't know why Tzila Ruchel had to send them to *such* a strict school. Did her daughter want to be praised for being the most religious in the entire family? Or was this some kind of distancing, some way of signaling to the community that Tzila Ruchel's family wasn't really connected to poor Lipa? Surie's four daughters had all gone to di alte cheder on Marcy and Keap and that had been good enough.

She opened the icebox and took out milk. Tzila Ruchel, at thirty, had just had her seventh baby and needed help in the afternoons, which Surie was usually only too happy to give. She peeled the metal seal off the glass bottle and poured milk into a pot. She pulled the girls' arms from their raincoats, hung the dripping garments on the nails above the window. The children exclaimed over their cookies and pushed against her in the small kitchen, and she stroked their heads, kissed their cheeks. Such darlings.

"Did you know," she asked them, "that Rabbi Shimon ben Shetach captured eighty witches all at once? Are you curious how he did it?" The witches ate human beings in their caves. There must have been human skulls on the floor, covered in moss. The smell of the cooking milk made Surie gag. The girls would be ashamed that their old grandmother was pregnant. *She* was ashamed of herself, of her traitorous body. When she found out, Tzila Ruchel, that mefunek, wouldn't send her daughters upstairs to Surie after school. Even if by some miracle the fusspot did let them come, their grandmother's house would no longer be a peaceful haven. It would be filled with the screams of hungry infants.

"Your Feter Lipa loved the story of Shimon ben Shetach and the witches."

The little girls had been trilling about the new dresses they'd be wearing to that night's sheva brochos, but now they looked at Surie with frowns. They knew the names of all of their uncles. Who was this stranger, this Lipa?

Lipa stood next to her mother's clock, his hand on the ivory escutcheon, turning the key back and forth, the edges of his body moving like a curtain in a breeze, filling and turning and collapsing. He'd been standing there for several minutes, not speaking. It had been him outside the hospital too. She glanced at him for a moment, her heart beating faster and faster. He slowly looked up at her.

"Your uncle . . . ," she said. "He was here. But now he's not."

The girls smiled uncertainly and switched to being excited about the boats Yidel was making them from his newspaper. They didn't care about Rabbi Shimon ben Shetach and the witches, and they thought maybe their grandmother was teasing them about this uncle. They hadn't noticed that their bubbie was the size of a small car. They had no knowledge of the facts of life. The rain struck the windows as if small pebbles were hitting the glass.

"We can go downstairs and sail them in the alley," Yidel said. He gave Surie a look with a question mark in it. She was gripping the edge of the table. Her fingers were white, but Lipa was no longer next to the clock. "Go ask your mother. But don't wake her up if she's sleeping."

They'd all been up late the night before. The newly married girl had fallen asleep at the meal in her honor, her mouth hanging open, and Tzila Ruchel had stood hurriedly and tapped Gitty on the shoulder.

The children threw on their wet raincoats and ran down the stairs, yelping and shrieking. Yidel's father and mother, both blind, lived on the first floor of the building. In the fifties and sixties, the third floor had been rented out, but after Tzila Ruchel was married, it had become her new home. Surie had been living on the second floor ever since the day she'd married Yidel. She'd switched apartments with Tzila Ruchel so that her daughter wouldn't have to pull the heavy baby carriage up three flights of stairs. But at this age, Surie wouldn't be able to pull a carriage upstairs, and Yidel, though he'd want to, shouldn't do it either. Would they have to switch apartments again? She didn't want to go back to her old place. She loved the view of the river and the bridge from the third floor. She hoped that something would change. That somehow, two new babies wouldn't join her tainted family. The midwife had said as much. Seventy-five percent of women older than forty-five miscarry. Her stomach clenched. She wasn't excited about the twins, but she didn't want to lose them either. A soul was a precious thing.

But what if the babies were born with Down syndrome? Women even younger than her left sickly infants at the hospital rather than bringing them home. She couldn't blame them. Most of those mothers were old and already had ten or twelve or fifteen children. They simply didn't have the strength left to raise a child with special needs. But what did they tell themselves about the preciousness of souls? She had no strength either. What would she tell herself if it came to that?

———

During the appointment two days earlier, Val had forgotten that Surie lived in the same building as her daughter's family and her in-laws. "What's the difference between in-laws and outlaws?" she'd asked, and when Surie shrugged, she'd finished the joke: "Outlaws are wanted." The midwife, who was not a womanly person, laughed in a hoarse bark and then covered her mouth with her giant hand. "Sorry," she said. "I'm embarrassing myself!" Surie knew what an outhouse was, but she wasn't familiar with the word *outlaw*. Did it mean cousins?

"My cousins came for the holidays," she said carefully. She hated when people thought she wasn't intelligent or couldn't follow a conversation in English, even though she often couldn't. Some of her guests had stayed on after Sukkos for the wedding. "They slept in the sukkah on the roof." There was a tiny air well between the buildings, protected by a sloping tin roof that was only accessible from the kitchen window. Despite the difficulty and his age, Yidel had climbed out the window before the holidays and slowly nailed up boards to make a room. He'd covered the bamboo rafters with evergreen boughs. The cousins all brought sleeping bags and said they were going camping. It was easier than going down three flights of stairs to Tzila Ruchel's sukkah each time they wanted a glass of water.

"Uh-huh," said the midwife, wrinkling her nose. "With that many people in the house, I hope you left the windows open every morning for at least half an hour. It's . . ." She left the sentence hanging.

On the wall of the office, a baby floated head down in a narrow frame of white scaffolding.

The midwife followed Surie's eyes. "That's at nine months," she said about the poster. "Don't you remember? When the baby's head is well down in the pelvis." Her gestures were large and immodest. She was hard to look at. Surie felt a little sad for Val, whom she imagined might have been the butt of unkind jokes her whole life.

Surie had never seen an image of the inside of her body. Her bones. Her parts. Prior to this pregnancy, the midwife had always come to her and she hadn't brought along pamphlets, photographs, diagrams, and maps. Surie would have burned such obscene literature. If one of her sons saw it!

Imagery of any kind was forbidden in her house. Photographs. Paintings. Sculptures. There were a couple of needlepoints of flowers in the dining room, a piece of black velvet painted with the Western Wall and sewn with spangles. She'd barely convinced Yidel to allow their wedding portrait to be hung in the privacy of their bedroom. Now, flustered, she mistook the word *pelvis* for peltz, a fur, and thought Val was talking about the way goyim liked to pose their naked babies on bear rugs.

"It's not our way," she said. "We take a photograph of the firstborn child on the thirtieth day. We cover it in gold necklaces and dress it in white clothes, a nice knitted outfit."

"Isn't that interesting," said the midwife, who vaguely remembered such events from other births. Covering a newborn in jewelry couldn't be sanitary. It puzzled her that even very old Jewish women like Surie looked young. Was it their wigs and their quaint hats and scarves or because of some strange innocence they all possessed? Maybe it was the lack of makeup? Maybe she should allow her orange hair to revert to gray? "You'll probably have to borrow extra necklaces since you'll have two babies instead of one."

"It's only the first baby that gets redeemed. The cohen doesn't want the others."

Val snorted, picked up a chart, and penciled in a few words. "That's nice," she said. She could never get this stuff right. Every time she thought she had it down, every time she thought some woman would appreciate her cultural understanding, *poof*, another kink.

The button on the front of Surie's blouse came off and fell to the floor. Surie fished around in her handbag and took out a needle and thread. She pulled off a little of the thread, put it between her teeth, and began to chew. She bit down on the thread as if it were the threat of Down syndrome. She bit hard. She wanted to chew right through it. Then she picked up the needle, threaded it, and with a few stabbing stitches reattached the button to her shirt.

"That's a quick job," Val said. "Maybe I should hire you instead of one of the surgical nurses in the clinic. They have five thumbs, both of them."

Surie, startled, smiled. She'd attached buttons almost every day of her adult life and not once had anyone ever said a word about her skill.

THREE

That night after the sheva brochos, when Surie's grand-daughters had run back downstairs to their mother, Surie washed all the extra dishes and dried them and put them away. She decided to wear a nightgown she'd been given by a friend as a joke when she had her cancer surgery. After peeking inside the scandalous box at the hospital, she'd squealed and blushed. It had been hilarious at the time, just the thing to give her a little bolt of naughty energy when she felt at her lowest ebb. She should have thrown it away, but she hadn't. In the back of her closet, she found the box and opened it. A sleeveless white nightgown with a pink silk bow. She pulled it over her head and then covered her bare arms with a cardigan. Under the clingy sheer fabric, the bowl of her belly was visible. When she came out of the bathroom, her husband lifted his head and looked at her. "Nice dress," he said.

Her twin bed listed as she climbed in. She didn't im-mediately cover herself with the blankets. Earlier, after her periods had stopped, they'd decided to put their two beds together at night. Each morning, she rolled the beds apart and pushed a little nightstand between them. Lying on her back, close to the crack between the joined beds, she pulled the fabric tighter over her belly and glanced at her husband out of the corner of her eye. He was staring at the ceiling.

"Yidel," she said, "do you really like this?"

He didn't look.

"It's not a dress, you know."

"It's a good thing you are such a refined role model for the einiklach," he said. "Their bubbie is always so elegant." He was staring at the ceiling, biting the hairs of his mustache. The ticking of the old clock in the living room seemed abnormally loud.

She pulled the fabric tighter and lifted her hips, willing him to notice.

Was he blushing? He was! And she was too. The nightgown had been too much, too transparent, too immodest for him. She jerked upright and leapt off the bed with a clanging and crashing of springs and rushed to change.

"I like this old flannel one," he said when she returned. It had long sleeves and a high collar with rows of lace. He put his arm around her and put his lips against the back of her neck. "It smells like you."

"What do I smell like?"

"Bleach. Maybe that powder you use to scrub the sink? And silver polish."

She sighed and pulled the blankets up over her shoulders. Once covered, she tucked her knees up inside her nightgown. Her thighs pushed into her belly and she could feel the twins fluttering deep within her.

"How romantic," she said. "Cleaning fluids."

"I love being a grandfather," he murmured. He loved a lot of things. He would love the twins too. Sometimes it was tiring to listen to all of his enthusiasms and to trip over the clutter from the castoffs in the basement. The mosaic tiles. The sock-knitting machines. The pile of tools he used to create parchment; the rotary sander that had destroyed his hearing. The half-finished cans of paint. At least he tried. Some men could barely get out of bed in the morning. And there was something endearing about how childlike he was when he was in the grip of one of these enthusiasms. "Being a zaidy is the best thing that has ever happened to me. I wish it had happened when I was young enough to enjoy it more, instead of having such a hard time getting down in the gutter with the girls this afternoon."

"You're ancient," she said softly, laughing. It was on the tip of her tongue to tell him about the babies. She pulled his hand down over her belly so that he could feel the twins' movement, discover the pregnancy himself.

"Decrepit," he said, pulling her closer. But then he moved his hand a little lower. "And so are you, Madam Clorox."

"Creek, eek, creek, groan," she said, pretending to be his joints. "Or perhaps I should say splish, splash." She leaned back against his shoulder.

When the twins were born she would lose this most precious of all things, the quiet love that had arrived after the children had become less needy, when she and Yidel finally had a little time to discover each other. Her mouth tasted like rust.

On the window ledge, just beyond Lipa's green glasses, two pigeons huddled out of the rain, making strange gurgling sounds. Their eyes were closed and their feathers seemed almost turquoise in the light from the nightstand.

"The new Pathmark that opened up is probably cheaper than Greenstein's," he said.

"I'd rather give my money to a person. Someone who knows my name."

"Yes," he said. She could tell he was smiling at her from the warmth in his voice, the way the *s* was drawn out. She had known when the children lied from the sound of their voices. Couldn't Yidel tell when *she* was lying? Perhaps he needed new batteries for his hearing aids. Tomorrow, she'd buy some. She pulled away from his warm hand, reached forward, and turned out the lamp.

"You are a good man, Yidel," she said. He untucked his sheet and blanket and tossed the edges onto her bed. He fell asleep quickly with his face against her back, his knees tucked under hers.

No words distracted her now. No rush of grandchildren demanding drinks and succor. No husband with warm and gentle hands. There was nothing in the room with her except the loneliness of knowledge. Soon, there would be a time when, like it or not, the whole family would know that she was pregnant, not just with one baby but with twins. Such recklessness, they would think. Didn't that poor excuse for a mother fear for the health of those new children? Why take unnecessary risks? What kind of mother would bring a damaged child into the world if she could prevent it by exercising a little self-control? And such children, *damaged* children, would cause terrible problems for their older siblings. When it came time to get married, their family would be marked. More marked.

Surie turned over in the bed and moved away from Yidel's faint breaths. The white hairs over his lips were just visible, rising on each exhale. A stream of minute bubbles rose from deep within her and she squirmed. The baby! The babies! By what bizarre miracle of internal engineering had she fallen pregnant?

Once, when they'd been in Florida on vacation, a little old woman in a wheelchair had loudly counted Surie's children and then said, as Surie passed, "Oh honey, don't you know how that happens yet?" Of course she knew how. Those times with Yidel remained as pleasurable as when they'd both been younger, more flexible, more energetic, more starved for it. When their bodies had all their parts and they were all in working order. Now, though it took longer, they still enjoyed one another. They'd adapted a little, changed positions, used a lubricant recommended by the doctor, but he had not lost his touch and neither had she. His hand between her thighs was just as exciting as the first time.

But look where it had gotten her. On that same Florida vacation, she had seen a dolphin leap into the air and fall back with a tremendous splash. A lady with a microphone taped to her face had said that the dolphins leapt out of the water to dislodge the orange lice that were embedded in the crevices of their bodies. If only. If only.

"Why are you awake?"

It was as if Yidel had an antenna specifically tuned on her. He almost always knew when something worried her or even if her foot ached. The silent language at which he was so adept. But he'd missed every sign of her pregnancy: the ongoing morning sickness, the crying jags, the painful varicose veins and swollen feet, the rushes to the bathroom, the afternoon naps, the pimples, the avoidance of gefilte fish, the swollen belly, the babies' movements, the unbearably itchy skin.

She couldn't tell him about the dolphins and their lice. She'd couldn't even tell him that she'd lost the key to the clock and had to buy a replacement from an antiques dealer in Borough Park, so how could she tell him that she'd almost, not quite, prayed for a miscarriage? "I've been thinking about your mother," she said instead, to blot up the silence.

Dead Onyu, her mother-in-law, was getting older and was blind, but there was no fooling her. Every day, when Surie visited the first floor, Dead Onyu held her hand for a minute too long, clearly waiting for Surie to say something.

"The state of her apartment. It's getting to be too much for her. Maybe we can send down one of Tzila Ruchel's girls to help? Miryam Chiena?"

She needed, at least until she told Yidel, to avoid his mother.

"But if we aren't careful about how we do it, she'll be so hurt, and then your father will be upset and you know what happens when he gets upset."

Dead Opa, Surie's father-in-law, used words, swear words, from before the time such language became unacceptable in the community, and his voice would be so loud that the neighbors could hear and sometimes there was talk. She snorted, thinking of the far worse talk there'd be when news of the pregnancy got out.

"The walls are stained with soot from her candles. The lampshades are literally made from spiderwebs and dust."

"No spiders, I hope." Yidel's voice was sleepy. He rolled closer to her and pressed his chin against her shoulder.

"No. Yes. There are. Lots. I saw her vacuuming one up the other morning, thinking it was a bit of yarn. She told me she doesn't understand it. She thinks the vacuum is malfunctioning because she keeps on feeling these same bits of yarn all over the place."

"She touches the spiders?"

He tickled the nape of her neck. His body was very warm, lying against hers. Would it be so terrible if he found out? Yes! It shouldn't happen like this! Despite how confused she felt, her body began to respond.

But when he lifted the hem of her nightgown, she pulled away from him. She wasn't ready. She was too tired. She had a headache. The truth was this: If he lay against her, hip to hip, he'd know she was five months pregnant. Fat in the belly was soft. A child, children in the belly were not. She didn't know what she'd been thinking when she put his hand on her skin. She hadn't allowed him to touch her for two months, the longest they'd ever gone. Yidel looked like he might cry.

They lay on their backs with their eyes open, staring through the darkness at the pale plaster rose on the ceiling. Spreading behind it was a water stain that looked like a map of Europe. They'd told each other that one damp patch looked like Romania. Hungary, Romania, Hungary, Romania again. Who knew which country their homeplace belonged to now. Sighet was on the border with Ukraine, they'd said, pointing. Yidel's father and mother had lived in Sighet before the Asten displaced persons camp in Austria, before Brooklyn. Half of the population was Jewish, eight thousand individuals. Now, no Jews lived there, but that didn't stop Dead Onyu and Dead Opa from wishing, daily, to return. But what could they see if they did return? They were both blind.

The Tisa River, as real to Yidel and Surie as the East River, appeared as a dark brown streak between the stain that was Ukraine and the stain that was Romania.

After a long silence, Yidel said, "What would have become of us if there hadn't been a Holocaust? Would I have married you? Would our children have been born?"

Surie wouldn't have been born. Her mother had given birth to Surie at an age when most of her friends had long stopped. She had told Surie that each child she gave birth to after the Holocaust was a poke in Hitler's eye, may his memory be erased. It was strange to think that her mother, at thirty-five, had been considered old. What would her mother have thought of Surie?

She and Yidel could almost see mayflies hovering in their great mating dance over the Tisa. The blue blush of dawn crept up over the walls. From somewhere nearby came the unearthly sound of the huge crane in the Navy Yard turning on its axle.

Half a block from their house, Division crossed Kent to dead-end at the East River. Surie's three youngest sons, waiting for their yeshiva buses, often wandered down to sit on the railing and swing their feet and throw pebbles and Popsicle sticks into the river. The water was the color and texture of avocado skin. There might be a man, a stranger, not one of them, sleeping in an abandoned car. There usually was. The board fences of Certified Lumber were covered with graffiti. In the backyard, the chickens screamed their egg-laying screams. Passing boats blew their horns. In the room directly underneath theirs, Tzila Ruchel's newborn woke up from the chiming of the big clock and began to cry. At their front door, black plastic bags awaited pickup by trucks with great rounded shoulders. On warm days, the river smelled of ashes and decomposing fish. That morning, Monday, it smelled like the thick scales that formed on the top of a baby's head, a combination of sweat and oil and exhaustion.

What a place to bring up a child! But she had done it for thirty years and never thought twice about it until this moment. Images came to her of the first time she had given birth in this house, the room dim, smelling of freshly dug earth, of rain and mold and forest, of growing things. She had thought she would die that night. She remembered Dead Onyu's tears at the appearing and disappearing sliver of infant scalp, and how she had wanted to push then, had wanted to see the face of her child, and she remembered when her mother-in-law put the raw child into her arms and kissed her and the child turned its head and began to suck. She remembered it as if it were happening right then and she cried the same tears she'd cried then, of wonder and fear and pain and something cold and thin and silvery that she had no name for, and she put up her hand to touch her breasts, but both were gone to the cancer and so she placed her hand on her chest instead and her fingers walked the thick, curving scars.

Her chest had been tingling and sore for months. She had not chosen to do reconstruction. Even if she had, she would not be able to nurse the new babies, but the surgeon must have left something behind, some cells that knew she was pregnant. She remembered waiting for the school bus on the corner of Kent and Division, wearing a heavy woolen coat that she had wrapped around the heads of her five children to protect them, the pressure of their small skulls against her thighs and her belly, the redbrick cobblestones, the wind. The children chanting, "Der roite godeh! Der roite godeh!" The street made of red bricks. She had thought she should remember the moment. Had known it was something worth remembering.

The emptiness in the house when they were all at school, the unbearable ticking of the clock, the almost explosive chimes. She remembered sitting on the lip of the bath in the middle of the night with the shower running, her son Lipa coughing and blue from croup, the steam smelling of mildewed socks and fear gnawing at her as a rat gnaws at a steel garbage bin. She remembered the lines of diapers flapping in the wind on the top of the building, her children playing "ships" in the empty laundry baskets, and she, pregnant again, stretching, bending, pegging out an endless row of wet linen.

She put her legs over the edge of the bed and lifted herself into the semidarkness. She was so tired. Even first thing in the morning, her ankles were swollen and her legs burned. Outside, it was still raining and raindrops glistened, caught in the mesh of the screen. From beyond the window, there was an almost constant sound similar to the scraping of chairs. Every so often, a metallic crash as something was let fall. Who knew what they did in the Navy Yard these days? Once, it had been the city's car pound lot. Now, it was businesses she didn't know anything about. A film studio, they whispered in the butcher shop.

In the kitchen, she lit the fire under the kettle and began toasting bread for her youngest sons, still unmarried and living at home, seventeen, fifteen, and thirteen, all of whom she had borne in her forties, the greatest risks she thought she'd ever take.

How will I manage? she asked the toaster and the kettle and the stainless-steel sink.

Tomorrow morning, they replied, you will tell Yidel and he will be so happy and surprised. He won't be angry or hurt or sad. He will cook so you build the babies properly, and he will make you suck umeboshi plums so you do not vomit so much. He will ask Tzila Ruchel to send her girls up to help you in the house, to clean, to sweep. Dead Onyu will stand in the street in the morning, waiting for the cheder buses with the little children. Yidel will buy pressure stockings for your tired legs, and when you are resting, he will massage your feet and feed you calcium for the cramps.

"The cramps," she said, and she shuddered.

She did not wish to remember her last birth, which had gone badly, very badly, and taken many days. She did not wish to remember the way she had put her hands around the midwife's neck and screamed that she wanted to go to the hospital. There had been a blizzard and the midwife had come in covered with snow, wheeling an oxygen tank. It left thin black lines of wetness on the wooden floors that did not dry.

The work required to sustain life in the world! Was it doubled for twins? She did not have the energy even for one newborn. No matter how she tried to distract herself, her mind circled back again and again.

In Romania, there had been small caves on the banks of the Tisa, and within the caves, if you dared to climb inside with a flashlight, you could see drawings made of ocher, of cows and lions and bears. Dead Onyu, as a fifteen-year-old girl, had climbed into one of these caves with her sister and that is how they had been missed when everyone from their town had been rounded up. The paintings weren't old. They had been the work of local schoolboys, one of whom was Dead Opa. He had also hidden in a cave. Now both of them were blind from when the flame in their portable gas heater had blown out while Yidel and Surie were in California. The old people had nearly died of carbon monoxide poisoning. As if losing Lipa weren't enough punishment.

At six, Surie's youngest three sons came into the kitchen from the mikva, pulling off their long coats. They washed their hands in silence and sat down to toast and eggs and coffee. Their jackets were wet from the rain. They wore plastic shopping bags over their beaver felt hats. They smelled like damp wool and spray starch. Through the closed window, she could hear the wind buffeting between the buildings, howling down the passageways from the Wallabout Channel and, before that, from the East River. Gulls rode the wind, cawing.

Somewhere, in the future, were two new children, maybe boys like these ones. Instead of almost sixty, feeding teenagers, she would be almost eighty. The new children would be ashamed of her, of her terrible age, of her frailty, of the way she still used occasional Hungarian words even though their friends' parents all spoke pure Yiddish. They wouldn't bring their classmates home to

48   GOLDIE GOLDBLOOM

taste her kokosh cake. She would look and sound and think like Dead Onyu and Dead Opa. To distract herself from this image, she stood still, trying to remember all that the midwife had told her about the pregnancy and the births. Val's hoarse smoker's voice, trying to be friendly, failing:

You know this already, but most babies are born head-first, Mrs. Eckstein. If they come with their feet first, it is known as a breech. It's far more common with twins. Don't you remember what happened with your third kid? I don't have to tell you what labor feels like. You know better than me! Even if the cramping is tolerable, usually the sensation during crowning, when the baby's head is delivered, feels very intense. Burning. You won't have too many problems with that. We already know you know how to push them out. That last one, you screamed. It's best not to scream. Moaning is okay with me. My ears, I'm getting old, know what I mean?

Never, during any of the births before her youngest son, Chaim Tzvi, had Surie screamed or even moaned. She had endured, the best that could be said of the experience. She had traveled, in her mind, to the place where Dead Onyu had played in the river, a river quite unlike the East River. The Tisa was unpolluted, shallow at its edges, and except during the spring melt, children could stand with their feet in the water and a small net in their hands and try to catch the minnows that swam just below the surface. Tiny yellow snails crawled over their feet, and long, pale green weeds twisted around their ankles. When Chaim Tzvi's head crowned after three days of labor, Surie was plunging into the icy water of the Tisa, making a victorious shout as a net full of squirming fish was held aloft.

———

At sixteen, a newly married Surie had come to live in the three-flat apartment building of Dead Onyu and Dead Opa. And still sixteen, she had her first child, a son. Dead Onyu, a young and sassy thirty-eight, had just given birth to her seventeenth child a few days earlier, so she wasn't available to assist. "Your family is keeping me hopping," Val had said to Dead Onyu. It had been Val's first year in Williamsburg and she didn't have a handle on the community *at all.* "You'd think an old pro like you would know how to avoid this by now," she'd said. "Don't you think it's time to give it a rest? Haven't you shown Hitler enough times that you won't be killed?"

During her labor with Chaim Tzvi, Val had told her she should make sounds. Heck, she could go ahead and scream if she thought it would help. Sweat broke out under Surie's turban and streamed from her body. The midwife had encouraged Surie to moo or bellow or cry. Something. Anything. But Surie had remained silent until almost the very end. "What is it with you women?" Val had asked.

Surie, laboring with that tenth child, paced from the living room at the front of her apartment all the way down the narrow hall to the back bedroom, where four of the five older boys were sleeping. She'd always hoped to have seven sons and gain free admittance to Paradise. Around and around she went. She stood in front of the big clock, each tick running through her like electricity, and she'd begged her long-dead mother to ask for divine intervention. From downstairs came the crying of Tzila Ruchel's new infant, Surie's first grandchild, the oldest daughter of her oldest daughter. Tzila Ruchel had gone to the hospital. She'd wanted a doctor.

Returning to the midwife after several circuits, Surie had said, "Why should I scream, why should I moan, when I am doing the exact thing I was made for? When I am fulfilling my part in creation? Thank God, I know my place in the world. The Torah speaks about many things, but always, always it talks about the children that come forth, the children that one is to sacrifice for. Every part of my life is turned towards children, the having of children, the raising of children.

"The strollers standing in the synagogue on yontiff, they are the Jewish people. And the yellow school buses that clog the streets in the morning, that is the Jewish people. And all of the crying babies under their father's white prayer shawls during the priestly blessing, that is the Jewish people. Their small hands, their feet, their shaven heads, their long curling payos, the singsong of their voices, at the end of the Holocaust when we thought no children were left, the sound of one child's cry was enough to fill every heart to overflowing. Families that didn't have money for blankets had money enough to bear children because that was the true and only wealth of the Jewish people. When the nations of the world say that we have stolen all the riches, there is no denying it, for aren't our places of worship full of gems, and aren't our schools full of diamonds, and aren't all the beds in our homes filled with gold and silver and onyx? When they say we have the blood of Christian children in our matzos, it is not true. We have the blood of *Jewish* children in our matzos. We have the blood of Jewish children in the air we breathe. It is all that we live for."

It was more words than the midwife had ever heard any of these women say and she was ashamed. It would be many months before she would again ask a laboring woman wearing a scarf and seamed taupe stockings, in the face of her stoic silence, her lack of curiosity, her denial of exhaustion, "What is it with you women?"

It had been more words than Surie had ever said to the midwife, and a few minutes later, she would barely remember saying them. Without any warning, she grabbed Val around the neck and began to scream that she wanted to go to the hospital, and Val laughed and said, "Looks like we are having us a baby!"

Her last son, her Chaim Tzvi, was born and placed on her chest and she thanked God and hoped that she was finally done, that there wouldn't be any more children, and then she retreated into that place where new mothers go when all of the violence is done. And that was thirteen years ago. Yes. She'd said what was true for her then. Until that birth, she had been excited about each new pregnancy. Now, she had white hairs in places unmentionable. She no longer needed to wear a bra. Her doctor was recommending a knee replacement. The crying of her grandchildren sometimes set her teeth on edge. And she did not want to be pregnant. Not this time.

FOUR

On a Friday morning in December two weeks after the visit to the clinic, Surie and Yidel rose at dawn. After rushing through breakfast, they parted: he to go to the synagogue for the psalms club, she to polish the candelabra for Chanukah. The rain had stopped, the temperature dropped, and the wind swung around to the northwest. The sky, a tight crisp blue, suggested snow later in the afternoon.

"Take a scarf," she said to Yidel, and tucked one of the dozens of plain black scarves they owned around his neck. It was permitted to touch him. The boys had already left for their yeshivos. There was nobody to see this intimacy.

Yidel put on his rubber overshoes and pushed the ends of the scarf into his coat. "Goodbye," he said. He put his palm against her cheek and she cupped his hand with hers. "I'll bring back olive oil."

"Enough for everyone. At least two large cans. Hurry!" she said, and he nodded, glancing at the big clock, then slipped his hand from under hers and went out.

He was such a decent man, a better-than-good husband. He'd always loved their babies, held them in his lap, staring into their slate-blue eyes for hours. He'd been the one who painted their bodies with calamine lotion and ran oatmeal bath after oatmeal bath that year they all had chicken pox at the same time; he'd helped drag the enormous baskets of laundry downstairs, twenty or twenty-five baskets a week, and then hauled the heavy loads up to the roof for her to peg out. Before his daughters' parent-teacher conferences, he'd prepared a list of questions, and on the night, he'd squeezed his bulk behind the little desks, one of the only fathers to come to the girls' building. On his bedside table, under the glass sheet that protected the wood, sat his favorite item in the house, a note from Tzila Ruchel written when she was six or seven, saying that he was the best father in the world. A tiny note covered in crayon kisses. Why was she worrying? Yidel would be *thrilled* to be a father again. So what if he was ready to retire? When she told him, he'd leap into the air like one of the chickens. He'd squawk and flap. They'd hear his cheering in Crown Heights. It wasn't fear of Yidel's reaction that was holding her back. It was something else. But what?

—

While Yidel was gone, Surie worked on the old silver menorah. It had come all the way from Romania. Dead Onyu's only living sister, who had since died, had given it to Surie for her wedding. Surie, at sixteen, had worn her hair in two long braids down her back. When she'd met Yidel a few weeks earlier, she'd worn a dark green rayon dress from the 1930s. She'd found the bias-cut dress in one of the charity bundles people had started leaving at their door when her mother was diagnosed and her father had to stop working. It had a little bow at the waist and pleats over the bust.

Yidel had been clean and presentable. He'd worn new clothes that didn't smell like mothballs. He hadn't looked at her as far as she could tell. She sometimes joked about that brief meeting with him. "I took a peek at you at the b'show," he always responded, smiling. "Ooh la la."

"No, you didn't," she replied. "You thought I had red hair. I remember. You thought I wore a pink dress."

The legs were attached with screws that had been stripped, and the menorah stood shakily. Like me, she thought as she rubbed the rouge cloth in circles. Her feet were swollen, dark purple at the ankles, the skin dimpled and coarse. Thick blue veins snaked down her legs. It was way too late for the special pantyhose of pregnancy. Yidel, had he known, would have made her wear support from the first day, not because he wanted his wife to have beautiful legs but because he wanted to lessen her pain.

She polished the window with vinegar and a sheet of newspaper. When it was sparkling clean, she covered the windowsill with aluminum foil to protect against drips and fire and then lined up a row of tin candelabras on the ledge. There was no more beautiful sight than all of the windows in Williamsburg lit with menorahs, snow spiraling softly down just outside. There was no worse sight than the flashing of the red and blue lights of the fire trucks outside a burning apartment.

She set a twenty-pound gogosha dough to rise on a

shelf behind the stove. She brought a third load of laundry to the basement and folded the second. She peeled potatoes for latkes and left them soaking in a pot of cold water in the sink. She polished the brass menorah from Hungary that had been her own father's, and then she polished the menorah she had bought for her son Lipa at his bar mitzvah. It was silver-plated but had an embossed design of lions holding a shield. She put that one back in the breakfront. Afterward, she took a yahrzeit candle from the drawer and put it on the windowsill together with the menorahs. And then it was lunchtime.

Her six married children climbed the stairs, laughing and calling out, with their wives and their husbands and all of their children. Surie had thirty-two grandchildren, and every Friday night, she lit a candle for each one of them and said their names in a long, prayerful chant. Her oldest son, Eluzer, was forty, not a child but still a child to her despite his height, his age, his seriousness, his long beard just beginning to go gray. Her son's daughter, the first of his ten children, was already married. Within a few months, Surie would be a great-grandmother.

Dead Onyu and Dead Opa groaned as they were lifted, one at a time, into the motorized chair that climbed the stairs to her apartment on a toothed track. Surie's children and grandchildren all looked alike, with their long, narrow faces and their navy-black eyes and their dark clothing.

She had many names. Surie. Onyu. Mamme, Mommy, Shviger, Tantie, Bubbie. Soon Surie would be called Dead Onyu, Great-Grandmother, and Dead Onyu would be called Ook Onyu, Great-Great-Grandmother. They all spoke together in their Hungarian-inflected Yiddish, and her children and her children's children hugged her and kissed her hand and told her what they'd brought for the family meal. This one day in the year, for the past four years, her family cooked and she didn't. Her daughters took over the tiny galley kitchen and began grating the potatoes, and her second son, who liked to cook, began frying the doughnuts. The house filled with the smell of hot oil and onions and children's diapers. The table was covered in delicacies, each of her daughters and daughters-in-law trying to outdo the others with delkelach or dobos torte or aranygaluska, krumplileves or cheesy papanași or walnut-apple-poppy-seed flódni.

It was a small apartment, narrow and lightless. The children set up a bowling alley in the long hallway and took turns rolling balls, knocking over plastic seltzer bottles filled with sand. The girls' group took a turn, then the boys' group.

As the oily smoke drifted through the apartment, the smell began to overcome Surie, and she felt sick despite her efforts to close her nose. In a moment, her stomach would turn upside down. In this apartment, there was only a small bathroom with two doors, one leading to her bedroom and the other into the hall where the children were playing. They would hear everything. They would worry about her and run to their parents for reassurance, and one of her pregnant daughters-in-law would make a whispered joke to another daughter-in-law about morning sickness. She could picture their horror if she told them she was expecting twins. The silence, the flaming faces, the shocked eyes. Nobody would say, "In a gite sha'a." Nobody would ask her when she was due. They would glance from her to Yidel and back again and everyone would be thinking that some crime had been committed, to make a great-grandmother pregnant.

She had to get away from the smells! Surie turned to Dead Onyu and said, "You look cold." The room was insanely overheated. Perspiration was running down her face.

Dead Onyu gripped her arm and sniffed the air. "What is wrong, Surie? Will you tell me?"

Surie shook off her mother-in-law and announced that she was running downstairs for her sweater.

No one would let her. "Today is your day off, Mamme," said Eluzer, leading her to a chair and drawing up a foot-stool. "I'll catch the cardigan." Tzila Ruchel brought her a glass of hot cocoa with marshmallows floating in the cream. A granddaughter climbed into her lap. Was it ter-rible that she couldn't always attach each child's name to the correct face? Small droplets of sweat stood out on Surie's forehead. She licked her lips. The salt tasted good. But she was afraid she might vomit on the head of the child. At last, the feeling passed and she was able to lean back against the upholstery and breathe again.

Someone had opened a window and the cold wind blew over her, bringing the deep green scent of the river. Through the window, she could see clouds piling up above the tops of the tallest plane trees. Hundreds of Canada geese flew past in a V, honking, heading someplace warmer. In the nearest tree, crows shuffled on the branches, hunched against the wind. The big clock's gears ground, a click, a moment of suspense, and then the tolling. It was three,

only an hour before Shabbos. A single white flake passed
the window and then another.

"It's snowing," one of the girls called, and everyone
cheered and crowded around the windows. "Der Oibershter is emptying out the feathers from His feather bed!"

Surie walked into her bedroom and looked up at the
map of Europe on the ceiling. Coats covered her bed, a
mountain of black woolen cloth lined with black silk. She
wanted to lie down. She felt very tired. Her legs hurt. She
scratched the nape of her neck, the inside of her wrist, her
jaw. If she wasn't careful, she would draw blood. She took
off her nice scarf and her short wig and covered her head
with a cotton turban. She looked at herself in the mirror.
Some bubbie. Then she took off the turban and replaced
it with the scarf and the stiffened piece of false hair again.
This might be the last year her children came for Chanukah. Next year they would know what she kept secret this
year. She should try to enjoy. Who knew what next year
would be like? Who knew if she'd even be alive? To be
pregnant at fifty-seven . . . She should go and sit with the
family.

"You look beautiful, Bubbie."

Surie jumped. Seated behind the mirror, just inside the
old-fashioned wardrobe, was her oldest granddaughter,
Tzila Ruchel's daughter, who had been born at the same
time as Surie's Chaim Tzvi, thirteen years earlier. The girl
sat on a folded coat with a book on her knees. This child
had thick blond hair parted into two braids. She was
known to be very smart. She was much smarter than
Chaim Tzvi, who'd been affected by his long birth. Everyone worried about her. Being too smart was not good.

Instead of the girl's face, Surie saw her sixth child's face, her son Lipa with his dark eyes and his sad expression and the strange green glasses he had come home wearing once. As a young child, he had also liked to sit inside the wardrobe and read. Sometimes he'd fallen asleep in there, and she'd had to lift him and carry him to his room, his dear little head bobbing on her shoulder, his soft payos cushioning her cheek. This, the first night of Chanukah, was Lipa's fourth anniversary. If only he were here. She wouldn't say anything about the strangeness of his glasses.

Lipa faded slowly. Surie touched the green-rimmed glasses in the pocket of her apron. She was alone with the girl again. She walked to her granddaughter and put out her hand. "Miryam Chiena," she said, "shall we go and join the others?"

They walked hand in hand out to the dining room and everyone was eating the special foods prepared in honor of Chanukah, though it wouldn't be Chanukah until the sun set. Yidel leaned back in his chair, his hands crossed over his belly, humming an old wordless song. This was their custom, to eat early and light the candles and then walk down the streets, looking at the menorahs in the windows and calling to their friends, many of whom would also be walking in the streets.

One of the little boys sat crying under the table because he hadn't received the last lick of the cheese crowns.

"Come," Surie said, and she bent over her belly, gasping, to lift him out and get him one of the chocolates that were supposed to be only for the grown-ups. "Aren't you special, my lamb?" And he gloated and licked the chocolate slowly in front of the other children, taking his time, tormenting them.

Lipa had always been the child crying under the table. His cousins had picked on him. He had no backbone. He could never hit the plastic seltzer bottles with the ball, and he preferred to sit in her room, organizing her shoes in the wardrobe. He never wanted to wear the black clothing they all wore, and from the time he was five, he'd asked for brown shoes, navy trousers, blue-striped shirts, a maroon yarmulke stitched with a gold star. She had said no. Such small things he had wanted. Why couldn't she have said yes? Why had she been so afraid of what others thought that she was unable to see how much these small concessions meant to her son?

In San Francisco, four years earlier, they had been taken to see him. On a metal table in the middle of a white floor was a body covered with a piece of plastic. Yidel lifted the sheet and looked at their son's face and said nothing. Fat tears fell from his eyes and into his beard. "This boy is not my son," he said. She had run to the table and pulled the plastic out of his hands. It was Lipa. He did not have his payos. He had a tattoo on his chest and a metal ring through one nipple. Around his neck was a dark purple line that came to a V in the front, like the neckline of an undershirt, and in the gray flesh of his neck were dozens of small cuts.

"My little boy," she said. "My lamb." She covered him with the plastic and tucked it in under him. She stroked the plastic over his head.

"Come on, Surie. We have to go," said Yidel.

"No," she said.

"He was never like the others. He had his problems from the start. Look what he has come to. It wasn't anything to do with us."

"They shouldn't have whispered about him like they did," she said.

FIVE

The community had found out about Lipa when he was arrested on nine felony counts of malicious mischief involving infected body fluids. Heads of the community had paid the quarter-million bail. Out loud, the rabbis said they didn't believe such lies about one of their own. The details weren't something to talk about. Sha, shtiller. No one in the community was like that; such behavior didn't happen among their own men; the arrest was some kind of scam. The story was a filthy stinking lie made up by anti-Semites, a new kind of blood libel. But despite what was said out loud, the news had spread like wildfire. The morning after the arrest, when Yidel entered the mikva, the room fell silent. His oldest friend came over to clap him on the back and display his solidarity but swerved at the last minute, afraid to touch Yidel, afraid of contagion. A few people pretended to talk about something else, but then the silence rose up again.

When he'd called home after his arrest, Lipa told them the accusation was true, though he hadn't known he was sick or that there was any risk to anyone. At twenty-two, he still didn't know the names for the things he did. The police didn't believe him. What kind of person *couldn't* know? Did the kid grow up on Mars?

Surie felt ill, and when a social worker came on the line, describing the medical routine and precautions that would be necessary, she handed the phone over to Yidel. He leaned against the wall, his face white, holding the phone away from his ear. As a result, they were both unclear about the details of infectious transmission.

Lipa, confused, exhausted, filthy, sobbing, was released into the care of his family. Surie was afraid to let him in the house. She put a pillow and a blanket they'd planned on throwing out onto the plastic-covered couch. Yidel told his father and his sons and nephews and grandsons that they shouldn't be alone together with Lipa. Surie told her grandchildren that if Lipa touched them or breathed on them, they'd die from a very bad kind of cancer. Lipa's old friends didn't visit. Their Ruv didn't visit either.

When Lipa went out to buy cigarettes, storekeepers stared at the hand holding out money until he put the cash down on the counter. Then they used a pen to knock the bills into the register. Men who'd known Lipa all his life jackknifed their bodies away from him and couldn't meet his eyes. His own family jumped whenever he came into a room, and for the first time ever, the door to Tzila Ruchel's apartment was closed and locked. His mother, Surie, took the china and the silverware she served his food on and, wearing rubber gloves and a mask, threw them into the incinerator. When he tried to return to Manhattan, he found he'd been locked out of his shared apartment. Even the gay community treated him like a pariah for not disclosing his HIV status.

He'd had no idea he had an illness, no idea about precautions, protection. Before the arrest, he'd never heard of the AIDS crisis. He'd thought condoms were a kind of apartment you owned instead of rented. He hadn't known the English word *gay*. He hadn't known the names for what he felt or what he did and so he had remained an outsider. A few weeks after the arrest, he emptied Surie's purse, jumped bail, and hitchhiked out to California. Without a high school diploma, a driver's license, or even a Social Security card, he'd been unable to get work. He'd lived behind a dumpster for a couple of months. Then he was found hanging in a tree in a public park one evening, the first night of Chanukah, by a jogger. Surie had to ask what it was, a jogger.

"For God's sake," Yidel had said on the way out of the morgue. "He was a fag. He deserved to die." But he choked on the word *deserved* and more tears fell and he turned and wiped his face on his sleeve.

They couldn't bury him in the community plot in the Kiryas Joel cemetery. The rabbis wouldn't permit it. They couldn't bury him in Israel. The rabbi in San Francisco took pity on them and said that perhaps a vigilante had strung up their son; that he was not, after all, a suicide, and could therefore be buried in the Orthodox graveyard. The rabbi was young and he said the words beside the deep hole in the earth very fast, and, intimidated by their old-fashioned appearance, by Surie's scarf and Yidel's earlocks, he did not come to comfort them at their hotel. None of their children came out to California for the funeral, and she wasn't clear, even all these years later, which of her children knew what had become of their brother. He was never spoken about. His photographs had been removed from the albums by the time they returned home.

It seemed that suspicions about Lipa had spread beyond Williamsburg, because recently they'd sent their Gitty to London to find an appropriate match, but even there, she'd had difficulties. She was a pristine and perfect child who should have been able to marry a kollel man, one of the best, and instead, at twenty-two, almost on the shelf, she'd had to settle for a boy in business who didn't want to wear white socks on Shabbos. Who knew what people were saying about their family! And this new embarrassment—everyone would think she was covering up a granddaughter's illegitimate pregnancy by pretending the babies were hers. She'd be lucky to be able to marry off the youngest three boys at all.

Lipa had HIV. He'd been ill. He had warts. He hadn't taken care of himself. It was clear that he had not eaten in many days. He had weighed less than eighty pounds. He was twenty-two years old. The coroner handed her the green-rimmed glasses in a plastic bag and asked if she wanted the ring from his nipple. She took that too.

The small cuts on his neck, the coroner said, were from his fingernails. In the end, her boy hadn't wanted to die.

She wanted to tell the body to hurry on to the next life, that this life had been one full of sorrow and that next time would be better. She wanted to hold on to the body and not let it go. Yidel took her hand and stroked it for a long time. He stood close to her and inhaled the scent of formaldehyde. The room was very, very cold. Her hands turned blue. "Come with me, my love," he said several times before leading her gently out of the room.

After their furtive shiva, on the drive to the San Francisco airport, she'd wondered aloud what it must have been like to be Lipa, to have held such an explosive secret tightly for so long. Had he wanted to tell someone? Had he been swamped with fear? Had the secret and the fears that clung to it like fog changed the ways he behaved? Were the green glasses a symptom of the secret or a symptom of his desire to tell?

Yidel didn't understand why Lipa couldn't just pretend. Be like all their other sons, marry a woman, have children, settle down. Forget the stupid secret. Bury it somewhere. He was sure he'd known young men with a similar secret and they'd all married, they'd all had children and done what was expected of them. Why had Lipa needed to be so stubborn, so visible?

Nobody was asking her, Surie said, but what, after all, was so terrible about loving a man instead of a woman? Did the Torah forbid loving? She did not know, did not want to know, what Lipa had done behind closed doors. But then, she did not know what her friends, women she had known for fifty years, did behind closed doors either. None of them spoke about such things. How she wished the veil of secrecy had remained drawn for Lipa too. Would it have been different if he could have brought home a young man he had met and introduced him to the family, shown him the family photograph albums, invited him to their Chanukah dinner? Would Lipa still be alive if they could have just loved him as he was?

For the first time in their entire married life, Yidel

shouted at her and said she must have been reading the secular newspapers or maybe she'd been listening to the evil radio broadcasts of the secular leftist destroyers, and she said she would never do such a thing, and the taxi driver had turned around and told Yidel in English to shut up, even though it was obvious he had no clue what they had been fighting about. The driver had ranted about how religious people were fakers and perverts and domestic terrorists, and Yidel had blushed bright red, not really following the conversation but shocked by the tone. He'd apologized, first to Surie and then to the driver. He'd asked in a whisper where she'd gotten such an outrageous idea. She'd wanted to say, "From my heart," but instead had stared out of the window at the water just below the highway, a wide gray expanse of chop.

Lipa's lifestyle hadn't been a perfect secret, Yidel said then. Lipa had told Yidel that he was gay. Yidel had been kind, hoping that his son might one day change his mind, and for that reason, Lipa kept on coming home, even after he moved out and lived somewhere in Manhattan, selling things. Surie had let her friends think he'd gone to some advanced yeshiva in Israel. She remembered Yidel taking Lipa out walking along the hidden stretch of river between Division and Clymer, how they would return, red-eyed, sniffing, blaming the wind and the cold. It seemed they had both decided that Surie wasn't ready for the details, that she might tell a friend who would tell a friend.

Surie felt a sour sensation in her throat, as if acid had risen up and burned her esophagus. Why had Lipa gone to his father instead of to her? Tears pricked her eyes. What kind of a mother was she?

"You should have shared the secret with me. He was my son too! I wouldn't have told!" she said. "When did I ever tell any of our secrets? Who would I tell?"

Yidel stared at her. He did not look away. It was as if he could pin her with his eyes. A police SUV approached with its siren blaring. The taxi pulled over and then, as the police car passed, raced into the empty space behind it. But really, who could she have told? Not her classmates, who would have been scandalized and distanced themselves. Not her only sister, who had been diagnosed at the same time as Surie but, unlike her, had not survived the chemo. Not even Dead Onyu, who had a taste for the salacious, who would have wanted details that Surie couldn't wrap her brain around.

Though occasionally she thought it might be nice to do something different, to step outside of the community norms the way that Dead Onyu often did—refusing to wear the Shabbos apron, going down to Florida and swimming on the beach, reading books in Hungarian—Surie was afraid to risk it. If she'd allowed Lipa to wear the yarmulke he craved, maroon velvet with an embroidered gold star, her other sons and her grandchildren wouldn't be accepted at the local schools. Goyishe kop, that's what the other children would have said about Lipa and his modern yarmulke, a *girly* yarmulke, with its decorations. Their parents would have said even worse.

"How could you?" she'd hissed when Lipa had shown up that last Passover before his arrest, wearing the green glasses. "You look ridiculous. Like some kind of . . . goy. Like one of those men with pink shirts. Take them off and put on your normal ones." He hadn't changed his glasses. He had kissed her hand and, without saying goodbye, walked out. And that was the last time she had seen him as her son, a healthy, normal child. It would be easy to say that it was the community whispers, the change on the counter, the plastic-covered couch, but Lipa had been stubborn. A few stares, some plastic, they wouldn't have driven him out of the world. But to lose the love of one's mother? It was her fault, all of it. California. The cutoff payos. The nipple ring. The tattoo of God's ineffable name. The awful diseases. The rope in the park at dawn.

———

Surie stirred in her chair. A wave of coldness ran from the crown of her head down her ribs and all the way to her feet. She was acting just like Lipa, holding on to an explosive secret, one that had the potential to rip her from her community, even kill her. Like Lipa, she wanted to tell someone but was deathly afraid to do so. Lipa had been such an honest child. He was the one they had gone to whenever they wanted to know who'd eaten the last ice cream or broken the glass. And yet for years he'd lied about where he was and what he was doing and with whom. She had never lied to Yidel, but she was lying to him every day. She had wondered what it felt like to be Lipa. Well, now she knew. It hadn't been deliberate. And yet it was as if she could feel Lipa standing in the room with her. She could smell the shampoo he used, lime and mint. In her ear, the beating of Lipa's heart.

———

"Bubbie," said Miryam Chiena. "Bubbie?" She stood next to Surie's chair and stroked her wrinkled face. This child was fascinated with bodies. She must never go near a public library. It would be the ruination of her. "It's Chanukah. Wake up."

Surie sat so still, the way the river seemed on a hot day, still on the surface and, underneath, full of broken things and rocks and garbage. Miryam Chiena lifted her spotted hands and let them drop. Surie's pale blue eyes didn't flicker. The child leaned forward and pressed two fingers against the carotid artery, as she'd seen Yidel do. Without warning, heat flooded back into Surie's face and she leaned to one side and was sick on the floor.

Then there were many voices, loud and angry, but coming as if from under a pillow or from a faraway place. A strange knell that must have been the clock. Three strikes. But hadn't it been three o'clock hours earlier?

"It's too much for her, this big of a party. We should have it at our house."

"But she loves when all the grandchildren come here. And her house is the closest to the shil."

"Well, then let Tzila Ruchel host it. She is just as close."

"She shouldn't go out walking tonight. Let the men go to the Rebbe's tish. But the women should stay here with her. Maybe she is coming down with something."

"We should say psalms for a recovery."

"Is nobody going to help her?"

Yidel brought warm cloths and put them in front of Surie. He took a bottle of seltzer from the table and poured it on the rug and then scooped up the mess with paper towels. "Bubbie will be all right," he said to Miryam Chiena, who was crying. "She's hard like iron." And then, when the child didn't stop: "I'll let you listen to her heart with my stethoscope on Sunday, to prove she is fine."

"I want to lie down," Surie said. Tzila Ruchel maneuvered her through her dozens of grandchildren and her anxious sons and daughters and back into her bedroom. Yidel carried the coats out into the living room and shushed all the little children.

"She's tired," he said. "But perfectly fine. Don't worry."

In the bedroom, he leaned down and whispered in her ear, "You gave them all a scare," and she laughed softly.

"About time," she said. "They've been scaring me for years."

In her eyes, there was a strange light that he had not seen in a very long time, and for the life of him, he couldn't remember what it meant. He looked at her for a minute. Two. It was something terribly familiar. What was the meaning of that expression? He knew it. He was sure he did. But he couldn't name it. With a sigh, he kissed her forehead and brought her a turban and looked away when she took off the scarf and nylon wig. He pulled the blankets up and asked if she wanted a cup of tea.

"Not unless you want to see me perform the same trick again."

Yidel had been a volunteer emergency medical technician with the private Jewish ambulance service, Hatzolah, until his hearing got bad. Married men were allowed to do those kinds of things, as long as they used a pager instead of a cell phone.

He took out his kit and looked in Surie's eyes with a flashlight, still hoping he would recognize what it was he had noticed earlier. He asked her to open her mouth and say ahh. He checked her reflexes and everything was fine. "I think you are very sick," he whispered. "I may be forced to perform CPR on you." They laughed softly together, afraid the children would hear them. He stood up and quietly locked the door. Surie smiled. For the first time in four years, she felt some whisper of her former strength flood her spine. It had been a long time since Yidel had been so playful with her.

They missed the Chanukah lighting. They lay, instead, under the warm blankets looking out at the snowflakes swirling past the windows and neither said anything. The door to the scuffed old wardrobe was open, and in its mirrored door, Surie could see the snow. And even if she turned all the way over, she could still see the snow reflected in the glass over their wedding photograph.

"Oh, love," Yidel said, and he held her hand in silence.

It was the night of the yahrzeit. What better time? She wanted, more than anything, to talk about Lipa. Her son lay wedged into the crack between the beds, without his payos, his face mauvely smooth, glancing from his mother to his father, somehow smaller, thinner than he'd been even on the steel table. How could she talk to Yidel about the twins when they still couldn't talk about this thing that had ripped through the fabric of their family?

"I miss him," she said.

"Who?" asked Yidel, knowing.

"Lipa."

Yidel sighed. Parents were not supposed to have favorites. They weren't. It might not have been written down in the Torah, but favorites were strictly forbidden. But in a corner of Yidel's heart, there was a shred of some feeling for Lipa that he did not have for his other children, a protective, tender, numinous love that could not be spoken of without destroying it. He understood Surie's wish to talk, but he couldn't bear to risk losing this last little ghost of feeling for Lipa.

"I'll say kaddish." They made a minyan at home on the first night of Chanukah so that Yidel would not be confronted by people walking out on Lipa's kaddish.

"Yuh. I'll answer Amen."

"Thank God."

"Thank God."

After an hour or so, they rose and Surie lit the Shabbos candles with her daughters. Yidel sang in his rich bathroom voice and Surie clapped her hands, her cheeks glossy red, and all of the little ones joined in off-key and behind the beat. On the window ledges were dozens of menorahs and each one held a single flame and, just above, the shamash candle that had lit it. Lipa's yahrzeit candle stood burning by itself.

Her seventeen-year-old, Mattis, began to sing a wordless tune that had come with their family from Romania. Then he sang Lipa's favorite tune, a Yom-Tov Ehrlich song, "The Resurrection of the Dead": "Dos iz Chaim, dos iz Nissim . . . men iz geven by alle brissim." Outside, the snow batted against the windows and melted and lights blinked on in the apartment buildings across the park. Behind her, Surie felt a cool breeze and she put her hands over her stomach to show Lipa where to look, because she wanted to share her secret with him.

"In the time of the Hashmonaim," Yidel said as he said every year, "there were great dangers that troubled the Jews. Hellenists wanted the Jews to be like the Greeks, to accept their modern way of life and take on their customs. But Yochanan Cohen Gadol forbade the Jews from behaving like the non-Jews. Then the Hellenists were furious at Yochanan and slandered the Temple, saying that it contained a great wealth."

Only the wealth of children, she thought. That is all we have, ever. Later, she could not remember all of the details of that Chanukah. Just a few parts remained clear: the face of her husband, Yidel, as he leaned down to her; the faint earthy scent of Lipa; the small pinpoints of light shining against the black openings that were the windows; the singing of the children as they went down the stairs and out into the road, to walk the frozen streets of Williamsburg.

And the words she said to herself as they went were the words Jewish women have said with a hand on the mezuzah for thousands of years. "God will protect your going and your return from now until forever." It was a small and lovely prayer and she had never allowed it to feel stale in her mouth and her heart, and she felt comforted and at ease and stood at the window watching her family, her whole family including Lipa, walking in the darkened street. Though she was not with them, she felt that she was a part of them, and traveled with them in some way, and she was grateful for the blessings in her life.

When she lay down in her bed she could hear, through the vents, Dead Opa talking quietly with Dead Onyu in their beds. They were speaking in Hungarian, which she could not fully understand. She heard her name and then the name of Lipa, and she knew that her in-laws must think her ill from remembering the Chanukah of four years ago. Morning sickness, she whispered to the vents, though it wasn't even close to the whole truth. Yidel had left a bar of chocolate and a small flower next to her bed. It wasn't anything special. One of the tiny red flowers that formed on the tips of the cactus in winter. The chocolate was her favorite kind, though, and he must have hidden it from her sons and daughters because it was their favorite kind too.

He couldn't have any clue about the twins. The one thing she couldn't stand whenever she was pregnant was chocolate.

SIX

A week after the wedding, when Surie left the high-risk clinic, there was a conference between the midwives, the doctor, the physician's assistant, and the dietitian. They somehow all found themselves in the break room at the same time, and the head midwife, Val, said what they'd all been thinking when they saw Surie's curved shoulders and her pinched face: "She hasn't told her husband!"

The doctor, retrieving a container of bhindi masala, said, "It's not reportable yet, but Val, you've spoken with her. Does she seem in the right frame of mind to make good choices for her health and the health of the fetuses?"

Val sipped her tea. "She's already refused the amniocentesis."

"Lots of women refuse that."

"Not in their fifties," said the physician's assistant.

"No. Not in their fifties," Val agreed.

"She will blame us if anything goes wrong." The doctor frowned at Val.

The ultrasound technician found them clustered around the coffeepot, their arms folded. It wasn't a birthday party. It was much too solemn for that. The technician waited for the doctor to speak, but he was searching for a packet of salt in his locker. His white coat was spotless. He wore five-hundred-dollar shoes. She'd been working on him for several months and hoped he might ask her out soon, despite South Indian tradition and the lack of a family go-between.

"Maybe we should make a note on her chart, just in case something goes wrong," said the physician's assistant, who had the most to lose if they were blamed. She was a recent graduate with massive school loans. She stabbed at her cold noodles. Metal chimed against the side of the steel bowl.

The ultrasound technician looked around. They were all nodding their heads. The doctor was making some notes on a piece of paper. She rubbed her fingers together. She looked at the doctor and then she looked away. "How can you say that? That's not right," she said. "That woman is a good mother. She's just been surprised. That's all. You'd be surprised too, if you were fifty-five and suddenly pregnant."

"Fifty-seven."

"She couldn't even point to her uterus."

"And?" said the technician. "Do any of you know the names of any of her children?" She didn't want to make a guess at the number. "Do any of you know how to speak Yiddish or Hungarian or Hebrew?" Maybe Surie couldn't speak Hebrew. She'd read about that kind of Jew in the Sunday paper. Anti-Zionist flag burners. "Do any of you have any idea how many grandchildren she has living in her house?" She didn't know either. She'd been too scared to talk to the woman with the silk helmet and the oddly unfashionable clothes stretched tight over the enormous tummy. But nobody else had even tried, not even Val. They barely looked at Surie. Especially the doctor. "This would be unforgivable racism if it were aimed at any other minorities, but it is acceptable when it comes to religious people?"

There was a long silence in the break room. A couple of the midwives pushed past the technician and left.

"There's no excuse for ignorance," said the doctor.

"Yours? Or hers?" said the technician.

———

Back in her office, Val was eating a turkey-and-mayonnaise sandwich, pondering her next move. She liked to introduce these Chassidic women to modern culture, to an appreciation for their bodies, to the terms for things they had no name for before her intervention, even though it never seemed to stick. The younger midwives deferred to her. They had not laughed when the technician berated the doctor. They'd watched Val's face and imitated her calm, even when the doctor left, slamming the door.

"What can we do to support Mrs. Eckstein?" they'd asked in respectful tones. Most of them were twenty or twenty-one.

"Birthing videos," Val said. Or the loan of some of their books. Or prenatal yoga. More vitamins. Or hypnosis.

"She's ashamed of her body. It's going to negatively impact the birth if she's holding back."

Val was about to say, "I'll suggest labor classes," but then she thought how foolish that would be, since the

Chassidic woman had already delivered ten infants and raised them to adulthood. To see that heavy old woman squatting on the floor with the thirty-year-olds, the yuppie mommy crew, huffing and puffing in her orthopedic shoes, her scarf falling down over her eyes! She would frighten all the hipsters away. "I don't think she is," she said to the younger women, "ashamed." It wasn't quite the right word for the way Surie held herself. Perhaps the word was *private*. In a world in which everything was common knowledge, there was a fence around Surie that said KEEP OUT.

In the demonstration kitchen, the dietitian smiled as she remembered the doctor's defeat. She had grown up in Williamsburg, in an Orthodox home, though she wasn't part of the Chassidic community. Her family were Oberlanders, Vien people. Punctual, educated, more worldly. But she knew enough about the community in Williamsburg to be able to picture the clean simplicity of the woman's kitchen and the orderliness of her home. The dietitian was one of the oldest women on the staff. She thought she knew everything there was to know about Surie, what the Chassidic response would be to anything unusual. She knew how unlikely it was that Surie would sue anybody. "God's will," was what the Chassidic woman would say. She'd do her mourning if anything went wrong, but she wouldn't come after the doctor or the midwives. The dietitian was the one who had brought a little sealed cup of orange juice to Surie after she'd gotten the news about the twins a week earlier. She'd seen her old neighbor perched on the examination table, crying and trying to hide the tears. She'd torn off the lid and held the juice out to Surie, who didn't take it.

"It's kosher," the dietitian had said, offering the juice again. "I took it out of my own lunch."

———

The mental health counselor, peeling radishes, wondered if it was too soon or too inappropriate to bring up the subject of adoption. It was too late, of course, to discuss abortion. She'd grown up in Brooklyn, in Bed-Stuy. Though they'd talked about Judaism briefly in her college classes, she didn't really know much about Jews. She didn't know why, but she had the feeling that those women in their silk scarves were secretly laughing at her. Mrs. Eckstein seemed perfectly nice, but still, there it was. Her very young clients were often convinced to give up their infants, and she was sure it was for the good of all concerned. She wasn't sure what the protocol was for very old clients. Surie was her first Chassidic client and her first pregnancy over fifty.

———

On the second floor of the apartment building in Williamsburg, Tzila Ruchel woke up from a bad dream and wondered if it would be terribly rude to slip her mother a brochure for Weight Watchers. Her mother was large, but lately things were getting out of hand. There seemed always to be a wedge of petticoat exposed between her mother's shirt and the waistband of her skirt.

———

On the third floor, Yidel also awoke. He had a scratchy
throat, and he went into the bathroom, where he found
Surie's bottle of kosher prenatal vitamins. She'd torn off
the label. Without turning on the light, he unscrewed the
lid and popped two pills without reading the container.
He thought they were vitamin C with zinc. Then he went
back to bed and patted Surie's haunch. "Thanks for picking up more vitamins," he said.

———

Sometime near dawn, Miryam Chiena dreamed that she
had a new auntie and uncle. They were younger than her
and they stood in the middle of the room holding hands.
"Hello," they said in unison. They were blue. Somehow
she knew that they were her grandmother's children. She
woke up sweating and crying out for her mother, but when
Tzila Ruchel came, the child swatted her away and began
to cry for her grandmother.

———

In the cemetery in California, Lipa lay in the ground, staring up at the stars. He didn't know where he was. He
didn't know where his mother was. But he missed her.

SEVEN

The Tuesday after the Chanukah party, Surie stepped out into the bright cold light of winter. She pushed a lone chicken back inside the entryway with her foot. The air was still and Williamsburg rested in the peaceful moment just after the school buses departed. Dead Onyu, bent over a straw broom, swept the strip of concrete between the house and the street. The rosebush the old woman had brought with her from Romania sprawled across the entire front of the house. A few rose hips dangled from the empty branches. The children were in school and most of the women were inside, avoiding the cold.

Surie walked down to the end of her street and looked out on Wallabout Channel. A tugboat was towing a barge full of garbage. It sounded its horn and the echoes bounced between the decrepit warehouses and the cement walls. The hum of traffic came from the Williamsburg Bridge and a helicopter passed overhead. She nudged a spray can with the tip of her shoe. As often as she could, she came to look at the river, endlessly moving, a different color every day. Twenty feet below her: black, turquoise, hell green, teal, olive, lime. A few flakes of snow came down out of the bright blue sky and melted on the water. The wind was fierce. That night there would be a Hatzolah party at the Eden Palace. The following night her niece was getting married.

One particularly cold winter evening fifteen years earlier, she and Yidel had taken Lipa and his older brothers down to the frozen inlet with borrowed ice skates. They'd climbed down to the ice on a ladder and wobbled around, falling over, throwing snowballs at one another. Her heart had been in her mouth: What if the ice wasn't thick enough in the channel? She had never seen the East River freeze. Lipa, who was surprisingly good at skating, had taken her hand in his little mittened paw and towed her under an overpass and back to the end of their street again. How she'd laughed and laughed! Was Yidel beset by memories like these, or did he go through his days closed off to the pain? She didn't know. It seemed impossible to chip away the ice that had formed around Yidel's heart to find the tender man, the grieving father she knew he was inside.

Everything seemed impossible. When she'd tried to open the hood on the old carriage, the waterproof woolen fabric ripped in the folds. She couldn't find the screws that held the spare cot together. And when she took out the box of cloth diapers she'd pushed behind the washing machine to use as rags, they'd been ruined by moths. Her fingers rested on the thick scars left after her mastectomy. Just to feed these new babies would be a constant labor; to bathe and clothe and comfort them would occupy every minute. There would be no leisurely walks to stare at the river.

She went upstairs to Tzila Ruchel's apartment and stood in the doorway. Her daughter. It should have been easy to tell her about the pregnancy. They'd become best friends. There were no secrets between anyone who lived in this building. She wondered if Tzila Ruchel had already heard her vomiting each morning and guessed; if her daughter was in the kitchen, waiting for Surie to make an announcement. But there was a ring of dirt just above the wainscoting, fingerprints on the doorjambs, toys lying everywhere on the floor. The apartment was silent. Tzila Ruchel must have gone out.

Her daughter's apartment had no curtains and no decorations aside from children's drawings taped to the walls. In the kitchen, all of the cabinets had child locks on them that Surie no longer remembered how to open. She had thought she'd make herself a cup of coffee while she waited for her daughter to return, but instead she began to fold and put away the piles of infant clothing that spilled off the chairs. When she finished, she washed the dairy dishes left over from breakfast, dried them, and left them in stacks on the counter next to their cupboards. She'd always wanted, more than anything, to be a good mother, but something about that simple wish felt strained. She wanted to be a good mother for the children she had already birthed. She wasn't sure how she felt about being a good mother to the twins. And she suspected that if she were a good mother to the twins, she would be a bad mother to her older children. Or they would think she was.

She'd been helping Tzila Ruchel for years, but that would be one of the first things to change. After the twins were born, Surie would have to get up even earlier every morning, to stand outside with the other mothers, in the rain, in the snow, in the sleet, in the unbearably hot sun, and wait for the school buses to arrive and depart, twice a day, forever. When would she and Tzila Ruchel ever again find a moment to share a cup of coffee? The companionship, the familiar jokes and ready assistance and frank comfort that had slotted into place between them would be thrown out of sync. She was glad that Tzila Ruchel wasn't home. She wanted to enjoy these last few months with her daughter before it was all lost. No need to rush.

After she'd wrung out the blue-striped dishrags and hung them on the security gate outside the kitchen window, she went upstairs and looked over her own apartment. She had three bedrooms, one medium and two very small, a kitchen barely large enough to hold a refrigerator and a tiny table, a dining room, a living room, and a bathroom. The walls had been painted many times with dark green oil paint about two-thirds of the way up, and above that, they were cream. The plaster bulged in the center the way she did. The corridor ran almost straight back, but where it made a slight dogleg, an iron ladder went up to the roof. She hung bananas on the rungs to ripen. Underneath the skylight, the wood was dark and the grain was raised like black and furry velvet from the rain that seeped through and dripped onto the floor. No matter how many times she scrubbed the walls with bleach, ferns of mold grew up from the skirting boards in that corner. From the front end of the corridor, a steep staircase zigzagged past Tzila Ruchel's and Dead Onyu's apartments and ended in the claustrophobic foyer. Scooters, a triple stroller, a folding wheelchair, and their shopping carts took up most of the space in the marble-tiled entrance. The stairwell was made half as wide by the automated chair and its tracks.

Though she had a reputation for being a baleboste and her apartment was always clean, it was falling apart. She wanted the rooms to be light filled, painted in the kinds of pastel colors babies are dressed in, fresh and sanitary and safe. The size of the clock and its dark wood, though beautiful, made the atmosphere in her front room solemn. Heavy. She couldn't imagine asking Yidel for help. "I'd like a paintbrush. I'd like several gallons of paint." How long had it been since she'd stenciled the walls in the hallway and polyurethaned the floors herself? The last time must have been just before the birth of her youngest. Nesting. That's what Val called the impulse to tidy and rest and clean and repaint. But maybe there was something toxic in paint that might not be good for the babies?

She put on her slippers, sat down on the couch under the window, and began to say the daily psalms. She added some extra verses for people who were sick, one for a friend whose daughter needed to get married, one for Lipa, who would have been twenty-six on the first night of Chanukah. When she said the chapter for Lipa, something grew in her throat, and she swallowed and swallowed but it would not go down. Did she really want to imitate his secret-filled life, all that running to Manhattan?

When she completed her psalms, she asked God, "What will I do?" She didn't expect an answer and didn't get one, but while she was sitting on the couch, she watched the dust motes floating in the slanting winter light, a constant eddying and turning, the rhythms of which she found calming.

"Mamme?" called Tzila Ruchel, startling her out of a sleep she hadn't known she'd fallen into. Tzila Ruchel had a brochure in her hand. Surie had fallen sideways on the sofa, one round and dimpled thigh exposed above the top of her stocking, her slippers off, a wide gap between her waistband and shirt through which could be seen a white slip stretched tightly over the bowl of her belly. She pulled her skirt and her shirt down and readjusted her turban.

"I want to show you something."

The moment Surie saw the Weight Watchers brochure in her daughter's hand, she had a vision of a particular beggar who sat on an upturned bucket outside the grocery. Though she usually gave every beggar whatever coins she had in her purse and smiled at them and wished them well, this beggar's legs were sunset colored and her toenails curved like golden scimitars. Her flesh was everywhere. There was no containing it. The beggar was a vast desert of despair, waiting for assistance from others instead of working to find her own solutions.

Surie jumped from the couch and jammed her feet into her slippers. "I don't need that silly old thing," she said to Tzila Ruchel as she briskly swept the floor.

There was a smell, much too sweet and catching in the throat, of burned caramel. She had swept the nylon broom too close to the space heater that had almost killed her parents-in-law. If only her daughter had been home earlier, perhaps they could have sat with their heads close, whispering, and her daughter could have put her arms around

Surie after all the secret telling was done, and together they would have figured out the best way to tell Yidel.

"It was all the kigel over Tishrei. And the cake. I won't freeze any next year. I don't need to open a bundt at every meal."

"Oh Mamme, I've upset you."

"Not at all. Just reminded me that I need to be more careful of my weight in the future. Thank you, darling." She swept so vigorously that the air was full of sparkling particles. "I can diet on my own. No need to waste money to have other people weigh me! I'm perfectly capable."

How her daughter would cringe when the twins were born and she remembered this day. Surie swung the broom through the air as if she might be able to sweep away the airborne dust. Her daughter took a step backward. The green linoleum in the kitchen creaked.

"It's not Pesach yet," said Tzila Ruchel, who tried to leave holiday spring-cleaning until the last week and then mostly called it quits after tossing a pillowcase of Legos into the washing machine and bleaching the floorboards. "Why so much fuss today?"

"That's *my* job," said Yidel, coming up from his parents' apartment and reaching for the broomstick. "You hear better, but I see better. You miss the ants on the floor when you sweep."

"You're a good looker," Surie said in English, smiling at him, "but not a good finder." They both laughed. Her body tingled all over and she began humming a wedding tune. He always had that effect on her. Such a lovely man. She knew she was lucky, luckier than many of her friends. She held out the broom and said, "Ready for the mizinkel dance?" At the wedding of the youngest child the parents dance with a broom to sweep out the house after the last of their children leave. For them, there never would be a broom dance, a home without young children. They would likely die before the twins left home. She wished she could spare her children the loss of their parents at a young age. Her parents' deaths had devastated Surie. Her only sister became moody and remote. And her brothers had up and moved to Belgium as a group, to "get away from this depressing place," they'd said.

So Yidel and his family were really the only family she had. He smiled at her slyly, then glanced over at Tzila Ruchel. He took one end of the broom she was holding and began to sway and hum along. "Don't tell your siblings about the shameful mixed dancing you are witnessing in your own home, eh, Tzila Ruchel?" he said. "Family secrets."

"Remember that Purim with Lipa?" Tzila Ruchel said, giggling. Lipa had dressed in Surie's ponzhelo and turban and come out and danced with Tzila Ruchel in full view of all the guests and then quickly scurried back down the hall. The cousins hadn't known it was him, but the family had whooped and chased after Lipa, banging on his bedroom door, begging to take another peek.

"Nobody remembers Lipa," Surie said.

"Stop," said Yidel, holding out a hand as if he could literally stop the flood of memories the way a policeman stops cars. "I don't want to have this conversation."

Surie dropped her end of the broom and went into the bedroom. She opened her purse and looked inside, at the bundle of pregnancy pamphlets. One for each month, detailing the growth of the baby, the new abilities, when the fingernails grew, the hair, the irises of the eyes. Now, the baby was the size of a lemon. Now, a butternut squash. Now, a watermelon. All this from a single seed carelessly tossed into her fallow field.

EIGHT

The next morning at five, down by the river, Surie watched the gulls rising and falling on guts spilled from a tuna cannery. They plunged their heads below the waves and then rose in the air, their backs arched, screaming. Two fire trucks raced by, their sirens blaring. It was probably the matzo bakery. The ovens, on the second floor, were always catching on fire. The gulls plunged underwater again.

Surie couldn't swim. She couldn't fly. She didn't even have the skill of a New York cockroach, which could flatten itself to the thickness of a blade of grass and crawl between two slabs of drywall, exist for months by nibbling the paste that held the wallpaper to the wall, lay a thousand eggs even as it was crushed under a boot. The simplest, coarsest natural thing mindlessly performed its role in life better than she could. If she could end the pregnancy somehow, in a way that wasn't too dreadful, in a way that was rabbinically sanctioned, she would. Would jumping up and down help? Or lying facedown on the floor? Praying? She didn't know. She was afraid to try. She didn't want to do anything forbidden. And the thought of harming a child, any child, turned her stomach.

The gull did not try to change its destiny. It knew only the river, the fish, the stale crust of bread. The cockroach did not fight what it was given. It knew only the wall, the paste, the boot. What did it matter if she was afraid about the birth, the strength she had left to raise the babies, the length of her own life? Why should she keep anything from Yidel, who had only ever been kind? She should be a seagull, brave and determined. She should be a cockroach.

———

When she returned to her apartment, she watered the leggy geranium that grew in a plastic pot in the window and she threw out some of the containers of food that had been too long in the icebox. She made her youngest son's bed and slipped a love note under the seventeen-year-old's pillow, then she took a chocolate cake out of the freezer and went to stand in line for the 8:00 a.m. bikur cholim bus that would take her into Manhattan. Lipa had taken a different bus, or maybe a train, when he traveled to Manhattan. The city scared her. Had he also been afraid?

On her way to be weighed and measured, she paused with her hand on the granite receptionist counter and gave a large slice of the chocolate cake to the secretary, who the previous week had seemed tired and melancholy. "It's probably not the most healthy thing to eat in the morning, but it does taste good," she said. "Chocolate lifts the spirits."

A few minutes later, the secretary—not a small woman

herself—brought Surie a hospital gown in a 5X that would actually cover her bulk. She also brought a spare sheet to act as a shawl were the garment to fail.

When Surie climbed onto the midwife's table and leaned back, Val noticed the gown. "I didn't know they made them so large," she said, plucking at the aqua cotton sprinkled with mauve hippos.

"Live and learn," said Surie, being a cockroach, being a gull. "Maybe you will have another large woman come into your clinic and you will know where to find something that doesn't make her feel like a sardine can wearing a sardine." The midwife laughed, partially because of the strange image and partially because there was a new note in Surie's voice. And Surie had looked her in the eye.

"Why *haven't* you told your husband about the twins?" Val asked. "You're not worried he might . . . hurt you?"

Surie looked over the midwife's shoulder. Lipa sat, watching, on a high stool in the corner, as the midwife listened to the heart tones of the babies using a long wooden ear horn. His own heart beat as fast as an unborn child's. She felt the long silence burning the inside of her lips and she knew a little of what it had been like to be him. Lipa was there and then he was not there, though Surie did not look away from him.

"We are both very busy," Surie said finally. "I'm waiting for the right time to tell him." And to herself, she said, After we talk about Lipa, we will talk about the babies.

The doctor, meanwhile, had been making plans about the best way to keep Surie from the worst obstetric disasters. What if it were his grandmother who had mysteriously fallen pregnant? Naani, who couldn't read a watch but always knew the time anyway? Or worse, his beautiful mother! What wouldn't he do to protect them from harm! But the thought of his elegant, reserved mother having an intimate moment made him squirm and blush, and though he would, of course, be compassionate to Surie and treat her with the respect he'd been trained to give to the elderly, when he saw her in the hallway, he felt his hamstrings tighten, the muscles along his jaw contract, parts that he didn't like to reference during work hours shrivel.

He stopped her. It was imperative, he said politely, that she undergo amniocentesis immediately, perhaps even that same day, before it was too late to make any important decisions.

"The hospital has never had such an aged mother. The oldest mother until now has been a woman who was fifty. And she wasn't delivering twins. It's not an exaggeration to say that it is a matter of national medical interest. I've been discussing your case with my colleagues." The specialist, in fact, had almost bitten Dr. Bhatnagar's head off. He'd been furious not to have been called in from the first day. Naturally, he didn't tell her about the specialist, but Dr. Bhatnagar *did* think Surie would like to hear that rather than an embarrassment, her pregnancy was of interest to many important people.

Surie looked beyond the doctor. She glanced at the doors along the corridor, but Lipa was not there. She

opened her purse. Her son's green glasses were still resting in their Ziploc bag.

"Sometimes . . ." The doctor hesitated, as an unwor-
thy image of his mother floated up in his mind. He felt
like a boy again, crying in the school bathroom, trauma-
tized by the first whispered tidbits about sex. "Not my
mother!" he'd said, and the circle of boys had jeered at
him. He blundered on, telling Surie what the specialist
had said, all the while folding and refolding his hands in
front of his crotch: "We have a film crew on hand for unusual births." Her face was frozen. "And"—he had told
the specialist that no Chassidic woman would agree, but
the man had shouted at him—"newspaper coverage."

She shut her purse with a click.

"Maternal age being such a risk factor these days, and
yet more and more common. New York mothers would
be reassured to think this hospital could manage such
high-risk pregnancies."

She unsealed the Ziploc bag and took out the green
glasses and opened their arms and slid the spectacles up
onto her nose. It was a strong prescription. Her eyes began
to water.

"I wonder," Surie said, pulling the glasses down lower
so that she could look at the doctor over the lenses. The
huge frames in that lurid green looked incongruous on
her pale face, tucked under her modest scarf. "What it
might be like for you to have a film crew there while you
struggle to remove some piece of surgical equipment
you left inside a patient by mistake?"

The doctor's face collapsed like a cake when the oven
door is slammed. Moisture oozed from his cheeks. He

writhed inside his tailored jacket. He was most sorry, but he had forgotten to mention something, he told Mrs. Eckstein. She was this close to preeclampsia. She could die. The babies could die. It happened regularly and to people in much better health than her.

Surie nodded and thanked him for the information. She smiled at the doctor and then handed him the neatly folded gown. She did not wish him a good day, because one does not wish doctors good days. A good day for a doctor means a day with many seriously ill patients.

When she was seated on the bikur cholim bus at 2:00 p.m. to return to Williamsburg, she opened her plastic Harrods bag, broke off a large piece of the leftover chocolate cake, and ate it with relish. Then she offered a piece to the woman sitting next to her. The woman seemed petrified. Her eyes looked at Surie's face and looked away, over and over.

"Are you sure this is the right bus for you?" the woman said. This, though Surie was meticulously dressed in the fashion of the community and spoke the familiar dialect of Yiddish with her companion. It wasn't the glasses. She'd taken them off and put them back inside her handbag.

They didn't know each other—the community had close to a hundred thousand members, and many of the mothers stayed at home. But it seemed that the other woman could not believe that Surie was part of the community at all.

"What is wrong?" Surie asked her. She had taken this bus many times before, and no one had ever challenged her right to be there.

"Where are you from?" the woman asked. "You don't look like anyone I know."

Surie glanced at her reflection in the dark window. There was something unfamiliar about her posture, the way she was holding her head, the set of her lips. And there was some loosening that she felt in her lungs, her chest, that had begun the moment she opened her mouth to the doctor.

"You are quite right," Surie said. "I must have made a mistake. I don't think this *is* my bus." Before the bus could leave, she gathered up her package of cake and her handbag and stood up. She did not feel like the same Surie who had come into Manhattan earlier in the day. She did not feel the same as the woman who had cooked five omelets and brewed a huge urn of coffee that morning. But she could not say in which way she felt different. She thought only that she would walk across the bridge rather than ride in the bus and that the fresh air would do her body some good.

At the center of the Williamsburg Bridge, fifteen minutes into what had turned out to be a steep walk, she turned and peered through the faded red girders. She didn't know much about New York, despite having lived in the city her entire life. Far below, the river moved like a scarf rippling in the wind, rolling over and over itself. It did not look like the familiar tame water at the end of her street.

A lone tourist pointed her camera at a distant building and said, "The Empire State Building!"

Surie pointed her finger down at the water and said, "The East River."

The tourist asked her twice to repeat herself and then, still frowning, walked away. I love you, East River, Surie thought. She broke off a piece of cake and fed it to the

river. "I am trying to love you, babies," she whispered,
and she sank her teeth into the cake.

———

The next week, when she went into the clinic, she asked
the secretary how to correctly pronounce the East River
in English and she listened to the young girl carefully, and
then tried to say it. When Surie spoke, it sounded like *di
est drivver.* "The East River," said the secretary over and
over. She had an accent too, maybe from Jamaica, a little
singsong patois from her part of Brooklyn, the *t*'s strong
and clean. "The Eeeeeeeastt. Rivuh."

For the next couple of weeks, after her checkup, Surie
decided to walk back over the bridge instead of rid-
ing in the stuffy bus, whether it was snowing or a cold
wind blew from the north, with her hands inside the
pockets of her good wool coat and her knitted scarf up
near her mouth, humming a little lullaby for the twins,
"Rozhinkes mit Mandlen," and each time she stood next
to a tourist or a hipster or a cyclist and pointed down at
the river and said, "The Eeeeeeast River." If she looked
out from one side of the bridge, she could see the Empire
State Building. And she could see the roof of her own
building, where, in the sixties, Dead Opa had installed
washing lines for the diapers and racks on which to
stretch the hides and a low iron fence painted red so
that no Ecksteins would accidentally fall down to the
sidewalk.

One Shabbos afternoon in the beginning of her second trimester, Surie invited her family to walk with her
over the Williamsburg Bridge. Her children knew that

sometimes she walked home over the bridge after visiting sick people in Manhattan.

"But is it permitted?" Yidel asked. "To pass from one island to another on the holy Shabbos?"

Tzila Ruchel's husband, a rabbi who taught in the kollel, said that it was allowed. He was much stricter than Yidel in such matters and so they deferred to him. Tzila Ruchel no longer wore a wig under her scarf like Surie and instead wore the holier shpitzel, a piece of unraveled brown silk over padding that looked nothing like hair. She always wore sleeves down to her wrists; she wove rubber through her collars so that they would stand up higher on her neck.

Tzila Ruchel's little daughters grinned and ran for their matching rabbit-fur hoods. They rarely went anywhere besides school and home. The new baby and the two-year-old stayed behind with Dead Opa, who couldn't walk far. Surie held Dead Onyu's hand and led her to the bridge and up the entrance ramp. "Lift your foot higher. There is a curb. A puddle. A dog. A bag of garbage. Bend to the left a little. There is a girder. A cyclist. There, Onyu. Below us, the river is so far down! You can't imagine how far down the East River is."

This was the bridge Lipa had taken on his way to some foreign part of Manhattan, to that glittering stainless-steel-and-glass life he had lived. When he had crossed the bridge, had he looked back toward his house with its crown of red fencing, or had he only looked forward?

"I can smell it," Dead Onyu said. "Like onions and cabbage and the ocean." She smiled. "Like the Tisa! Tell me what you see down there. Are there caves?" Her mother-in-law had walked next to the East River when she could see. She knew there weren't caves, but Surie told her about the long, narrow barges and the stumpy little tugboats and the way the water rippled like a flag in a strong wind. When they came to the middle of the bridge, she pointed down at the river and slowly enunciated, "The Eeeeast River," and Surie's grandchildren copied her pronunciation and giggled.

Afterward, she sat in her armchair and Dead Onyu sat next to her in Yidel's armchair and Yidel sat at the table together with Tzila Ruchel and Tzila Ruchel's husband and their children, and everyone was talking all at once, and laughing, and their faces were bright red from the cold and their ears were red and their fingers were itching, but they were happy.

Dead Onyu leaned forward and sniffed Surie and tilted her head.

"I am not so blind that I can't see," she said. "I've been thinking it for a while, but now I know. How could I forget that smell?" And she smiled at Surie, and Surie was relieved that the old woman somehow understood that she was pregnant.

"Don't say anything yet," she whispered in her mother-in-law's ear. It was an ordinary request, because all of the women of that community withheld the news of their pregnancies from their friends until past the fifth month and even afterward didn't refer to it directly. "Not even to Yidel."

Standing closely so that no one could see, Dead Onyu pressed her wrinkled palm into Surie's belly.

"It's too early," Surie said, "to feel them kicking."

"But you are very large," Dead Onyu said. "*Them?*" She frowned and smiled at the same time.

"Twins!" Surie said. How good it felt to speak about the pregnancy! The East River sweeping New York's garbage out to the sea. She leaned forward and pulled her mother-in-law against her, and for a moment, Surie rested her head on the old woman's shoulder.

"But I can't do it this time," she said, turning her head and whispering into Dead Onyu's ear. "I can't. It's impossible. I'm too tired. I need time. I want to rest." She began, very quietly, to cry. "I'm too old."

"If you don't want to be old," Dead Onyu said, "hang yourself when you are young."

Surie pulled away with a gasp.

"It's just an expression my mother used to say! I'm sorry, darling." Dead Onyu stood up and pulled Surie to her feet. "I wasn't thinking."

"Nobody thinks," Surie mumbled. "Nobody ever thinks . . ."

"Take me downstairs, darling. I need to rest." In a whisper, Dead Onyu added, "Sha! It's Shabbos! No crying." She handed Surie her handkerchief and Surie guided her out into the stairwell.

"Listen, my little lamb, you and Yidel are wonderful parents and that won't change just because you are old." Dead Onyu snorted. "You'll pull yourself together when you need to. Stop that sniffling or the others will be out here in quick time." She slipped the damp handkerchief inside the sleeve of her cardigan. "Didn't your own mother have you very late? It must run in the family."

"After Lipa . . ."

"Shhh, shhh." Dead Onyu put a finger on her lip. "Less said, sooner forgotten."

"Do you have any photographs of Lipa?"

"Why would we keep something we can't see?" Dead Onyu snapped. "Opa and I had already lost our sight when Lipa . . . after California . . . it must be an atonement so that no more bad should ever come our family's way. You know how I loved Lipa, but really . . . such a thing . . . such an evil decree he brought down on us! God forbid the punishment for his actions should land on one of my grandchildren! Opa and I accepted our blindness with gratitude to the will of God for all of your sakes. So let's not talk about that anymore. You'll do a better job this time round." Lipa stood behind Dead Onyu, his face long, his eyes closed, earth falling from his beard. If Surie just reached out her hand, she could hold his jaw in her palm.

"I hope so," she said, her hand skating the nothingness that shimmered where her boy had been. "I just don't know. And I'm so afraid of dying. That's all the doctor ever talks about. Me. The babies. Every single time I see him he tells me some new way I could die."

"And so? What if you do? Dying is not the worst thing."

Surie shook her head. "It is! All I can think of is Lipa on that table. The smell." She had spared Dead Onyu the details.

"Is that why you haven't told Yidel? Because you think you might give yourself an evil eye? Somehow cause yourself or your babies to die? Oh, lamb. You're more likely to have something go wrong if Yidel *doesn't* know. He's so capable. He'll help you through it."

"But the women . . . they'll talk about me behind my back. They'll *laugh* at me. And Tzila Ruchel will be ashamed of me. *All* the children will." Surie sniffed. Yidel stuck his head out the door and raised an eyebrow. She gave him a watery smile and waved him back inside.

"Let them, the yentas!" said Dead Onyu, who still made her own old-fashioned padded scarves out of scraps she cut from ripped curtains and used-up housecoats. She put clean white sheets on the tables every Shabbos instead of the embroidered Swiss cloths everyone else used. She'd never cared what the community thought of her. "Feh! If that's the worst thing they could find to say about you . . ."

Surie leaned in to hug the old woman again. "I love you, Onyu. I feel like you just saved me from . . . I don't know what."

"The eyes are useless when the mind is blind. It's been years since the thought of a pregnancy was on his mind. Yidel won't know unless you tell him. So for heaven's sakes, tell him already!" Dead Onyu patted Surie back into an upright position, as if she were molding a clay model of a proper Chassidic mother. "Make sure you eat your vitamins and a little bit of meat every day, darling," she said. She looked sternly at Surie as if she could see her. "You can kill yourself later."

———

"What a day," Surie said to Yidel as she lay in bed that night, warming her feet between his.

"I can't remember one like it," he said. He touched her cheek. "You're all rosy from the wind. Glowing."

"What do I look like?"

Again, he looked at her and wondered what it was that he saw. Again, he couldn't name it.

"Beautiful as the seven worlds. My wife." Somehow he imbued these words, *my wife*, with great meaning.

"Silly man." She blushed but pressed herself against him. "If you dress up a broom it looks nice too."

"Broom? Who's talking about a broom? You look like a sweet little lobster. Like you've been boiled. That can't be normal." He patted her cheeks. "So red! Are you blushing?"

At the day's end, to talk like this, quietly, before Yidel took out his hearing aids, was unbearably precious, one of the great joys of her life. She knew it. Her belly rose slowly, remained extended for a minute, and then twitched back to its normal shape. Far too early to be able to feel kicks, and yet. And yet. Twins. They were a whole new parsha. She put her hand in Yidel's beard. If he didn't notice the twitch, she would tell him in just a moment.

"You're so patient with me."

"Why wouldn't I be?" he said.

"There's so many things one person can never know about another person."

"Have you been up to mischief? Should I be worried?"

"Always," she said. "You know me. Nonstop trouble. But I'm the one who should be worried. What kind of religious Jew sleeps with a lobster?"

They laughed, but then, instead of telling him about the pregnancy, she began to tell him about what she'd seen at the hospital that Friday, the old woman who had fallen and who had been placed on dialysis, the little child with no hair, the boy who had been hit by a car service and now wore a crown of iron bolts. Just as she got to the end of the tale, she felt the soft puffs of his sleeping breath on her chest. The following morning, by the time she woke up, Yidel had already left for morning prayers.

NINE

Often, in those January weeks, Surie tried to say something to Yidel about Lipa, and then, when she couldn't, when something held her back, her anxiety about the twins increased too. Never before had she kept a secret from Yidel. Never had she felt so lonely or so powerful. Her mouth tasted like ashes. Lying in bed at night, awake hour after hour with the routine aches of pregnancy, she held herself back from speaking, from reaching out to Yidel, who had always been her comfort. Again and again, the words rose into her mouth, and again and again she swallowed them down. Sometimes she knew that Yidel was awake too, but they didn't turn to each other. What kept *him* awake? What were the worries of a slightly-beyond-middle-aged man? She had no way of knowing.

Dead Onyu asked her every day if the babies had moved around overnight, going on and on about what a blessing it was to have twins and how every lady on the street would be jealous of the little bubbelahs in their matching outfits and the brand-new carriage that she, Dead Onyu, wanted to purchase in their honor from the nice shop, the one that sold the European models, and after saying that, she spat three times on the ground to ward off the evil eye. "But why haven't you told him yet, darling?" she asked and asked and asked, and Surie didn't have an answer. Every day, Tzila Ruchel thumped up and down the stairs, glaring at Surie's belly, her mouth in a prim little line. Even Surie's modest sons raised their eyebrows when they caught her picking at a piece of chocolate babka.

The day before Tu Bshvat, right after the children had left for school, she asked Tzila Ruchel what she'd done with all of the photographs of Lipa. It seemed to her that if she didn't find some way to talk about Lipa soon, she would never be able to speak about the twins.

"Who?" said Tzila Ruchel, her face reddening.

"I'd just like to see . . . you know . . . one photograph of my boychik. Where did you hide them?"

"Mommy."

"Is it so much to ask?"

"What we don't talk about ceases to exist."

Surie wanted to strangle her own daughter. If the family talked about Lipa, which rarely happened, it was only sideways, in whispers, when no one else was around. If Surie picked up his prayer book by mistake, she knew it was his because the front page, where his name had been, was torn out. Lipa's tefillin had been given to one of her grandsons after Lipa's embroidered name had been unpicked from the velvet tefillin bag and replaced with the name of the new bar mitzvah boy. But it didn't matter if every trace of him had vanished. Lipa still existed. He was still her little boy. Nothing could erase that.

"Give me the photographs."

Tzila Ruchel wiped her hands down the sides of her face. She took Surie by the elbow and led her down into the basement, to the incinerator. She opened the door and pointed inside at the red flames and the ash rising up the chimney.

———

Surie ran up the stairs and threw all of the photo albums off the shelves. On almost every page, there were empty rectangles under the clear plastic sheets. She turned the pages so quickly that some of them ripped out of the binder. There had to be one image left! Tzila Ruchel stood in the doorway, frowning, her hands on her hips. "Why is this so important to you?" she asked.

"I need them!" Surie wailed, not able to put into words how a single photograph could be a key to life, to health, to a peaceful home.

But there were no photographs of Lipa, not even the edge of his back or a glimmer of his bright eyes peeking from between the other children.

"You're being silly," Tzila Ruchel said, but still, she helped her mother up and into the kitchen and made her a cup of tea and patted her hand, and after she'd taken a few sips, her lovely daughter whispered, "Do you remember when Lipa used to get up in the middle of the night to make gingersnap cookies because he had a craving?"

Surie smiled. Photographs would have been nice. But this was where Lipa really lived. In stories. "He used to make a dozen and take them all into his bed and hide under the blankets and eat them. His payos would be covered in molasses."

"The other boys would be so jealous!" Tzila Ruchel
was still whispering and looking around, making sure
that no one overheard, though who would, in the middle
of the day? "They'd tear his bed apart, hoping to find
crumbs!"

Surie put the molasses and the ground ginger on the
counter. "In his honor," she said.

"Just this once," Tzila Ruchel said.

Lipa, watching from the doorway, licked his lips.

———

On Friday mornings throughout February, when Surie
went to the clinic for her appointment, the midwives
greeted her with a cool familiarity. They still felt, as she
felt, as she *intended*, the distance between their lives, so that
when she saw how they greeted the other mothers with
hugs and high fives and laughter, she felt even more iso-
lated, as if she wore a shroud over the person she knew
herself to be.

Weeks and weeks passed like this, and then, the Friday before Purim, something changed. She had urinated
in the cup an orderly gave her and stood, in stocking feet,
on the scale, waiting for someone to come and record the
numbers. She'd successfully avoided discussing with the
dietitian the amount of cake and chicken fat she was eating. Most of the other women had already checked out
and gone home, but it wasn't yet lunchtime. Val brought
Surie to take a three-dimensional ultrasound.

They waited for a free technician in silence. Every wall
was covered in posters of babies at different stages of their
development, and on the counter was a pink, bulging,

knitted uterus with a doll's head emerging from the neck. The doll smelled of vanilla and did not look like any of Surie's newborns.

"I already took an ultrasound," Surie said when she grew tired of waiting.

"It's a different kind," Val said kindly. "It's not so much for me to see the babies as for you. I think you need a little boost."

"I can wait by myself."

"True. But it seems to me that maybe you do a lot of waiting by yourself." Val turned to look at Surie. "I canceled three clients so I could wait with you."

She put her hand on Surie's shoulder and it took everything Surie had to stare at the floor and close off the well that had opened up inside her chest.

Lying on the table in the dim room after someone finally came to do the ultrasound, Surie drifted toward sleep. As the technician waved the wand over her belly, though, a moving image appeared on the screen. First one baby's face and then the other's. These babies somehow looked like their grown siblings. They looked real and alive and human, unlike the kind of ultrasound she was used to. Their familiar faces lay close together, and one was sucking the thumb of the second, their movements small and slow and somehow sweet to her. Surie was wide-awake and paying close attention to every detail. One baby's legs kicked out and the other baby moved away and flailed with its arms. She could see the movement on her belly. She could see what the movements meant on the screen. The babies flinched and frowned and pouted and smiled. And then the technician wiped off the wand and

turned off the machine and it was over and Surie had not
wanted it to end.

"They can hear me now," she said softly. "I sing to
them sometimes. Do you think the sound from the wand
could ruin their hearing? They made tumblesauces away
from it whenever the technician tried to get a closer
picture."

Val leaned forward and for the first time she smiled a
wide and genuine smile. "How did you know that?" she
said. "Have you been reading one of those pamphlets I
gave you?"

"No," Surie said. She hadn't even taken the pamphlets
out of the plastic shopping bag. She'd dropped them into
the incinerator when no one was looking. "We believe
that unborn babies hear and see everything the mother
does, and mothers try to listen to peaceful things for the
sake of the new child. I would rather limit what waters I
sink my child in. The sound of a bird singing, yes. Looking at private parts, at kishkes, no."

The midwife nodded. "We are the same, you and me,"
she said. "Because I want to protect babies from unnecessary interventions. I remember delivering your children
by candlelight. It was very peaceful. Those were good
births. And your babies were very calm babies. I miss it."

Surie was surprised. The midwife had delivered all of
Surie's other children at home. This time she'd been told
it wasn't an option. *High risk.* She'd assumed Val still delivered other women's children at home. But Val had
stopped doing home births entirely! "Why did you stop?"

A shadow blew across the midwife's face. Her lips
puckered and darkened. The policy change hadn't been

her choice. As the most senior midwife, she was required to work in the high-risk clinic. In one more year she would retire and she would be glad never to see another cesarean, another mother bent over a pillow, her back bared for an epidural.

"By law, all babies in New York City are supposed to be born in the hospital."

Surie, still lulled by the semidarkness, turned over on the technician's table to look at the midwife. "You did not answer my question."

"Babies are supposedly more likely to die when they are born at home."

"You didn't tell me that when you delivered the others in my bedroom. And babies die here in the hospital too, I'm sure. With children so small, the Angel of Death has easy pickings." His sword was always raised, ready to harvest, and not just the weakest. Oh, how she knew that now. Ever since Lipa. How quickly death came.

"If it were up to me, I'd prefer to deliver most of the women at home, but it's not up to me anymore. The hospital where I had my backup doctor went bankrupt. The medical association is very powerful and convinced all of the local hospitals not to support home-birth midwives, and these days, women who want a home birth have to do it illegally, underground. Parents who have bad outcomes sue. The doctors go after the midwives for practicing illegally and take away their licenses. The cost of malpractice insurance is crazy. Bottom line, I want to help pregnant women and I have to eat." Val sighed. She picked up a pen and put it down again. "But even if I could, I wouldn't deliver you at home, Mrs. Eckstein. At your age, there's too much that can go wrong. You need to be near an operating room and a good surgeon."

Surie gripped the railing of the table and pulled herself upright. "I didn't realize how many rules you have."

"Did you think you were the only one with strict rules?"

Surie almost laughed. "I see you looking at my scarf, my clothes. This." She brushed her hand across the nylon bangs. "I don't know why it makes me like you more, to know you have all kinds of crazy rules too, but it does."

"Misery loves company," said Val, and then Surie did laugh.

That morning, fully dressed and on her way out the door, she'd stopped to pull two trays of kigel from the hot oven and the steam had fused one side of the fringe into a sticky brown mass. The bus was leaving and it was either go out with a melted front or stay at home all day. Just wearing a scarf was not an option. A scarf with a front was her family's custom. She wore it. Dead Onyu wore it. Except for Tzila Ruchel, her daughters wore it. Her daughters-in-law did too. Marriages were made based on adherence to this custom. People would stare at her, but they stared at her anyway. "I never said I'm miserable doing what I do, but"—she batted again at the melted wig—"sometimes . . ."

Val glanced at Surie's forehead. "I wish I knew more about your world."

Surie didn't know how to respond to this invitation. It was forbidden to proselytize non-Jews, to tell them details about religious practice. Maybe it would help another woman, though? Maybe it would make Val kinder and more understanding toward the newly married ladies from the community who came to the clinic? And though she could barely admit it to herself, it had been a long time since Surie had felt seen. It had felt good to laugh a little about her burnt wig with somebody who knew she was expecting twins.

"If you want," she said, and then she bit her thumbnail very hard and tore off a chunk, "you could visit this Sunday. It's a holiday, Purim, a good day to come." She felt a chill rush of heat, thinking about this merging of her two worlds, and then an additional flush as she remembered the difficulty involved in inviting the midwife to her home. "If you do come, though, say that we volunteer together in the main part of the hospital. Please."

Val, seeing Surie's red face, frowned. "You still haven't told Rabbi Eckstein?" She began to giggle. "Is he on night shift or blind or what?" She spread her hands to the sides of her hips to suggest Surie's enormous belly.

"I told his mother, my shviger. She actually *is* blind, but she figured it out herself."

"I'm not going to tell you your business, but I think you're digging your own grave if you don't say something to your husband soon." And then the midwife said a harsh word that Surie knew was obscene, so she erased it from her mind.

———

That Sunday, a crisp early March day, the midwife dressed carefully in opaque tights and a long skirt and a black turtleneck and she took the B44 bus from the leafy, single-family Victorian houses of Ditmas Park, through Flatbush's narrow, dark red two-story duplexes and up Nostrand, along the edge of the gracious brownstones of Crown Heights. The bus bumbled through Bed-Stuy, with its street vendors and boarded windows and mothers walking to church with their children, the little girls with dozens of brightly colored plastic baubles in their braided hair.

In Williamsburg, the streets were full of men pushing baby strollers and children in costumes towing wagons full of food. Music blasted from trucks and vans. One group of about thirty young men, all dressed in gray lab coats with bright orange hats, grabbed some policemen and danced with them in the middle of the road. Cars beeped their horns, trying to pass. The young men ran to the cars and gestured for the windows to be rolled down and then extracted donations from the drivers. Laughing children sat in the front seats of the private ambulances that lined the roads and pressed the buttons that worked the sirens. On every corner, there were clusters of men and boys holding out plates with money on them and passersby quickly dipped into their wallets and threw down coins as they passed.

Val, who had scribbled Surie's address on an appointment card and thought she remembered roughly where the Chassidic woman lived, had to ask for directions multiple times. Everyone, it seemed, knew the Ecksteins. She rang the bell and climbed the three flights of stairs that Surie climbed every day. Ten years earlier, she would have visited a pregnant woman several times by the fifth month. She would have seen the track of the lift chair. She would have noticed the steepness of the stairs and that they smelled of oil soap and weirdly of chickens and something dead or decomposing. At the top of the steps, Surie waited for the midwife. She wore a long white apron over her usual black skirt and a light pink cotton turban instead of her silk scarf. Without the strip of fake hair, the many lines of her face and her gray eyebrows were prominent. Here, in her own house, she stood straighter; the fabric ran smoothly over her body, her eyes were full of laughter. Surie and Val stood on the landing together for a moment. Val wasn't sure if a hug was appropriate or wanted. The building was full of sounds. Children's voices, the calls of the elderly, telephones ringing, the clunk and hiss of the steam.

"Have you ever been in a Jewish home on a holiday before?" Surie asked, and Val said she had, but not the home of a Chassidic person. In the foyer on the ground floor, Val had noticed a sign from the local rabbinic organization banning children from owning bicycles and another one with an edict against noisy high heels.

They went into Surie's apartment and a grandchild dressed as a bride jumped up from the couch and came and put her arms around Surie's leg. "Tsatskeleh di bubbeh!" Surie said, kissing the child's head. What did it mean? Val asked, and was told "toy of the grandmother." So strange.

Someone who could only be Surie's daughter, for she looked exactly like her but in a more trim, less neat version, gave Val a cellophane package of fruit and cookies, saying it was something that sounded like "shuluch muh-nes" from her mother. It was strange to think that at some time in the distant past, Val must have brought this woman into the world as a naked infant. And was she supposed to open the package, eat the fruits? She looked around. There were literally hundreds of wrapped packages on every surface. None of them were open.

In the narrow kitchen there was no space for an extra chair, so Val leaned against the counter, staring at Surie's grossly swollen ankles. Surie could almost hear the midwife checking the boxes for eclampsia: Elevated blood pressure—check. Water retention—check. High percentage of body fat—check. Swollen extremities—check. But Purim was a time for joy, for happiness without limit. God would not allow her to die on such a happy holiday.

Surie stirred several huge pots on the stove. She threw a handful of salt into one that was full of a bubbling red sauce. Cabbage rolls and chunks of apple bobbed on the surface. The room filled with steam, the window was open; there was no electric range hood, but a box fan was brought in and propped up in a second window. The cupboards were the metal kind, from the forties or fifties, still spotlessly clean. A girl who looked about ten years old carved produce at a tiny kitchen table using a razor-sharp knife, but she worked with a skill that Val herself did not have, cutting tomatoes into royal state carriages, carving apples into swans to draw the carriages, radishes into rolypoly infants. She turned curiously as her grandmother began to speak in English.

"Soon, everyone will arrive. My whole family comes to me for the holidays. We bring Dead Onyu and Dead Opa upstairs." And then, seeing Val's puzzlement, Surie added, "My parents." She looked up, searching for the correct phrase on the ceiling. "In-laws. They do not speak

English and they are blind, so they will not speak to you. Don't be insulted."

Today, even Surie—disconnected, anxious, exhausted Surie—looked happy. Three teenagers in long coats and plastic cowboy hats—Surie's sons?—came into the kitchen firing off cap guns. One called out, "Giddyup!" and they all burst into laughter before noticing Val and falling silent. They gathered up armfuls of the wrapped packages and left again. The doorbell rang and rang, and costumed revelers arrived to sing and dance and perform small plays for the family, and when they were finished, Surie's husband wrote them checks and handed out shots of whiskey. Outside, hundreds of sirens went off, police and fire trucks and other unfamiliar ones; a wild cacophony of beeping and wailing and roaring rose up from the street. Inside, Val startled when the enormous old clock at her back loudly struck the time. Women climbed the stairs and handed Surie's daughter elaborate baskets of food that she gave to her mother, and then Surie gave her daughter small baskets of home-baked treats to give to the women. It was obvious that she was important in her community. Some of the younger women—it was hard to say if they were relatives because they all looked so alike—asked Surie questions about the laws of the day and she gave her answers in simple language, clearly and well.

"The children are wild animals today." She did not seem upset about it. "Full of sugar and high spirits. The women get to show off their baking. The men, though they do not drink the rest of the year, drink glasses of the brown stuff, the white stuff." She gestured at inexpensive bottles of whiskey and vodka. "Today they all have flies in their throats and want to drown them. They sing and hug each other and tell the story of Purim, which is the story of the survival of the Jews. The same story from the Holocaust, the same story from the Cossacks, the pogroms, the Spanish Inquisition. But fresh, somehow, in each generation." Val asked why Surie didn't hand her guests the parcels directly but instead had her daughter hand them over. Surie smiled but didn't offer any explanations.

Soon, Surie's oldest son arrived with his family, and he banged on the door to the living room and yelled at the women in Yiddish. He'd said for them to tame down because he would be reading the megillah, Surie translated. Then there came a chorus from the young men standing in the dining room. "Nushim, zeit shtil!"

"I need to learn them some manners," Surie said, laughing, when she saw Val's face. "They have no geduld." Surie herself seemed infinitely patient. Val was already exhausted from the noise and the crush.

Some of the women and girls moved toward the door to the dining room, but Surie put her hand on Val's arm. "Stay here with me. I already heard it, and you can hear from the kitchen if you are interested." Val was relieved because the dining room and the living room were crowded with children dressed in costumes and identical pregnant mothers and terrifyingly identical fathers, and even the elderly all looked the same, as if the community consisted of black-and-white cookies made by a machine on a conveyer belt. *Chunk, chunk, chunk.* They all looked at her when they thought she didn't notice and then looked away when she turned to look at them. Surie must have felt like this each day when she came into the clinic. All those women in lipstick and jeans. The midwife, intimidated, thought about excusing herself and going home.

Val took a deep breath and looked around again. There was not one pregnant mother over the age of forty-five. Poor Surie. No wonder she hadn't said anything. In this community, in this place, everyone followed an invisible pattern. Surie didn't fit in at the clinic either, but pregnant at fifty-seven, she'd be anathema in this community that so valued sameness.

They were not alone in the kitchen. The terrifyingly thin grandmother crouched like a gargoyle over the counter, braiding dough. When they were introduced, the woman's face turned fifteen degrees away from where Val was standing and she smiled at the empty air and nodded her head and put out her hand, and Val remembered that the old woman was blind. Dead Onyu, not dead, just the name for "great-grandmother" in Hungarian. Then she was introduced to Miryam Chiena, the granddaughter, who was picking thrips off strawberries with a pair of tweezers and drowning them in a glass of water. And still Val did not have a chair or anything to eat, though every room she had passed through was full of food. Despite the bounty, nobody was eating or drinking. Not even a glass of water. And she saw that Surie was watching her, waiting for her judgment. Sure of rejection.

From the other room came the song of the scroll, the megillah, so strange to her ears, an unearthly wail, more in keeping with the call of the mu'addhin than with the Lord's Prayer. The children, even the babies, were silent, listening to this ancient story. Without warning, the room erupted in hisses and clangs and shots and horns and boos.

The granddaughter banged the heel of the knife on the board. Several babies burst into tears and were shushed. The grandmother smacked two cans together and cackled. She had no teeth. Surie wrote something on a notepad and pushed it across to Val. "They are drowning out the name of Haman, who tried to murder the Jews."

At lunch, when everyone was seated around three long tables, Val felt comfortable for the first time. It was a feast. The windows were open to the cool breeze from the river. Simple white muslin curtains bellied into the room. The men sat at the table in the living room. The women sat with the children at the two tables in the dining room, closer to the kitchen. Four courses came out and a dozen different desserts. The children ate everything and then lay on the floor, playing the games that children play when they are utterly content. The doorbell rang, people arrived and left. The family laughed and told jokes and sang long songs without words. Surie, seated next to Val, translated some of what was said into English so she would understand.

"Missus Val from the hospital came to see us, how it is to be us," Surie announced in English after they had sung the final blessings. There was a long silence.

Then Miryam Chiena, the girl with the knife, said, "It's good to be us."

Dead Onyu, the great-grandmother, upon hearing a translation, said in Yiddish that she was too old to figure out what it was like to be herself. She just was. And if you were going to be like someone else, then who would be like you? She stood up with a groan and said she was going to go downstairs to sleep off the big meal. Surie led Val to the south-facing front windows and Miryam Chiena joined them after helping her great-grandmother go to her apartment. They all stood back from the glass to avoid being seen from outside and looked down into the street.

The road was blocked and no traffic could get through. Shopping carts and strollers were pushed straight down the middle of the street by people dressed in all kinds of elaborate costumes. There was a wheelchair that had been decorated as an old-fashioned popcorn cart, and inside it, surrounded by the popcorn, the head of a small child turned and laughed as people approached. A young man covered in purple balloons like a cluster of grapes wheeled a barrel full of bottles of wine. A father led six daughters all dressed identically as brides into the new apartment building opposite Surie's house and then they reappeared briefly in a window on the second floor. A real beggar in a broken hat and fallen stockings came down Division, weaving from side to side. Every Jew went to him and put coins in his hand and gave him food.

Later, they saw men performing a kind of line dance to raucous klezmer music from a boom box. "It's a wedding dance. That boy"—Surie pointed to a boy with a few tufts of red beard on his cheeks—"just got engaged. He's my brother's wife's cousin's nephew." One group pretended to be the young man, awkwardly meeting his bride. Another group pretended to be the blushing girl. The groups ran at each other, making their twin gestures of shyness, the "girls" twirling their braids, tugging at invisible dresses, the "boys" stroking their beards; the two groups almost but not quite touched hands, retreated. Then they were at the wedding. Then they were married.

Then they were pregnant. And then they had a baby in a carriage. The men laughed. Surie laughed. But Val suddenly felt annoyed by the restrictions of the religion, as if she were somehow being forced to believe as the community believed, live as they lived.

"Even your dances are about marrying and having children," she said. "Is there nothing else to look forward to?"

"What else is there?" Surie asked. "The whole life of a Jew is devoted to family. There is no end to that cycle. Think of Dead Onyu. In another community, she would be in a nursing home, alone. No one would know that she makes excellent poppy-seed jam. Instead, here, she is loved. She is treasured. Her great-grandchildren sit in her lap every day. She will never be moved to a nursing home because there will always be someone to take care of her."

"Are you sad to have another child?" Val asked.

"Children?" And Surie's face flushed carnation pink as she twisted around to see if anyone had overheard.

"*If* I could have another child, it would be a blessing. Every child I am given is a blessing from the Oibershter," Surie said. "But of course I won't. I'm much too old." She glared at Val, who looked at her watch and then out the window.

Surie's granddaughter Miryam Chiena, who was standing with them, said, "I want to be a teacher *and* I want to be a mother *and* maybe I'll be a lady Hatzolah person too, but so far they don't let girls, so I probably won't, but I definitely want to be a teacher and a mother. Are you a mother?" And when Val shook her head: "Are you sad?"

Val looked at the child. Surie thought that the midwife's apartment must be silent. She smelled faintly like empty rooms. Even the people who lived on either side of her probably didn't know her name. What a life! Surie was relieved that her grandchild had not understood the midwife's comments. She leaned down and kissed her granddaughter and her face was hidden. "When I am old," Surie said to the child, "you are the one I want to take care of me, as I take care of Dead Onyu and Dead Opa now."

"Everyone wants to take care of you, Bubbie. We fight over you! But I will be the one who wins."

On the way to the train station, Surie and Val did not speak. When Val was about to go through the doors, she felt compelled to turn and face Surie. The Chassidic woman's confidence in her world was troubling. Did she really think that it was enough to just be a mother? Didn't she ever have questions she wanted answered? Didn't she ever want to get out of her chicken-scented house and discover the real world? "Miryam Chiena, is that her name? She's so bright. Don't you want her to go to college? Have a career of her own? She could easily be a doctor, never mind an EMT. And what about your new babies?"

"Miryam will always be surrounded by people who love her and so will the new children. That's something special." Under the overpass, a group of men sat on the cold concrete, bundled in blankets and newspapers. One of them was erecting a tent that flapped wildly in the wind. A tall, thin man in colorless clothing held up a piece of cardboard on which he'd written HOMELESS VETERAN. WILL WORK FOR FOOD. Surie walked over to drop a quarter in his cup and then, when she returned, she said, "My children and grandchildren will always have homes."

"But what if," said Val, "what if one of your children turned secular? Or turned out to be a Hitler or an Osama bin Laden?"

Surie grimaced. "So extreme!" she said. "Can't you think of anything more reasonable?"

"Okay. What if you had a son who was gay?" Val said then. "Do you know the word *gay*? Could he live at home? Would you still love that child?"

Surie's face felt like a stone and a cold, sharp wind ran between her ribs. "He would still be loved."

"But isn't it true that your community in Williamsburg rejects children like that? That's what I've heard. Kids who stick out for one reason or another?"

Inside the pocket of her coat, Surie squeezed the lime-green glasses so that the metal hinge dug into the palm of her hand. She shook her head.

"They do! There are articles in the papers about it. There was something just the other day, a writer who said he'd been 'raised like a veal' and then slaughtered when he didn't fit in."

The glasses were cutting Surie's flesh. Hot wetness slid over her freezing-cold hand.

"If that's not conditional, what is? 'Be like me and you will be loved.' Isn't that your belief?"

Surie brought her hand out of her pocket and wiped the blood on the black wool coat. She coughed from the hard bite of the wind. "I had a child who was both gay and not religious, and though he pushed me hard, though everything he did felt like he took a razor to my flesh,

I could not stop loving him. And if I had the chance again, I would bring him home and put him to sleep in the best bed, and I would tell him to bring home his boyfriend and I would tell all of my children and my grandchildren to smile at him and to love him and never to stop. And that is because a parent's love does not end. Should not end."

"You have a gay son?"

"Had."

"What happened to him?"

"He is lost, farloiren, he has lost himself to this world and the next," she said, very slowly. "He is wandering somewhere, and I only rarely see him."

"Well, that's exactly what I mean. Your community spits these kids out."

"It wasn't like that for him." Surie wiped her hand again. It would not stop bleeding.

"Don't you want something better than a community like that for your twins?"

"I will make sure that doesn't happen to them," Surie said. "I don't know how I will, but I won't lose another child."

Surie stood like a pillar in the train station, someone people thought they knew everything about—a foreigner, a fanatic, an anachronistic joke, an uneducated mother. Even her family thought they understood her. The wind from the incoming train flattening the ugly coat against her round belly, tickets and gum wrappers flying into the air, the smell of ripped steel and rat dung and loss. She raised her hand and moved it sideways once and then turned and walked away.

TEN

In mid-March, the young men began to return home from their faraway yeshivos and mesivtas and kollels for Passover. School was let out from the beginning of Nissan and the streets filled with children pushing other children in strollers or carrying home dripping paper packages of fish for their mothers. Older girls who would soon be engaged walked hand in hand, their heads close together, their thick braids down their backs, swaying. The smells of bleach and polish wafted from the open windows. Tulips bloomed in the rough grass of the empty lots. Men ran through the streets, their tzitzis flapping, their arms piled with boxes of freshly baked matzos, and in the space created from their passing lingered the scents of well water and wood smoke and flour.

Hugely pregnant women in their ninth and tenth months rested on the benches in the weak sunshine without shame, talking amongst themselves as their other children played at their feet. Though she was already at the end of the fifth month, between visits to the clinic Surie often forgot that she was pregnant. It felt so distant, something that was both true and not true, her and not her. She'd started a story about Lipa at the Shabbos table and Yidel had walked to the front closet, taken out his overcoat, and left the building. Two weeks before Passover, when she was buying horseradish and potato starch and coconuts, she'd asked him what he wished he'd done differently with regard to Lipa, and he'd said the sort of obscene word his father sometimes said and asked her to stop, but then, when she hadn't, he'd left her with two heavy carts in the middle of Lee Avenue. As a result, the secret of her own pregnancy had become like a stubborn walnut that would not be cracked, no matter the pressure.

She could not imagine a time when she would ever tell Yidel. Even as she grew larger and larger, even as her feet swelled and she had to remove the wedding ring from her finger and slip it onto the necklace inside her shirt that held Lipa's nipple ring, even as she was no longer able to reach the faucet, no one noticed what seemed to her to be obvious. Perhaps it was her age. Or her large girth to begin with. But most likely it was because she had not said anything, and her family could not believe she would ever withhold anything from them.

In bed a week before Pesach, Yidel even felt the twins turn under his arm, but he only frowned and moved away from her, saying that she should not eat so many macaroons if they caused her gas and that there was nothing less romantic than a woman making a bad smell in bed. She hadn't said anything and the moment, like so many others, had been lost. And now she lay on the far edge of the mattress, turned away from him so he could no longer place his arm around her waist as he had always done.

It was odd, this dark thing, to hold herself away from the person she was forever bound to and loved. Lying on the far side of the mattress and rejecting Yidel's arms should have made her sad, but instead it filled her with a curiously tantalizing sense of power, something almost like a piece of meat stuck between her teeth that she could worry at all night.

"Do you love me?" he murmured into the darkness. It had been months since they'd lain together. He approached, she rebuffed with excuse after excuse. They'd never gone longer than a month or six weeks in the past.

"Love is good, but it's good with bread," she murmured. The expression accidentally made it sound like he wasn't a good provider, so after some little mew of disappointment from him, she said, "Of course I do. Love you."

The deep wish to tell him about the twins filled her, rushing into her like water into a jug held under the surface of a pool, but still she didn't say anything. There were two desires twisting within her, to tell and not to tell. To blurt out the secret and be free or to hold the secret and hold a shred of power. The stories about Yaakov and Eisav were alive for her then: Yaakov wanting to be born when his mother, Rivka, passed the synagogue; the other twin, Eisav, bearing down when she passed a place of idolatry. What had the matriarch Rivka done? Surie wished she knew how to study the Torah herself. But girls were not taught, and though she could read the basic story in her Yiddish, *Tzeina U'Reina*, the commentaries, where the helpful insights would be, were beyond her ability.

———

The final Friday before Passover, when Surie was about to enter her sixth month, Val told her that there was a woman from Israel in the clinic who required a procedure. The woman didn't understand a word of English and Val had not been able to make her understand. They had Hebrew translators in the hospital, but this woman spoke only Yiddish. Would Surie mind coming to help her?

Surie protested that her own English wasn't the best, but in the end, she agreed to translate for that woman and for another woman a bit later that day, and by then, she had already missed the bus, so she stayed and said she would translate for the last patient of the day. Could she please go to the room at the end of the long hall and ask for some basic information? "She doesn't have a file?" Surie asked, and Val said no, not yet. The patient hadn't been willing to talk to any of the less senior midwives and Val had not had a chance to try yet herself.

When Surie reached the closed door and listened from outside, she heard nothing, and when she entered the examination room she saw only a young girl dressed in the style of her own community, sitting with her hands folded in her lap, her fair hair held back with the type of padded headband used by very young children. No one was with her.

She was a refined girl, lovely even, her hair in a shoulder-length bob, her hands smooth with lavender-scented cream, her flat black shoes spotless. She sat with her back against the chair, her head high but her eyes downcast, and at first, Surie did not recognize her.

"Where is your mother?" Surie said. "Or your sister?" An older woman, a relative, must have gone out to the bathroom. But no mother in her community shared news about a pregnancy with an unmarried daughter. Who would bring a teenager to a prenatal checkup? She looked at the girl, puzzled, trying to figure out what was going on. The part of her that had been born in her community and would die there, the part of her that was connected to the oldest mores and traditions of Jewish life, refused to see what was right in front of her, just as Yidel could not see *her* pregnancy because he assumed she could not be pregnant. She stood at the doorway, waiting for the child to say something. There was only silence. After many awkward minutes, the child slipped off the chair, and in the strange twisting motion she made as she stood, Surie recognized her own gesture to balance herself, to offset the change brought on by a growing pregnancy. Inwardly, she complained to God. Was it not enough that you gave me twins? Was it not enough to take Lipa? Was it not enough to send me here, where I deceive my husband every single week? You have to send this child to me too?

The girl looked up because Surie had said some word of complaint in Yiddish. When she recognized the sofer's wife in her silk scarf and her dark taupe stockings, the old woman's bare face without a shred of makeup, the girl's eyes grew wide and fearful.

"Excuse me, Rebbetzin," she said in the mother tongue. She made as if to leave, and Surie silently cursed God and Val and men everywhere and the innocence of young girls in particular.

"Wait," she said, catching at the girl's arm. It had been years since the girl had come as an eight-year-old with her mother to buy new mezuzahs. She couldn't be more than thirteen now. "Don't go. It is braver not to go." What could she possibly say to this child?

Like a dragonfly hanging motionless above the hot summer pavement, the girl hovered between sitting and darting toward the door, both options equally possible. Surie sat down on the rolling stool next to the examination table as if she were sure the girl would sit too, and gradually the girl's fear subsided and she sat. She did not ask the girl's name because she already knew it.

"Does your mother know?" she asked. She could not see the girl's face now because the child had taken off the headband and twisted it between her hands and her hair fell across her face like a screen. And she couldn't quite picture the girl's mother either. Had there been something not quite put together about the woman? A dirty scarf? A crumpled dress? "Does anyone know besides you?"

The girl shook her head.

Surie was full of questions it was too soon to ask. Who could have done this to the child? How did the girl know that she was pregnant? How did she find the hospital? How had she enrolled herself in the clinic? How had she managed such a difficult thing when no one would have helped her with information? How had she gotten out of school for the day and paid for the train? What would happen to her when she returned to her school and her family?

"You must despise me," the girl whispered, and Surie searched around inside herself and realized that she did not. What she felt was closer to despair and a deep sadness for the child and for the child's family and for the community, for they would never be able to accept such a thing and would vomit her out.

"Here," said Surie, "I have some salt crackers left over from lunch. You feel sick to your stomach, yes?" She touched the green glasses she kept in her pocket, then pushed them aside and took the crackers and held them out to the girl.

"If I eat, I will get bigger," said the girl, "and then everyone will know. But when I don't eat, I feel so sick. Do you think it would kill the . . . could I kill it if I don't eat?" She asked this hopefully, unaware, almost, of what she was saying.

"Don't open your mouth for Satan!" said Surie. "No. No, I . . ." She hesitated, but this girl deserved nothing less than absolute honesty. "I am also pregnant." Such eyes she had, this child! "And, as you might imagine, I cannot tell anyone. Different reasons, but I know how it feels." The girl nodded. "When I found out I was expecting twins . . ." Those eyes again. "I hoped the same thing. I tried not to eat for as long as I could. But babies"—the girl flinched at the word—"are stubborn. You will harm yourself long before you harm the fetus. The baby." She touched her own belly. Translation. Always translation.

The girl pushed the cracker into her mouth, took it out again and said a blessing, then ate it quickly. She brushed the crumbs from her skirt and sat up straight and put the headband back into her hair.

"Twins! You're lucky! My mother always wanted twins. The babies will keep you young," she said. The traditional blessing for a woman who has children late in life. "Excuse me, but do you have any more crackers? I'm hungry all the time." Perhaps the girl had moved out of the first trimester and into the second. She was terribly thin, but beneath the loose school cardigan and the plain blouse, Surie thought she could see a roundness to the girl's stomach.

Surie went out into the hallway and came back with her Harrods bag full of chocolate cake. "Help yourself," she said. The girl took out a thick slab of cake and devoured it.

The babies *did* keep her young. Surie was far busier than she'd been for years. She woke up earlier, worked all day on her feet, and with it all, she felt lighter, healthier, more alive. She smiled. When they were born she'd be busier yet, but she'd built up some stamina in the past months. The hipsters wouldn't believe their eyes when they saw Surie taking daily five-mile walks with the twin stroller. And they thought *they* were fit! She laughed out loud and the girl looked up from her second slice of cake.

"Rabbi Shimon ben Shetach once tricked eighty witches into getting caught and hanged," Surie said. She wanted to offer the girl something better than crackers and cake. Better than the late confession of an old woman. "Eighty! Just think about it. Witches are so wily, so clever, maybe they even see the future. Yet one man who wanted to trick them into losing their own lives was able to do it. *One* man could trick eighty witches! For sure one man, if he wants something, will always find a way to do it."

"It wasn't one," the girl said. She swallowed some more of the cake. "It wasn't once."

"Can I get you some water?" asked Surie, who suddenly felt dizzy, as if the floor had tilted slightly and everything was at odd angles. "An orange juice? It's kosher."

But the girl had come to tell her story to someone, and

now that she had said something, she could not be stopped. The story spilled out. Surie listened. She felt frozen on the tiny, unstable rolling stool.

The father of the unborn child was an unlicensed therapist, a Chassidic man well-known in the community, who worked in the main girls' school. He was someone Lipa had gone to speak to about his own issues; she'd planned on sending Mattis to talk with the therapist about his problem. Mattis had been caught by the principal of his school, looking at the magazines on the racks near the subway station. The therapist had a good reputation, but this thing between him and the girl had been going on for months.

Could this man have touched Lipa too? Such a man would be capable of anything. Had he made Lipa gay? They'd forced Lipa to go to therapy once a week for years, even though Lipa had pleaded with them not to send him. Had he said something, once, about the therapist? That he'd made him undress? Or was she imagining that? It couldn't be right. Or was she only able to remember with this child in front of her, the proof of the therapist's wrongdoing permanently carved into the girl's tender skin? What a terrible mother she'd been. But it seemed she had learned something in the past four years, and though she hadn't treated Lipa with compassion, she could start with this girl.

She stared out the window, and of course it was raining. It was always raining. She could just see the tops of people's heads as they walked past, precariously balancing umbrellas and cups of coffee, their glasses steamed over so that their eyes were no longer visible. Cars hissed by, buses, and the sounds they made were hoarse and disturbing. In the fractured light under the clouds, their colors seemed unbearably garish. Their windshield wipers flicked sprays of water toward the pedestrians. One man walked past carrying a boom box on his shoulder. It was covered with a grocery bag, and the window shook to the bass of whatever growls it was making. It was as if the world had been shaken and refolded and now the dark inside seams were showing.

Poor Lipa. She had tried her best, but she had failed him in so many ways, ways she was only just now beginning to understand. He had definitely come in one day after therapy, deeply weary. Not the tiredness that all of the boys carried with them from long days in yeshiva studying, but a weariness that was inscribed on his young face, permanent. What made him look that way? She had known even then that she would never hear the whole story of his life. Of anyone's life, really. So much of a person's life is hidden from even her husband, her best friends, her children. A whole world of thoughts and images that no one ever knows about. Had Lipa wanted to be hugged? Had he wanted a kind word? Had he just wanted her to notice him? Had he wanted her to see that something was wrong? In just such ways had she failed him. Simple ways. If she had only taken the time to listen to him.

She put her hand in her pocket and touched the green glasses again. After a moment she took them out and laid them, folded, on top of her belly as if it were a shelf. The girl stared.

"Those are a nice color," she said. "Like grass, in the spring, when it's all new and fresh, you know? If I have a boy, I'm going to make him a onesie in that color. Can I touch your tummy?"

"I don't know. Maybe? Yes."

The girl put her small hand on the front of Surie's dress.

"It's hot!" she said in surprise. "And hard!" She pulled away her hand and touched her palm against her cheek. "Do they move around? Can I feel that?"

"They aren't moving right now," Surie said.

"Is that all right?"

"I think so." She hoped so. She should have Val check the heart tones after work. "I heard that babies move less when they are closer to being born."

"How do you know when the baby is going to come out? The due date?" The girl said "due date" as if they were words in Chinese and full of unpronounceable syllables.

"Do you know the date of your last menstrual period?"

Almost eagerly, the girl sat up and answered and then she listened and took notes in her school notebook. She was in the fourteenth week, due exactly two months after Surie. The conception must have taken place on Chanukah. Surie gave the girl a Ziploc bag of expensive kosher prenatal vitamins from the bottle in her own handbag and told her where to buy more.

"We could choose a name for your baby. A boy's name for a boy. A girl's name for a girl. You wouldn't have to tell anybody or even write it down, but it would be something to hold on to. Would you like that?"

The girl nodded shyly but said, "I thought we aren't supposed to name babies before they are born."

"It's not really naming. It's just imagining a bit. A nice kind of imagining."

"Did you do that for yours?"

Surie paused. "No," she said. "Not yet." She paused again. The girl looked toward the Harrods bag and licked her lips. Surie laughed. She was filled with love for this young girl and for the girl's baby and for her own twins. "We could talk about names together. We wouldn't need to say which ones we chose. How about that?"

———

"Where is the girl that came in earlier?" Val asked later, her big hands flapping. "I can't find her."

"She's gone. I spoke with her and she didn't agree to have an internal examination yet, and anyway, she needs an adult present, so I made another appointment for her and sent her home. I know where she lives. If she skips the appointment, I will bring her with me on the bus."

"I'm disappointed that you didn't ask me, but I'm also impressed," Val said. "No one else could get a word out of her. She'd been sitting there for an hour when I sent you in. Who's the father?"

Surie hesitated. The reputation of Chassidic Jews would sink lower if she revealed how the pregnancy had happened. "It is a miracle that she came in at all."

"Did you talk to her about the possibility of an abortion?"

Was that part of Val's job? Surie would never discuss such a thing with anyone. It was forbidden even to kill wasps on a holiday, flies on Shabbos, spiders. Even in her worst, most desperate moments, early in the pregnancy, she hadn't considered that word she didn't even like to think.

"Killing an unborn child is murder."

"But how will she bring the child to term? What is she? Twelve? Thirteen? Surely that will be worse for her?"

"She's already in the second trimester. There's nothing to talk about, so stop. Her parents will send her away to be a 'mother's helper' somewhere and the baby will be adopted, and it will be hard, very hard, on the girl. Or if her mother is young enough and fat enough, the family will say she is the mother of the baby. The girl will be able to stay in the community and she will eventually get married and have more children. It's not a perfect solution. But I don't think there is a perfect solution."

"But was it her father? Or a brother? An uncle? You shouldn't have let her leave the clinic until we made sure she was going home to a safe environment."

Surie shook her head. "It was a therapist. In the school."

"Oh my God!" Val cried. "I have to call ACS." Then, seeing Surie's blank expression, she said, "The Administration for Children's Services. They have to arrest this maniac before he hurts anyone else." She lifted the phone, but Surie put a hand on hers.

"Wait," she said. "Let me speak to the family. I'll call the community police too. He'll be watched."

And after speaking with the girl's mother, then what? Would she dare go to the home of the therapist, to make sure that he really wouldn't hurt any other children?

His innocent wife would let Surie in and offer her Passover cookies with a look of puzzlement. What's wrong? she would ask. Can it wait? And Surie would say no, it couldn't wait, and she'd take a bite of the biscuit, which would taste of dry potato starch, and she would have to gag it down before telling the therapist's wife and the woman would probably not believe her and would already be calling the police when the molester arrived home from baking his matzos, right as Surie would fly at him, screaming and crying. She'd scratch his face. She'd throw the yarmulke off his head and tear handfuls of his beard out in both of her fists. At first, she'd be yelling about the little girl, but in the end . . .

My son, she'd cry, my son, my son, my Lipa.

———

The clinic closed for the day and Val and Surie walked out onto the wet sidewalk, the awning dripping cold water down their necks.

"I told that girl I am pregnant," Surie said.

"She doesn't need to hear about your life, she needs help," Val said. "Listen, if the girl's parents know what happened and they are still sending her to the therapist, they are hurting her and will be liable in court. I need to know how seriously your community will take this—can the Chassidic authorities lock him up? What's the plan? How old is he, anyway?" She looked at Surie, frowning, but Surie looked away.

In his sixties. He'd been seeing Lipa when he was in his fifties, but now the therapist was totally gray. Most of his kids were married off. She regularly saw him walking down Lee holding one of his grandsons' hands. The filthy beast. Maybe Lipa would still be alive if she hadn't relied on him to fix her son. If she'd just listened to her son the way a mother should.

"I'm upset too, Val. To my knowledge, this is the worst thing that's ever happened in the community. You have no idea of the tumult it's going to make. I'm going to bring this girl's story to the rabbis and tell them the name of the therapist, but I'm scared. It's risky for everyone involved, and the last person I want to hurt is that little girl." The rain trickled down her spine, so cold. "Please don't tell anyone until I've had a chance to tell her mother and the rabbis." Though she wouldn't go to the therapist's house and tear out his beard, she was going to write a letter and leave it in his mailbox and she was going to ask what, exactly, he had said and done to the girl. And to Lipa. She remembered the way he had sneered, passing them, after Lipa had come home from his arrest. The hypocrite!

"I can't wait," Val said. "I am a mandated reporter and this is a matter for the police. The girl is so young. How would you like it if you sent your own child to this man and she came back pregnant?"

Surie's son, hanging from the tree, the rope tangled around the branch, the sun just rising over the mountains, the jogger running on the hard dirt path.

"Pregnancy," Surie said, "is not the worst thing." She had to hold her elbows tightly to keep from walking away.

———

It was getting toward evening and the bridge was empty of pedestrians. A strong wind was blowing, and the water in the East River was rough, and the tugboats rolled in the swell. The sky was dark gray and it was bitterly cold. The wind tore through her coat, which had been warm enough in the morning. She leaned over the railing and looked down at the black water. Could parents ever get it

right? If she failed her children, she'd always thought she
could send them to counseling or therapy or one of those
special schools. But you couldn't rely on other people to
fix your mistakes. It was better not to fail in the beginning. By the time she got home, it was well after dark on
Friday evening, too late to light the Shabbos candles, and
when she came in, Yidel burst into tears.

"I didn't know what happened to you!" he said. "I
thought you were, chas v'shalom . . ." After checking that
no children were nearby, he put his arm around her and
drew her close. "I couldn't bear it . . ."

"I was safe the whole time," she said into the cave of
his warm, familiar neck.

"Shabbos HaGadol, Surie! What were you thinking?"

"Yidel," she said, taking a small handful of his beard
and giving it a shake, "while I was at the hospital, something very terrible happened."

He'd been the head of a volunteer ambulance organization for years. What could be so terrible that he hadn't
already seen it? Until the moment she opened her mouth,
she thought she'd tell him about the girl. But how could
she have been a witness to such a thing? As a volunteer
food distributor?

In whispers, she told him about holding the hand of a
dying woman. Lipa, leaning against the wall, frowned.
One of the unlit candles fell out of the candelabra and
rolled under the breakfront. Lipa's outline faded. The last
part of him to disappear was his left eye, which watched
Surie for a while and then blinked and was gone.

———

Saturday night, Surie sat up late composing a letter to the girls' school that employed the therapist and a second one to the rabbinical court. She provided all of the details she'd heard from the girl, but she did not write the girl's name. Neither did she sign her own. She wasn't afraid of anyone recognizing her handwriting, since none of her family members served on the beis din. She put on her coat and walked up Division to drop off the letters. The school was closed, but the rabbinical court was swamped by Jews with last-minute questions about Passover. In the hallway, she sat on a bench and watched as her letter was plucked out of the mailbox by one of the gloomy male secretaries and taken into the inner sanctum. Men and women and children continued to flow in and out of the poorly lit waiting room. After an hour, a different secretary came out of the room, carrying a wastebasket. On a torn piece of paper, her handwriting.

She left the building, angry, and called the Community Watch from a phone box in the street. Holding her sleeve over the receiver and doing her best to imitate a Bobover accent, she reported the therapist to the Chassidic police.

———

Later that night, Val called Surie at home.

"I've already spoken to the Community Watch and the rabbis," Surie said. "And I'm going to see her parents tomorrow morning. Please wait on making your report until the community has a chance to respond." If only she'd had some warning before the cyclone that became Lipa's last months. "The mother deserves that kindness."

"Thank you." Val sighed with relief. "Listen, I'm really glad you are helping out here. It's awkward, you know. I don't really understand how things work in your world. And I know I can be a bit gruff at times. Truthfully, there'd be nothing to report if that girl hadn't stayed and spoken to you," she said. "In fact, today was the smoothest clinic of any in recent memory."

There was a long silence. Surie closed her eyes and waited.

"Would you consider doing this regularly? As many days as you can come in? I'm fairly sure I can get you about fifteen dollars an hour."

She'd been certain Val was about to tell her she'd called the ACS and that Surie was in trouble for failing to report the crime in a timely fashion. "Not next week," Surie said. "It's the holiday."

"You can't come in for a whole week? What about your appointment with the doctor on Friday?"

With fifteen dollars an hour, Surie could buy the twins some fresh outfits and a crib they could share. Maybe she could even put some money toward a helper for the girl, for after the birth. She wouldn't have to ask Yidel for anything.

But that Sunday, she was too busy with the last-minute preparations for the Seder to go talk with the girl's parents.

———

Surie, dressed in her holiday clothes, anxious and sweating, took a taxi to the hospital first thing on Monday morning, the eve of Passover, wondering what had happened over the weekend. Val had filed the report on Sunday afternoon, the moment she thought Surie had spoken with the girl's parents. Sunday evening, Surie had lingered near the windows, but she hadn't heard a commotion on the street. Yidel had not come home from the evening prayers buzzing with gossip.

Though it was scandalous to leave Williamsburg on erev Pesach, she felt a responsibility toward the girl. Yidel would not be able to find his freshly laundered holiday clothes; the boys would be fruitlessly searching for the cases of wine, wanting to open the bottles before candle-lighting; Tzila Ruchel would ask a rabbi if Surie wasn't to be fully trusted with the grandchildren, since she had gone to Manhattan for no good reason on the eve of a festival. *Like a goyta.* But Surie wanted to ask Val if other children had come in from the community with a similar prob-lem. If what the girl said was true, there must have been others.

Val's eyes grew wide when Surie walked into the clinic.

"I thought you said you couldn't come!" She smiled. "Isn't it Passover tonight?"

Surie had finished cooking a week earlier. She'd set the tables for the Seder the day before, and after sunset followed Yidel and her sons around the house with bees-wax candles and wooden spoons and feathers, searching for crumbs.

Around ten that morning, Val called her into an exami-nation room to assist with a secular couple, people whose first language was English.

"Why?" Surie asked. She didn't know anything about

science, about anatomy. Her only useful skill in this hospital was Yiddish.

Val said she didn't just need a translator. Really, she needed an additional physician's assistant, but the budget didn't stretch that far. The clinic needed many extra pairs of hands. If Surie was going to be here anyway, could she maybe learn to assist with some of the easier jobs? And more important, Val said, the patients seemed to relax more when Surie—awkward, old-fashioned, otherworldly Surie—was in the room. Val also wanted Surie to be around other pregnant mothers, happy mothers whose delight and acceptance might rub off on Surie herself, transform the pregnancy into the kind of joyous event that the others had been. But Val couldn't say that to Surie, so she said instead, "I don't really understand why, but the women like you so much."

"It's because I'm a mother," Surie said. "They trust me. That's why that girl spoke to me when she wouldn't speak to anyone else." The headband twisting between the girl's hands, such small, pale hands. "Nothing against you, but that orange hair doesn't exactly inspire confidence." Val almost shouted with surprise, and then they both laughed.

Just before lunch, she told Val, "I have to leave now, but in the future, I could come every day. If you want."

"Two conditions," said Val, holding up her fingers. "You have to tell your husband about the twins and what you are really doing at the hospital. No secrets. And I need you to keep on talking with the mother of that girl. They are all going to need a lot of support. Are you up for that?"

Surie nodded. Despite the lack of obvious response to her letters and telephone call, she still felt sure she could help the girl get the care she needed while somehow shielding her from the kind of idle gossiping that had killed Lipa. "Thank you for waiting to make the report. It's really helpful to the family."

Val was glad she'd waited and followed Surie's lead. She didn't want to set off a cascade of unpredictable consequences. "I'm grateful," Val said, "that you were willing to speak to her parents. What did they say when you told them?"

Surie glanced at her watch, though there was no bus scheduled for that day. "Oh my goodness!" she said. "The bus will be here any second! I have to run. Happy holiday!"

———

On Thursday morning, the first of the intermediate days of the eight-day holiday, Surie found the girl's address and walked up Division for fifteen minutes, to the far end of Havemeyer, where there were a series of Section 8 apartment buildings that were full of wailing music. Bizarre garments flapped out of the windows and smoke that smelled strangely like skunk filled the hallways. The girl's father was the janitor of one of these places. After asking a woman for directions, she found him, jacketless in the basement, sitting with his feet up on a pipe coming from the side of an old boiler. "Cup of tea?" he offered, and then poured some hot water from a tap he'd welded into the side of the tank. "It's Pesach'dik." He was nothing like Yidel or any of her sons. No one she knew would offer another man's wife a drink. "Is something the matter?" His face was almost obscured by steam. Being in this dark, enclosed space with a man she didn't know felt wrong. There were definite laws against it. She backed out toward the door and told him she was looking for his wife. He pulled a walkie-talkie out of the rafters and pressed a button. "Says to go on up," the man said. The entire time, he had not looked at her. He spoke quickly and wiped his dirty hands on his trousers, clearing his throat. Surie had never visited this family. They were far from her social circle, the kind of outcast family she might, because of Lipa, because of the twins, have to consider as matches for her granddaughters.

Upstairs, the girl's mother looked at her through the peephole for a few seconds before opening the door. "A gitn moed, Rebbetzin!" she said. "I'm so surprised!"

Surie didn't quite know how to open the conversation. She couldn't compliment the apartment, which had a yellow-gray ring around the walls a few inches above the baseboard, like an unwashed bathtub. She couldn't compliment the woman, who was wearing a speckled housecoat, a turban, and flattened felt slippers. There were no babies in the house to tickle, no food on the table, no curtains, no tchotchkes of any kind.

"I saw your daughter," she said.

The other woman smiled. "Which one?" she asked. "I have seven."

Surie said the name of the girl and the woman's smile faded. "What now?" she asked, sitting quickly on the corduroy-covered daybed. "What next?" She put a hand over her eyes. "Where did you see her? Was it a boy?" she whispered. "We sent her to see someone, but she won't stop. She tells me she's going to a friend's house to play, but she lies to me. She lies! I'm sure, honored Rebbetzin, that your refined girls never lie to you! She has to follow the rules, but she don't follow the rules, and she's a whore, I tell you. I catch my daughter on the phone past midnight, and women come to me, telling me such stories about her. The principal of the school . . . ach."

"She's twelve," Surie said. The little girl with her headband, her soft, fine hair falling in front of her face.

"Thirteen."

"Not yet. Her birthday is in two months."

The girl's mother nodded. "Sometimes I get the dates confused. I'm not that great with numbers."

"At twelve or thirteen, a girl's mother is responsible for where she is, what she's doing, who she is with, *what happens to her*." Surie paused. "I was at the hospital . . ."

The woman began to breathe very hard and she clutched at her throat. A thin whistling sound filled the room, like the scream of a boiling kettle. She fumbled for an asthma inhaler and took two quick shots.

"You sent her. Am I right?"

The woman's eyes darted left and right and she blinked rapidly. "Maybe?"

"Don't try to pretend you don't know that your daughter is pregnant. Just tell me if you stopped her going to see the therapist. Did you tell the school there was a problem?"

"What therapist?" the woman said. "She has a boyfriend. She's a bad girl. She doesn't know how to listen."

"It was him. The therapist," Surie said. What a world! It seemed it was more damaging to one's reputation to admit to having a therapist than to having a boyfriend!

She felt as if her skin were not connected to whatever was inside her body, and none of that was connected to the part of her that could think. She looked around the room again. Chair, table, laundry basket, pegs. Only then could she feel her toes inside her orthopedic shoes. Never in a million years had she imagined having this conversation with someone, and she felt, sorely, her lack of preparedness, her inability to help this woman or her child in any real way. "She doesn't have a boyfriend. She told me she told you but you didn't believe her. But it was the therapist. I am sure. She told me details . . ." The woman's face. Surie stopped. She put out her hands and took the woman's in her own. "But just tell me that you will tell the court what you know. That man is stealing the innocence of our children and if no one is willing to state the truth, nothing will change."

"He's the best," the woman whined. "That's what the school said. We didn't have insurance, but my husband took on another building and I was babysitting for a while, just so she could go to get psychologized and learn to be like the other girls. Normal." The woman pulled away. She picked up the asthma inhaler and turned it over and over. "What will happen to my other daughters? They will never get married! If anyone hears . . ."

"Every family has secrets," Surie said.

"But some secrets are worse than others!" the woman shrieked, and Surie had to acknowledge that it was true.

———

When Surie arrived home, she telephoned Val's private number. "The mother knew," she said. She didn't tell Val about the way the woman picked at the flesh of her wrist or about the smell of rodent droppings or about the sense she'd had that the girl was standing someplace very close, unable to speak.

———

The next day, on Friday, Surie went to the clinic, though Yidel had hoped to take a family trip to the Brooklyn Botanic Garden in honor of the holiday. The men on the floor panting with their wives in the labor classes reminded her of Yidel's sweating face as he'd pleaded with her. How would those women like their husbands panting in their face during actual labor? They would be screaming for the men to get out. Better to be honest from the start.

She wandered from room to room, picking up discarded items and putting them in their proper places. She wiped down counters and organized vials. Every so often, Val would call her into an examination room and ask her to help with something. Most of the time, Surie stumbled through whatever it was. Urine sticks. Fundal height. Due date calculations. "I'm training her," the midwife told the patients. "She's going to be the first Chassidic midwife in New York." It was a joke, but not a joke to Surie.

"They arrested that man, but I just got word that he is already out on bail," Val said at the end of Surie's first full day as they were sitting with their feet up in the lunchroom. "A million dollars' bail and your community raised it in a single night for a pedophile who has been molesting their children for twenty years. It's obscene."

"It's not him they are protecting. It's the reputation of the community." The emergency fund-raising party had been called that Thursday night, right after the school had fired the therapist. Surie had refused to donate any money, but she'd had calls from friends who said that her absence had been noted.

"And the girl has gone into hiding."

Surie nodded. It was true. The moment she had left the apartment in the projects, the girl's mother had called a distant aunt and spirited her daughter away. The child had missed her Friday appointment and now Surie had no way of knowing if she was getting prenatal care.

"That bastard won't be prosecuted if no one else comes forward to say, 'Me too.' It's the word of a young girl against a respected elder. No one will take her side. But I heard that the mother is going to court to support her daughter. The father refuses to have anything to do with it."

Surie was surprised. What had changed the mother's mind about the girl? Usually, no decent family would go to a secular court about such a thing. But the girl's family were already regarded as strange. They weren't related to anyone important; there were no rabbis or sofrim or teachers in their family lineage; the girl's sisters would marry garbage collectors, janitors, the children of the man who moved the Porta-Potties from place to place. There was no one lower in the system than they were already, so what did they have to lose? Nothing. Exactly nothing. Even today, if someone were to ask Surie to testify against Lipa's therapist, she would refuse. Though she had lost so much, there were still further depths of alienation that she didn't want to explore.

Lipa sat opposite her, his mouth open, his teeth showing, his fists up beside his head. It looked exactly as if he were screaming but she could hear nothing. She closed her eyes and opened them again, but Lipa was still there, his mouth still open. She shuddered. Was it true? Would she, through her silence, side with a molester instead of with an innocent child?

"So, you told him everything?" Val asked, and Surie faltered for a second and said yes, yes, of course she had. She had no idea what Val was talking about, but she knew the answer should be yes.

Val stared at Surie, her eyes sweeping across the other woman's face, and then she shook her head. "Here," she said, hanging an old stethoscope around Surie's neck. "Watch and learn. When taking a blood pressure reading, you have to listen for the slightest difference, a faint tapping. The change is so tiny, you might not even notice if you aren't paying attention."

Surie tried to pay attention, but her mind was elsewhere. The girl's mother had probably had a nervous breakdown. This was why she was willing to testify. The mother, the whole family, the girl, they were all damaged goods, like the crushed cans of beans Surie was afraid to open.

Before coming in to the hospital, Surie had gone back to the squalid apartment to try to talk with the mother and make sure the girl was getting prenatal care. "Just tell me she's seeing a doctor," Surie had said to the peephole. She could hear someone breathing on the other side. Down the hallway, a door opened a crack and a woman's face peered through. It was 6:00 a.m. "At least give me your sister's name!" The shwush of an inhaler. Surie banged again. "Where is your daughter?" Another door,

another face. Erev Shabbos in the mikva, the men would
be saying that Rebbetzin Eckstein broke down a woman's
door, that maybe the Rebbetzin needed a little rest somewhere upstate.

———

Surie had thought she'd have time over Passover to tell
Yidel about her own pregnancy and about working at the
hospital, but instead, she'd spent most of her free time
worrying about the girl. Working at the hospital was
ridiculous. Look what kind of horrors she was exposed to.
She couldn't keep this up. Why had she ever thought
working with Val would be acceptable?

But Tuesday night, immediately after she turned her
kitchen back to normal and trudged out to buy a bag of
flour from the non-Jewish grocery, Surie baked a chocolate cake to bring to the hospital the next morning. Yidel
told his friends that his wife was getting very active in the
bikur cholim—she went every day and didn't come back
home until after three!—and that there was no bigger
mitzvah than comforting the sick. By Wednesday evening,
Yidel arrived home with a new pair of orthopedic shoes
in her size and he gave her his old pager so that he could
reach her if needed. He left a little pile of her favorite
chocolates under her pillow that she flushed when he
wasn't looking. "You're like the Rebbe's wife," he said.
And upon his face shone his pride, a pride she didn't
deserve.

———

That Friday, after telling a Chassidic couple in their
forties from Borough Park that they were expecting IVF

triplets, Surie and Val sat down together in the break room. There were thirty minutes until Surie's own appointment.

"I feel ancient. And so tired." Surie eased her foot out of her new shoe and rubbed her calf. "I don't think I've ever stood on my feet so long. And definitely not when I am twenty-five weeks along!" She sipped from the little thermos of tea she had brought with her.

"You really need to eat more," Val said. "Your babies aren't growing very fast."

Surie barely noticed the weight of the twins. It was as if they were floating along together with her, buoyant. She thought she might call one Frimet, if it was a girl. If one were a boy, Hirshy would be a good name. Val peeled and ate an orange. The room filled with the bright smell of citrus.

"You were very good in there, Mrs. Eckstein."

"Really?"

"Yes. I think she was on the verge of hysteria, happy and afraid all together. And you were very comforting, with the Yiddish and the practical advice." Surie didn't know much. She often mixed up the vials, the labels, the paperwork. She dropped things. She mispronounced basic terms. But the pregnant women *did* love her.

They leaned back in the cheap plastic chairs and Surie tried not to look pleased.

"I bet it's the first time she's ever seen a Chassidic woman who is a midwife! She looked so surprised when I came in. She gave me the once-over. You know . . ." Surie looked from the top of Val's head down to her toes and back up to the top again.

Val smiled. "Did you just call yourself a midwife?"

"Yes. Yes, I did." Surie's face bloomed.

Val smiled even wider. "I'm proud of you, Mrs. Eckstein."

"For goodness' sakes," Surie said. "Nobody calls me that. It's Surie."

ELEVEN

The Friday after Passover, the high-risk doctor had insisted on meeting Surie for her preadmission checkup at the clinic. He was a new hire, a young man who was afraid to appear soft and less adept. After one of his first patients had asked him his age and when he'd graduated, he'd grown a mustache, decided it wasn't enough, and added a beard. The old doctor, his mentor, had retired after forty years and moved down to Florida. Initially, the new specialist had tried to flirt with the Chassidic women who came to the clinic. He was a good flirt, a handsome man who liked women, but they didn't even smile. Their little hats and the strangely stiff scarves they wore seemed like helmets, the women themselves like soldiers in some silent army. They wouldn't shake his hand, even though his fingers had been in far more intimate places. Why had he studied so long, practiced his bedside manner and received As, only to land in a hospital with people who would not speak to him or meet his eyes? He only wanted to help! He wanted to save lives! But these women didn't listen to his advice and they ran to their holy rabbis for

every little thing, and then they came back and said that
they couldn't do what he recommended.

He particularly hated their physical examinations.
Their stricken faces as he probed. He felt like he was rap-
ing them. With time, he became angrier and less talkative
and more brutal. Suspecting that half the time they didn't
even understand what he was saying, he no longer gave
warnings of what was about to happen, and from the
break room, where Surie was chatting with Val, she heard
a woman cry out, "Gottenyu!" Maybe she should go home
and miss her appointment? Inwardly, she cursed the
dreaded doctor with thunder in his belly and lightning in
his pants, before knocking on the door of the examination room. She asked if she might come in and translate,
which really meant explain to the woman all the things
that the doctor did not say.

Afterward, when it was her turn, she had to peel off
two layers in order to lie down on the table: the first, the
professional sense of capability and calm remove she had
in the clinic; the second, her fantasy that she was not really
pregnant, just getting fat in her old age, a belief that served
her well in her apartment in Brooklyn but was not helpful at the clinic in Manhattan.

She asked the doctor if she might remain dressed and
take off only her underthings, but he said no. From experience, she knew it would not make a difference to his
examination. Val always allowed her to maintain her modesty. "Everything off," he said from the corner where he
was washing his hands. He left the room for a moment
and then came back in while she was fully exposed, struggling to put on the tiny hospital gown he had provided.

Without asking, she pulled several yards of crackling white paper off the roll at the head of the examination table and used it to cover her arms, her chest, her backside. Then she sat on the end of the table, her feet dangling.

"There are many risks when an older woman decides to get pregnant," he said to the air somewhere over her head. "But you're not the oldest Jewish lady to get pregnant. There was a woman in New Jersey, a therapist, who was sixty and had twins just a few weeks ago."

"Dr. Frieda Birnbaum. It was in the newspaper. But I didn't do IVF. It just happened."

"Listen, Mrs. Eckstein, the likelihood is good that we will end up with gestational diabetes, placenta previa, preeclampsia." He squeezed her ankle. Yidel had also recently squeezed her ankle, but his touch had been so gentle.

"What is going on with your feet, dear love?" Yidel had asked. "Maybe your stockings are stretched out? Do you want I should get you some new ones? How about a massage?" He'd begun already and she lay back against her pillows and sighed with relief. Each dimpled foot had a turn in his lap. He'd walked his fingers around her ankles and then milked each bone, each toe, each tiny joint, until she'd tingled all over. And never once had he raised the possibility that she might be pregnant, and never once had she, either. He couldn't have missed the signs. He must know! He must be waiting for her to tell him, growing more and more disappointed as the days passed. Yidel was not as blind as his parents. It had turned into a silent power struggle, this wanting him to say something before she had to tell him. How well can you really read my body? How well do you actually know me?

"I'm pretty sure we'll be doing a C-section here. And we have to worry about an increased risk of ovarian cancer, uterine hemorrhage. Dr. Bhatnagar tells me we are still refusing amniocentesis. Well, what if our babies have birth defects? We're talking Down syndrome. And worse. Can we understand what is being said here? Should I speak slower?" the doctor said, speaking louder and just as fast. It was only because Surie had begun trying to read Val's books that she knew what the man was saying. She felt even more sorry for the woman who had gone before her. And she wished a sweet death—being run over by a sugar truck—upon obstetricians who used the collective "we" when they really meant "you." The doctor wasn't pregnant. She missed Val. She even missed the regular man, Dr. Bhatnagar.

The specialist tinkered around. A door slammed. He drew a line on her belly with his finger to show her where he would make the cut if (when) a cesarean became necessary. "After so many babies, your uterus probably doesn't have the coordination to push out twins." Overextended. Placental insufficiency. Geriatric pregnancy. Preterm labor.

It didn't matter what happened to her or to the babies. Their births, her own health, it was all in God's hands. Only those without faith worried about such things. Either there would be a disaster or there wouldn't, and stressing oneself, worrying about it, wouldn't change a thing. It might even be harmful to the babies. The doctor pressed his hands around the babies' heads and wiggled them from side to side. It hurt. Surie wanted to kick out, she wanted to grab his hand and push it away. But instead, she began to silently mouth one of her favorite psalms.

Val came in and reminded the doctor that Surie was helping them at the clinic, as an intern. He frowned and looked down at Surie in surprise. "Who decided that?" he asked, as if it had been a bad decision on someone's part. "I did," Val said. "We are woefully understaffed and the majority of our patients don't understand the medical terms we use." She stared at the doctor until he looked at his hands, which were still spread on Surie's belly.

"We should be gaining a pound a week from now on," muttered the doctor. "Maybe even more than that. It wouldn't be the worst thing in our case, because these babies are very small. Of course, with such a large mother, it's hard to tell exactly due to the panniculus. Place your legs in these stirrups, please."

Surie was rowing down the Tisa River. A thick fog blanketed the water and muffled the sounds of the villages she passed. The boat in which she lay wallowed in the swell caused by a larger boat going in the opposite direction. A foghorn. A dog. A herd of goats. Tinkling bells. Small wavelets plashed against the wooden sides of the rowboat. The water gurgled and chimed. Smoke from many woodstoves hung below the fog, wet and dank. She slid past a cormorant sitting on a pylon. He, like her, hunched over his belly, black, sinister. Her dreams, recently, had a darker edge to them. Underneath her bottom, a small amount of lukewarm water slid from one side of the boat to the other, wetting the back of her clothing. From far away, she thought she could hear men on other boats calling to one another, but it was faint and distant and difficult to understand.

"Well, there's plenty of room in there, at least," said

the doctor, wiping his fingers on a paper towel and snapping off his gloves, inside out. "Everything looks good."

"Can Val deliver me? When it's the right time?" Surie asked. The doctor was already halfway out the door. He turned back.

"This is a high-risk pregnancy," he said. High. Risk. Emphatic.

"Yes," said Surie. "But can she? You could be right there." She wanted Val's gentle hands on her children.

"Impossible," he said. "Dr. Bhatnagar and I will be delivering these infants. And we will make a public announcement about the birth if everything goes well."

"No, I already told Dr. Bhatnagar that I don't want that, and he said . . ." Surie didn't remember what he'd said. She imagined Yidel out with his shopping cart, stumbling upon a newspaper showing her with twins, two-inch letters announcing the birth in graphic medicalese. "I don't allow it! Any of it!"

"If that's your decision," he said. He flicked a finger against the frame of the door as if he were getting rid of something unpleasant and then left.

Sitting outside, on a plastic chair, was the girl. She was back in New York, recalled from wherever she'd been by ACS and the police and who knew who else. She was waiting for an appointment with Surie's doctor, and from the look on her face, she had overheard their conversation. She tilted herself to stand and then came over to Surie.

"Rebbetzin," she said, slipping her small hand into Surie's, "will you come in with me? Will you tell me what the doctor is saying?"

And though it pained Surie to see the slim body of the trembling child in the much-too-large gown, to see the twelve-year-old climb up onto the examining table and put her feet into the stirrups, though Surie had to wipe her eyes every few minutes, she sat there and rendered the doctor's words into something resembling kindness.

———

Shabbos came in after 7:00 p.m. in mid-April. After scrubbing down the counters at the clinic, Surie washed her hands and put on her woolen coat and tried but failed to fasten the buttons. She stood in the empty waiting room, and after a moment, Val came out to join her.

"Why are you still here, Nurse Eckstein?" she asked.

Surie had been upset since lunch. "I can't read those textbooks you loaned me. I read English like an ax swims."

"You don't have to. There's a program for lay midwives. Midwives who have learned by doing, rather than by studying. It's how I started, though I'm a certified nurse-midwife now. If I teach you and you keep on working at it, I am sure you could get a lay certificate."

Surie was afraid of certificates. Secular education had a stink to it—you give the devil a hair and he wants the whole beard.

"What's that face?" asked Val. "How far do you plan on going with your education?"

"No one will take me seriously. People do not think Chassidic Jews can read or even speak English. I see how some of the patients laugh at me. The way I pronounce words. I can't even say 'doctor' right." *Daktir.* "My clothes. No one will trust me to deliver a baby. And bottom line, soon I won't have time to do anything. I'll have babies to take care of." Surie sighed.

She would miss the mental stimulation. It was almost unbearable to listen to her old friends talking about the most effective ways to remove a stain from a tablecloth or the best methods for cooking a moist chicken.

"Then you won't do it. But in the meantime, until the birth and *maybe* afterward, you are learning something."

Coming to the hospital, learning midwifery, it was all temporary. Something like the way other women craved fried ice cream or pickles. To continue studying afterward would be to divorce herself from her community. And that Surie would never do.

"Aren't you enjoying yourself? I could be wrong, but you really seem happier. You helped that family today. You've been trying to help that little girl. You will help other women in your community either way."

It *did* feel good to get up each morning with somewhere to go and something to do that wasn't what she had been doing for forty years. Surie loved seeing the women come in deflated and leave pink and glowing. She loved to see the looks on their faces when they heard the heartbeats of their babies, the fast lub-dub echoing throughout the room. Women came into the clinic and signed in and sat down and other women left. Doctors were paged over the intercom, and just outside the windows, cars rushed past, their tires hissing in the heavy spring rains. Surie had even enjoyed her efforts to track down the aunt in Monroe and the missing girl, though they'd been unsuccessful. The police also couldn't find the girl. Surie wondered how she'd been caught.

It was the first time in her life that she wasn't afraid of everything outside her community. Instead of her usual terror, there was this new thing, a cautious curiosity about the world.

———

When she arrived home that Friday, Yidel had already heated up some soup and cut up hothouse tomatoes and laid everything out neatly on the table next to a glass of orange juice. He sat beside her as she ate and then put his hand on the back of her neck.

"I thought you might be hungry, so I made you an erev Shabbos snack. Schlepping around the hospital all day like that with heavy packages. It's a lot for a bubbie," he said when she finished. "I ordered you some of the good support stockings at the pharmacy."

Her great betrayal of this gentle man ballooned in her throat and she hung her head and began to cry. He might not have even known she was crying except that her tears spread like dark stains on the white damask cloth.

"What's wrong?" he asked, standing. "Is something the matter?"

She shook her head. "I'm just tired," she said. "And there's so much sadness in those hospitals."

"We are so lucky, you and I, to have our health."

She cried harder.

He put his arms around her awkwardly, from behind the chair. "Maybe you shouldn't go to the hospital," he said. "You've always been so sensitive. I know you love to help and to do kindnesses for everyone, but you have to take care of yourself as well."

"Oy, Yidel, loz mich tsu ru." She shook him off and put her head down on the table.

He paused, a long pause, and then very softly asked, "Is it that sickness? Did it come back?" The cancer. She laughed with anguish.

"Women in my condition," she began, "we are extra emotional. It's hormones. That's what the doctor said."

There had been a time, after Lipa, when she hadn't been able to get out of bed, and then, when she had finally emerged, the sight of the hipsters walking down Lee Avenue had caused her to burst into tears. "I killed him, just as surely as if I put the noose around his neck myself," she'd said to Yidel as he loaded her into the chair lift and followed her up the stairs. In those days, he'd thought that the slightest wind would blow her away. Or at least blow her into Bellevue.

"Are you talking about when black pepper grows?" he asked her now. It was their private euphemism for menopause. "Is that why the tears?"

"I'm fine. Really. You don't have to worry about me so much." Oy. It was all so complicated! Why didn't she want to tell him that, on her worst days, when she was tired and stressed and afraid, she saw Lipa leaning against a cabinet, walking down the street, playing his violin in the living room? Maybe if she told Yidel about the twins, or about Lipa, her son would no longer make his appearances. She didn't want to risk it. Seeing Lipa after all these years caused a sting in the back of her throat, a tightness in her chest, but she could almost feel the weight of her little boy in her arms again, the fresh scent of his hair. So though it was wrong, she couldn't help herself.

"Come on, tayerinke, a little sleep helps everything."
Yidel pulled her up from the chair and led her to
the candles and watched her light. Then he guided her
to the bedroom and eased her shoes from her feet and
turned away as she replaced her scarf with the cotton turban, before tucking the blankets around her and kissing her
forehead. And this, even though they were supposed to
go downstairs to Tzila Ruchel for the meal. He would go
by himself. He turned off the light and closed the door.

During the weeks of s'firah, the forty-nine days of
mourning when nothing new could be purchased and no
weddings celebrated, everything went wrong.

Each day she woke with cramps. The babies made vi-
olent jerky motions, unlike anything she'd felt with any
of her previous pregnancies. The roof leaked, and not just
under the skylight but over her bed and over the kitchen
sink, and the space heater shorted out and almost started
a fire. "I smell burning," Dead Onyu had shouted up the
stairs. "Surie! Something is burning!" Mold grew on the
walls and inside the kitchen cabinets. Lipa appeared to her
several times every day, and though his visits remained a
secret joy, the unexpectedness of them could also be startling. She received a letter from a lawyer, requesting her
to appear as a witness against the therapist, and a day later,
another letter arrived from the state prosecutor, demanding the same thing. That evening, hauling herself up the
stairs hand over hand, she'd pulled the wooden railing out
of the wall, and now it lay, waiting to be repaired, completely unusable, blocking the already blocked stairs, a

hazard. None of her clothes fit her, and she couldn't ask
Yidel to bring the box of homemade maternity clothes up
from the basement. And when she found a moment to go
and find them herself, to secretly dig through the box and
bring things up one at a time, she found the boxes full of
those kinds of centipedes that live in New York basements,
shivery, thousand-legged things that ran in every direction when she pulled out the first enormous dress. She
threw the clothes into the incinerator. "Of course," she
said savagely. "Everything is perfect. Everything is always
perfect."

"What is perfect?" asked Miryam Chiena, who had
come down to fold the long lines of washing zigzagging
through the basement.

"Everything," said Surie.

"If everything is perfect, then why are you so sad?"

"This isn't sadness," Surie said. "It's energy." She threw
another handful of her maternity clothing into the incinerator and swung the heavy steel door shut with a crash.
She wiped some soot from her face with her sleeve, blew
her nose, and then crushed a centipede under her orthopedic shoe.

By the end of her twenty-sixth week, Surie needed to
time the cramps. They built up painfully until they were
five minutes apart and then stopped. On Tuesday, she and
Yidel returned from grocery shopping. He was just pulling up the second cart of groceries when he caught her
looking at the stopwatch he used for his chemicals. "What
on earth are you doing?" he said, angry. "Are you timing
how long it takes me to bring these carts upstairs?" She
denied it, but he was hurt, and that Thursday when she

went shopping, he didn't go with her and she had to climb the stairs a dozen times, carrying two plastic bags in each hand. Exhaustion felled her. The boys came home later that night and found that the stove wasn't lit, there was nothing to eat, and their mother was on the couch, a book fallen from her hands and her scarf askew, asleep sitting up.

After dinner, Dead Onyu climbed the stairs to talk with her, worried. "Lipa?" the old woman said. She couldn't understand the connection between Lipa's secret and Surie's. "This secret keeping is wrong, darling. A true sin."

"I can't do it," Surie said. "I don't know what's wrong with me, but I just can't."

"I'll tell Yidel myself."

"Don't!" Surie cried. "I know I have to. I will. Just . . . not now."

"This is not the kind of thing to spring on a man. Especially not Yidel. He doesn't deserve this. I really don't know what's gotten into you."

Dead Onyu ran her hand over Surie's head, checking the scarf, the nylon bangs, Surie's bristly shaved neck at the back. She slipped her fingers inside Surie's collar, testing how high it came. Surie tried to pull away, but Dead Onyu held her tightly by the wrist. Then she pinched the fabric of Surie's cardigan, seeing if it was too tight.

"You've put me in the worst position," the old woman said. "Perhaps, maybe, you should stay upstairs and not come to visit? I don't want my son to be angry at me too when he finds out what's been going on."

Surie had been trying to go in to the clinic every day, even if only for a few hours, because she knew that once the twins were born, the opportunity to learn would be lost. But this saddened Tzila Ruchel, who missed her mother's company and her help. "Did I offend you?" she asked as Surie scurried past her landing close to midnight that same night, on her way to throw in a load of dirty towels.

"No, no," Surie said, but she couldn't stop to chat because she had a new textbook hidden in the laundry basket, and Tzila Ruchel would notice it and have words to say about that too. "I'll see you some other time!"

"You are not like I thought you were," Val had said to her that very morning, the day Surie left Tzila Ruchel crying on the stairs. "And by you, I really mean Chassidic women." How so? she'd wanted to know, and Val had smiled. "You wear different clothes and speak a different language, but you are just like me." Hardworking and curious. Deceitful, thought Surie.

———

Surie had began to know many people she would never have come into contact with before the clinic. She knew the young Mexican mother who had given birth to five children before finding out, in America, that she had two wombs. Surie told her that it didn't really matter. Cats also had two wombs and they gave birth without any problem, and she whispered in the woman's ear not to heed the words of the doctor, which were almost unintelligible to both of them, and they laughed and slapped their palms together. She knew the forty-year-old lawyer who lived by herself and who had one day decided that she needed a child, but as stretch marks appeared, began to regret getting pregnant and wanted to somehow end the whole process. "But you have to wait for the good part," Surie said. "Good things don't come easy." And the woman listened to her because Surie had nine living children and several miscarriages and was pregnant with twins and knew what she was talking about. She sat with the young woman who had miscarried for the sixth time and she said nothing. She was only a compassionate presence, and when the woman finally rose, she leaned down and put her arms around Surie's neck.

It was easy to lose herself in the work, to forget about her family at home and their concerns: Dead Onyu, Tzila Ruchel, Yidel. It was easy, too, to pretend that she had already told Yidel and that they were both eagerly awaiting this miraculous birth. She chattered on with the patients, gleefully telling them her due date, how much ice cream she was eating to help the babies grow, how grateful she was to God for such a surprise. Val, hearing these comments, turned to look at her with a frown but said nothing. It was only when Surie returned home that she was confronted with the reality of the situation. So she left for the clinic earlier, returned later, fell asleep right when she came home.

———

Earlier the same day, still struggling with the complex language in the books Val had given her, Surie had found a simplified nursing textbook on her seat in the break room. As she'd lifted it to return to the shelf, her hand made a slight jerk and she put the book on the table in front of her and opened it to the first chapter as if she weren't worried at all and put on her reading glasses and bent her head and realized she understood everything that was written there. Later that afternoon, Val had come in and seen that Surie was up to the sixth chapter and was humming away to herself, sometimes shouting in happiness, and then all the technicians had come in and the dietitian and the other nurse-midwives and they'd congratulated Surie on breaking through the language barrier, and she'd blushed and had to excuse herself to go to the bathroom.

She'd read the textbook secretly down in the basement, tuning out the clanking of the old washer and dryer, and, around 3:00 a.m., crept up the stairs and got under the covers. Yidel rolled over and opened his eyes.

"I think I'd like to be a nurse," she said.

There was a long silence and then he cleared his throat. "You are already. Dead Onyu and Dead Opa appreciate everything you do for them."

"I'm not making a joke," she said. "The wives of Williamsburg need a Jewish nurse."

"Next you'll tell me that you want to eat pork," he said. He didn't mention that the women in their community never went to college because she knew that as well as he did.

"If you're worried about someone in the family leaving the path of Judaism, maybe you should talk with your son." She meant their seventeen-year-old, Mattis. Surie had found a DVD under her son's mattress and shown it to Yidel. *The Forty-Year-Old Virgin*. A pornographic film. The word *virgin* itself was pornographic. Neither she nor

Yidel had ever seen a film. There'd been no film made of their wedding or at the weddings of any of their children. Tzila Ruchel had to tell them what the shiny disc was when she'd seen it on the kitchen counter.

"But how did Mattis watch it?" Surie had asked her daughter.

"I'd search the basement for a computer, a lep tup." At the clinic, there were lep tups with thick cables into which the doctors and midwives entered patients' information. Some Chassidic businessmen used computers at their workplaces, but it was forbidden to bring the Internet into one's home. An open sewer. It wasn't possible that her son had somehow brought such a terrifying device into their apartment. People were ejected from the community for less.

"Surie," Yidel said, "going to college is worse than looking into a lep tup."

"You were an EMT. It's okay for you to learn how to help people but it's not okay for me?"

He frowned and his mouth had opened and he moved his hand as if he were signing some response. He picked up his hearing aid and pushed it into his ear. "You sound like a goy," he eventually said. "Me, me, me, instead of we, we, we." He glared at her. "Aren't you afraid that because of what you are doing, all of your grandchildren will be kicked out of cheder?"

She shook her head and rolled away from him, disturbed and furious, not trusting herself to speak. It was the truth. That was the whole problem, right from the start. What had become of her? Instead of viewing her life, her home, her marriage, as sacred, as something whole and impossible to divide, she risked cutting them all off from what they valued most.

———

Spring was a very busy time in the clinic. Though they were always busy, many more women wanted to have spring babies and the hallways were clogged with extra chairs. Now, Val trusted Surie to do many of the basic checks unsupervised—the urinalysis, the weight, the blood pressure—and Surie rushed from woman to woman, amazed at herself for having acquired these new skills.

"I'm studying," she told Yidel when he found the textbook in the laundry basket. He'd thought to surprise her with a pile of freshly folded clothes. Her face had flushed. Miryam Chiena marrying one of those hipsters on the bicycles. Chaim Tzvi, an old unmarried man at fifty. A grandchild born with some terrible illness, God forbid. It would all be her fault.

Yidel had taken the filthy thing—such images!—and dropped it down the incinerator chute, but Surie dragged home another one, exactly the same, the next day. Afraid of what it meant for a woman to bring such a treif thing home, worried about the chill chemical smell of her words, he turned his eyes away from her and didn't ask her any more questions. Now, each night, when she went into their bedroom, the beds were pushed far apart, on opposite sides of the room.

They fought with Mattis and he denied having a DVD, despite the evidence. They didn't find a lep tup in the basement, and on the surface, the family was calm again. The lilacs along the chain-link fences bloomed, and then the red buds and the wisteria. Dead Opa was mailed a batch of day-old chicks in a cardboard house with little circular holes punched into the sides. Bright green grass grew long in each vacant corner and sparrows nested inside the streetlights.

Surie returned home by train or by foot to her neighborhood a half hour before candlelighting on Friday afternoons with barely time to wash herself and change into her best clothes. "Mamme," Tzila Ruchel said one evening just before candlelighting, "why are you coming home so late?" Usually, the family was dressed and ready for the holy day at lunch. "Where do you go? Tatie won't tell me, and"—she looked around as if someone might overhear her—"it's really time for you to start looking for a shidduch for Mattis." The seventeen-year-old lep tup pornographer. "It's not going to be easy to find him a good match. Please tell me everything is normal and that people won't have anything new to say about our family."

Surie looked at her daughter, that pale rose of a girl, her pride and joy, blocking the way to the candlesticks. As a child, Tzila Ruchel had wanted to wear her tights to bed as an additional stringency, and Surie, proud, had pasted gold stars on her daughter's mitzvah chart. Thank God she hadn't told Tzila Ruchel that she was pregnant with twins. She almost laughed out loud from horror. And imagine if she told such a stickler that she was studying to be a midwife! The less said, the better. Their family's reputation couldn't come to any harm if she didn't tell anybody what she was up to and was meticulous about dropping off cake each time she traveled to Manhattan. Once three people knew, it would no longer be a secret.

And so she tilted her head and smiled and said she was just busy with the bikur cholim, and Tzila Ruchel sighed and went back downstairs to her own apartment. Surie, full of adrenaline and self-loathing, rushed around the house, checking that all the lamps were switched on or off, the toilet paper was torn, the challos were on the table next to the salt and the spices. At seven o'clock, she was ready to light her candles, one for each child and grandchild. Each flame would be reflected in the bright silver of the candelabra and the trays and the old brass mirror that stood above the buffet cabinet, making it seem as if there were hundreds of candles, thousands.

Surie stood alone in her dining room. Her husband and her boys were at shil, praying. Tzila Ruchel and Miryam Chiena were downstairs reading to Dead Onyu. The whole room felt alive, shimmering in the last rays of light from the sun as it slid below the horizon. On the pol-ished floor, slowly moving rainbows of color. She could hear her own breathing. In her hand, she held the burn-ing match. It felt as if the room waited for something, and she too waited.

Just at that moment, she felt the twins move within her, both somehow turning as if to face the candles, as if they could sense light. There was such a silence. No noise came from the Navy Yard or from the street. Time stretched out. The match had barely burned. She reached into the top drawer of the buffet and took out two extra candles and put them into the candelabra. It was completely for-bidden to light candles for the unborn. Yet it felt com-pletely right to her in the moment.

The smell of late lilacs floated in to her from the open

window, and the smell of the East River. Something like the woods up in the Catskills, like ferns and duff and damp soil. Lights went out across Williamsburg and were replaced with the gleam of the Shabbos candles. The air-raid siren announcing the last minutes to light the candles rose and fell away to that same huge silence. Outside, the streets were empty.

She leaned forward and lit the two extra candles. It was as if she could hear the twins whispering to her. They were her children. She *did* want them to live. The way she behaved at the clinic was not a lie. She wasn't acting. It was how she truly felt, underneath the complications that beset her at home. She wanted to see their infant faces, wanted to sit them on her knees and teach them to read the alef-beis. She wanted to sing them the songs that Jewish children learn from their mothers. She wanted to knit them miniature matching cardigans and bonnets with pom-poms on the top. She wanted to put them to her breasts and nurse them, and at that, a little sob escaped her. To lie again drowsily in bed in the afternoon, bathed in slanting golden light, with an infant sleeping next to her, a trickle of milk at the edge of his lip, his soft, warm body curled up next to hers.

Yidel would again be a father, whether she told him or not. He wouldn't be angry. Thrilled, that's what he'd be. But he'd been unrecognizable when he'd thrown the textbook into the incinerator chute. His face livid, his lips tight. An entirely different man from the one who'd walked with Lipa along the river and listened to his story. Hearing a noise on the steps, she pinched out the two extra candles and shoved them to the back of the drawer.

It was nothing. It was nobody. Look how she'd startled, like a criminal! Tomorrow, after kiddush, she'd tell Yidel and Tzila Ruchel. She lit the rest of the candles, waved her hands, covered her eyes, and said a prayer for everyone she knew, for the healthy and for the sick, for the born and for the unborn, for the wise and for those who needed wisdom, for the adults and for the children and the grandchildren, for Yidel and for Dead Onyu and Dead Opa, and for herself, last of all.

TWELVE

Lag B'Omer came on a Sunday at the beginning of May. Surie had reached her seventh month. Many of the men and older boys traveled to Kiryas Joel, the community village in upstate New York, and those who stayed lit bonfires in the streets. Yidel broke rotting boards off Dead Onyu's old chicken coop and lit a fire in their backyard. Small children ran screaming through the streets, firing arrows from their plastic bows, and teenage boys carried legless chairs to throw onto the piles of wood that were accumulating in the back alleys and the abandoned lots. Groups of girls peered down from the windows of their school, pointing as men carried their dried-out palm fronds and the old green s'chach from the roofs of their sukkahs to the bonfires. Two- and three-year-old boys, dressed in their finest, had their long hair cut off and weighed and their payos shaped, and men danced around the fires and late into the night, the musicians played the old songs, and singers took the microphones to sing the new.

The first truly hot days had arrived and the hipsters—

the real Americans on their bikes—had begun to roll through the neighborhood, flashing their tattoos and their breasts, their voices loud and their music full of words and sounds that were forbidden. In the coming weeks, the young children would be kept inside and girls told not to walk out unless they were in groups of four. The teenage boys would spoil for a fight and occasionally throw rocks at the backs of the bikers when they were far enough away. But on that Sunday, they were all out on the streets together. When Surie walked up Division, she felt a strange wind blowing through her neighborhood, and when she stood on the edge of the huge communal bonfire, the women were whispering about this strange wind and the men whispered about it behind the smoke and some of the children inside the synagogue sat next to the barred windows and looked out at the street instead of toward the Torah scrolls, and this was a new thing, a thing that had never happened before.

In the afternoon, she spoke about it with Yidel. He was reading his newspaper over a cup of tea with lemon before he got to work on the Torah scroll, the last he would ever write. In two months, he would retire.

"What is happening to our community?" she asked.

Yidel put his newspaper down and looked at her. He picked up one of his hearing aids, turned it on, and screwed it into his ear. She repeated herself and he snorted. "You're one to talk."

"Forget me," she said. "Can't you please forget me?"

"If you're talking about the gonef who stole the silver atoros off the talleisim, the Shomrim will catch whoever it is. Or is this about Mattis?" Yidel jogged his cup and some tea slopped out onto the newspaper. He mopped it up and then poured a cup of tea for her and slid it across the table. "Has something else happened?"

"Nothing new happened," she said, though she had barely been home and wasn't sure. Many mornings, she did not make the beds. At night, she was too tired to spend time talking with her children. She couldn't remember the last time she'd sat down with Mattis the lep tupper. "I'm talking in general. We aren't the only family that has a son, a daughter, a grandchild who left. My friends blame the Internet."

"Books," he said. They stared at each other through the steam from the cups.

"I like studying."

"I hope you like when all your children bow down to idols and turn into apikorsim."

She was the same as she had always been. Even if she learned how to be a midwife, she would always braid the challos for Shabbos and prepare the chulent and shave her head and cover it with a scarf. She would always be a believer. She told herself that reading a midwifery textbook would not cause her children to deny their faith. Could not.

"Please," she said, placing her finger on the lip of his glass. "I am worried. Every summer it's the same craziness. The tattooed ones come out of their houses and they walk our streets. Most of our children turn away, but some are fascinated."

"Is Mattis one of the fascinated ones?"

"I saw him on the street listening to the way they throw words around. He wants to speak English like them. Didn't you hear him on Shabbos with his friends? Every second word was English. He is ashamed of his accent. He

is ashamed of us. He wants to wear deodorant and a shirt
with cuffs. He wants to brush his beard. He'll want to
have a say in who he marries."

Yidel winced. "It's Lipa all over again."

"I won't have another child die because I don't like his
glasses."

They both glanced up at each other, ashamed, then
looked quickly away. Surie was afraid to look in the corners of the room for fear Lipa would be standing there,
listening to them.

Yidel cleared his throat. "We must find him a wife.
Settle him in the community." His glass was empty, so she
put the used teabag back in and refilled the glass with hot
water from the stove. She sat down.

"He has time. He's only seventeen."

"Your own brother was married at seventeen."

"What if it's too late for marriage already? What if we
would merely be causing pain to more people—his wife,
his children, his in-laws?"

"What if it's you who are causing him to want to leave?
With your books, your . . . freedoms?"

Her face filled with color. It wasn't the textbooks,
really. It was her. It was the pregnancy. It was all the things
she wasn't saying, Lipa, the twins, the young girl, that
court case. She'd ruined one of her own children, and
now, it seemed, she was ruining another one. *Secrets.* She
looked out at the street and at the greenly flowing East
River and she said, "If I knew for sure? I would take my
books and throw them down the chute myself." She had
wanted to talk to Yidel, but she couldn't tell him when
they were arguing, so she opened the kitchen window
and, crouching, with much effort, climbed out to the little

platform between the roofs where they usually built their sukkah.

When she came in, she noticed that the midwifery textbook was missing from the kitchen table. She went looking for it and found it in the hands of her granddaughter Miryam Chiena. The girl was seated just inside the wardrobe in Surie's bedroom and she was reading.

"Is this what you are studying, Bubbie?" she asked, and she stood up and carried the book over to Surie and pointed inside to the photographs of the developing fetus. She did not seem upset. If anything, she was eager. And yet this was not a subject that was ever discussed with young girls. They went to their weddings, as she had done, with the barest of information about the process of procreation. The name for a leg was foot. The name for a toe was foot. The name for a thigh was foot. The name for the place inside their thighs did not exist. Front, her granddaughter said when she had an itch. Back. This place. That place. Here. There. Miryam Chiena, in her excitement, forgot to be modest.

"Is this what a baby looks like when it is in the mother's tummy?"

She did not know what to say to this child. They did not talk with children about mothers having babies in their tummies. Babies came from God. And yet, this lack of knowledge had contributed to the situation with the young girl at the clinic. Surie faltered. How had Miryam Chiena learned even this?

"Is this the place where the baby comes out?" her granddaughter said, turning the page and pointing. She was not distressed. She was curious, much as Surie had been, and at the same age. Thirteen. Maybe fourteen.

Not much older than Surie's patient, who would be five months along. Showing.

"It is," Surie said.

"Where is that on me?" the little girl asked, running her hand from her head to her knees.

Surie said nothing.

"And what is this?" Miryam Chiena said, pointing to another picture, and Surie gently closed the book, not wanting to frighten the girl, but also not willing to answer, and afraid of what Tzila Ruchel would say when she found out that her daughter had been reading about birth in one of her grandmother's books.

"I will give you another book," she said. "This afternoon." But when she went to get the book she had given to her daughters when they were twelve and thirteen, a plain pamphlet about the holiness of menstruation, she knew it would not satisfy Miryam Chiena. And she thought about her options. She could say that she could not find the book. She could tell the girl she was naughty for wanting to read such a thing. She could let her ask some questions. But if she quashed the girl's interest or didn't assuage her curiosity, what would happen? Is this what happened to the lost children in the community? If every place and every thing was forbidden, the tiniest shred of curiosity would automatically lead the children to forbidden things, and then the schools would send them to unlicensed therapists where anything could happen. The worst things.

———

That evening, almost everyone fell asleep early from the smoke and the arrows and the excitement, but Miryam Chiena came upstairs and sat down next to her grandmother on the couch. In her hands, she had a crayon drawing of a fetus floating in an orange-red ball. In the fashion of the textbooks she saw at school, the baby did not have a face.

"You drew the picture you saw this afternoon," Surie said.

"That photograph was so beautiful," Miryam Chiena said. "But where was the angel?" The angel who teaches unborn infants the Torah.

"May I see what you made?"

Miryam Chiena showed her.

"Why didn't you draw an angel?" Surie asked, sweating a little bit inside her high collar.

"I didn't draw it because I am not sure that people can see angels," Miryam Chiena whispered. "But if I did, I would have drawn the angel pale blue and I would have put it right here." She pointed.

The fetus was pink and headless. It was covered in fine gold hair, just like the picture in the book. Across its chest ran a blue-and-red umbilical cord.

"It's wearing a seat belt," Miryam Chiena said. "See?"

"For safety," said Surie. "May I have your drawing?" She thought she might be able to get rid of it before Tzila Ruchel saw what her daughter had been doing.

"I'm not finished," Miryam Chiena said. She did not release her hold on the paper.

"What if there were twins? What if there were two babies inside the mother? Could you draw that?"

What if she turned to this child, her favorite grandchild, and very simply said, "You know, I am expecting twins." From this child, there would be no judgment, just curiosity. She would want to put her head on Surie's belly and listen to the babies. She would want to feel them kick. But if Surie told Miryam Chiena about the twins, Tzila Ruchel would burn her own mother at the stake.

The girl was nodding. "I can draw anything. I'm an artist."

"Yes," Surie said, smiling, "you're a good artist and a smart girl."

"I'm going to give it to Mommy the next time she gets fat. Gets pregnant." She pronounced the foreign word carefully in English.

"You know, not everybody uses those words. I don't think your mommy would like it if you said that to her. And not everyone knows what babies look like before they are born either. It's specialty information."

"Why?" Miryam Chiena asked.

"You know how the most holy things are covered? Like the Torah? Like a mezuzah? Well, babies are very holy before they are born, so they are covered."

"Ketchup is kept in a bottle. Is ketchup holy? What about socks? We keep them in the drawer."

Surie winced. This girl. Too smart. She sat motionless on the couch, clenching and unclenching her hands. The babies within her were motionless too. She wondered how long it had been since they had turned or kicked. She couldn't remember.

"When I was a young girl, your age, maybe a little bit older, the non-Jewish women didn't look so different from us. They wore hats and gloves and skirts below their knees. The men wore hats and neat suits. The outside world wasn't so scary. But then, something changed and the whole world went crazy."

"Are you talking about the Holocaust?" How did she even know about that? They were all so careful not to mention it in front of the children.

"No. I'm talking about a kind of revolution that happened. People stopped caring about what other people thought of them. They stopped listening to their parents and the government and their teachers. They were called hippies. I was horribly afraid of them. Everything they stood for, every sound they made, terrified me. I did everything I could not to be like them. All of my friends were the same. One of the things the hippies did was talk about . . . the kinds of things you might find in my book, as if that was the only thing in the world."

The little girl leaned against her. "Bubbie," she said, "were you ever pregnant?"

"I'm pregnant now," Surie blurted, putting her hands on her enormous belly. "With twins." She snuck a look at the child. "Would you like to feel them?"

Miryam Chiena laughed. "I'm pregnant too!" she said. "I ate too much food. Just like you, Bubbie!"

———

Late that night, Dead Opa motored up the stairs to tell Surie that Dead Onyu wasn't feeling well.

She found the old woman sitting up in bed, her fist curled around a piece of paper. Her breathing was ragged and her face was purple.

"How could you?" she hissed. "You're lucky it was me and not Tzila Ruchel that Miryam Chiena talked to about her drawing."

Surie felt sick. She was mortified.

"I told her to give it to me and I was going to burn it." Surie hoped that Miryam Chiena hadn't told her great-grandmother about the textbook and the photographs she'd seen. Dead Onyu shook her head and muttered, "Gottenyu. The expression goes that one can't fool the children, but neither can you fool the elderly." She told Surie that Miryam Chiena had come downstairs and eagerly described her drawing and how she knew what to draw. She asked Surie what she was trying to do, get the girl expelled from school? All very well, teaching her something interesting, and yes, the girl was very intelligent, but to teach her something like that, something that no girl knew anything about, and then to send the child back to a school where everyone was ignorant, it was like firing a missile, first through her granddaughter and then through her own house. Are you crazy? she asked. Don't blame me if this child ends up marrying some wild, long-haired shaygetz with tattoos up his neck.

"And how could you tell her you are pregnant when you haven't even told your own husband? I used to think you were the smartest person in this house, but now . . ."

"Lots of Jews think there's nothing wrong with telling a daughter when you are pregnant. I see women in the clinic who bring their daughters with them to the appointments, five years old, ten. That's too young. But Miryam Chiena is old enough to know. She'll find out soon enough."

"Firstly, she's not your daughter. She's your grand-daughter and it's not your decision to make. And secondly, since when do we ever tell our girls that kind of thing? That hospital has infected you with some kind of crazy germs."

"Onyu, really. You grew up on a farm. You knew how things got born when you were much younger than Miryam Chiena."

"That book had a detailed description of what happens before a child is conceived. She told me she'd started to read it when you took the book away! If I thought you'd told her anything about that—"

"I didn't say anything!" Surie said quickly. Though she couldn't help thinking of the other little girl, the one in the clinic.

Dead Onyu snorted. "Now she won't be like the other girls in her class. She'll be different. And that difference will mark her, it will erode her sense of belonging. She'll be one of those who leave us."

"She's different already. She's so smart. When Mattis was learning his parsha, she knew the songs before he did. She had the words and the tune memorized the second or third day. And she was nine."

"When she is older, she will leave us. When there is a wedding, she'll call up and say she's too busy to come, and when she has her first child, she won't invite us to see it. She'll say to her husband, 'My family believes in the evil eye. When they see how beautiful our baby is, they'll spit on the ground and say she should grow with her head in the ground like a beet, and my mother will say she looks exactly like a little worm.'"

"Onyu. Stop. Miryam Chiena will never be ashamed of us," said Surie.

"Maybe," said Dead Onyu, and she shook her head. "But if there comes a time when we are ashamed of her, it will be because of what you did today."

"Onyu, do you know the story about Rabbi Shimon

ben Shetach? The way he caught eighty witches and brought them to be hanged."

"Whenever you change the subject, it shows you know you are in the wrong."

"I can't bear to think anymore. I just want it all to be over. The telling. The pregnancy. All of it," Surie said, and she took the old woman's hand. "I've changed my mind. Could you tell Yidel for me?"

Dead Onyu drew her closer. "I wouldn't be you for the world," she said, moving her hand in circles on Surie's back. "You've made a mess of it, for sure. And why does that make me love you even more? I'm a back-to-front old woman."

Surie breathed in the scent that was Dead Onyu, the homemade tar soap she used, the woolens, some smell that was indefinably old and from another country. She was closer to Dead Onyu than she'd been to her own mother, God rest her soul. She'd known Onyu for longer, and they'd gotten along. Dead Onyu had seen her through every one of her early marriage fights, through the rough days of nursing, through the trial of postpartum depression, through financial troubles, and through the hospitalizations of her children. Even newly blind, she'd been there when Surie came back from California and all she'd wanted to do was put her face down in Dead Onyu's lap and sob. She was calm and wise and honest and gruff. Other people complained about their mothers-in-law, but Surie felt blessed.

She knew that when she finally told Yidel about the pregnancy, Dead Onyu would be there to smooth everything over. Dead Onyu would glare at anyone who stared at Surie and the twins in the streets. She'd hiss a few choice words in Hungarian and the staring would permanently stop.

"I'm sorry, Onyu," she said. "I was just getting up the strength to tell Yidel. Practicing. Sort of. I'm ashamed that I said anything to Miryam Chiena."

They sat in silence until Dead Onyu fell asleep and her hand fell from Surie's grasp. Surie took Miryam Chiena's drawing and put it inside the incinerator, and when she closed the door she made sure to do it very quietly.

THIRTEEN

The last trimester was the time when all the customs must be kept and none forgotten: Surie kept canned chickpeas in the cupboard in case there was a bris; under her pillow lay the book *Noam Elimelech* and a knife to scare away the Angel of Death; she bit the end off an esrog; every knot in the house was untied to make sure that there would be nothing holding her back from an easy labor; she didn't lift her arms above her head; she washed her hands and ate a full meal on Saturday nights after Shabbos ended; birth amulets and copies of the 121st Psalm were hidden behind pictures in every room and especially near the front door; each morning she put extra coins in the old tin charity box before she prayed; she set up an appointment with a mikva in Far Rockaway where nobody would know her, so her babies' skin would be clear of pimples; she avoided looking at the dogs and cats that roamed the streets. When Yidel adjusted a tapestry of flowers Surie had made years before and an amulet fell out, he was puzzled and thought that perhaps it had been forgotten there, from before the birth of their youngest son, Chaim Tzvi.

Just before Shavios, in the first week of May, shortly after Surie had made up with Dead Onyu, Val told her she couldn't take any more days off. The clinic was too busy. She'd be paid the same wage as a nursing assistant. Now birth and its rituals dominated her home life and her work life. During the week, she was at the hospital, assisting Val. On the weekends, she rested at home with her family and studied increasingly more difficult sections of the textbook. Though she didn't look at the feral cats that yowled around the garbage bags outside her building, she looked at photograph after photograph of teratology, the disasters that can befall fetuses when there is slippage between their chromosomes or when environmental troubles break into the sealed room of the uterus. On Sundays, when Yidel and her sons came home from synagogue, they often found her at the dining room table, bent over one of these books, and Yidel would clear his throat and the boys would shuffle their feet and she would look up, red-eyed with exhaustion, and wipe her hands on her housecoat, close the book with a snap, and go into the kitchen to make toast and porridge and eggs.

Coming home from the hospital, rushing, late on Friday, Surie was brought up short by the sight of a woman standing in the vestibule of her apartment building, a gaggle of chickens around her feet. It was the mother of the little pregnant girl. Though she was hidden away somewhere out of sight, the mother must have wept over her daughter's swollen belly. The mother wore a neat maternity frock and a small black hat with a short wig. If Surie looked closely, she thought she could tell that the woman was wearing a pillow under her dress.

The building was very quiet. Usually, at this time on Friday afternoon, it was full of the cries of Tzila Ruchel's children, but even the sounds from the Navy Yard were absent. The children should have been out of school, but no one ran down the stairs and held her around the legs. No one was outside, playing with Zaidy. Where were they all?

"My daughter wants you to stay with her," the woman said. Mrs. Shnitzer, that was her name. She lifted one foot and kicked at one of the chickens. "When she has the baby. She says she doesn't want me to come to the birth."

"I like her," Surie said. "I could try to go to her. If she wants me there." Only after she said this did she realize she'd have two-month-old twins at home.

"One time, she painted her fingernails red. And the fingernails of her little sisters. Who does that?"

"It's normal," Surie said, though she would have spanked her own girls for such wildness. She was the older woman, a respected teacher and a grandmother. The younger woman would listen to her. "But let's not stand here talking about fingernail polish. Is someone taking care of her? A doctor, I mean?"

"If her modesty had been like the other girls, she wouldn't have been his victim," Mrs. Shnitzer said. She wanted to distance herself from her child. Surie understood. She had done the same thing with Lipa. She was doing the same thing with the twins.

"No," she said. "Your daughter is not a bad girl. She is only thirteen. That rapist is in his sixties. You sent her to him for help and this is the help he gives?" Hadn't Val said that the mother had sided with her daughter?

Val had said that the whole family would be receiving counseling. And the police would be provided some counseling too. But six weeks later, the mother still seemed ambivalent.

"Promise me you won't tell anyone about what happened. Promise!"

"I won't. I wouldn't do that to your daughter. Call me when she goes into labor. I'll try to come."

The woman leaned against the wall. She pressed her fingers against the green tiles and she sought out the lines of grout with her fingernails.

"She's not here." That little girl, all by herself. Surie felt herself fill with a cold liquid. "Afterwards, we will move somewhere else. Buenos Aires. Or Antwerp."

One of the pullets leapt up and pecked at the hem of Mrs. Shnitzer's dress and she flapped and squawked, a bit like a chicken herself.

"Your husband won't have a job there. You have other children. How will you eat? Just tell me where she is and I'll go, even if it means a plane flight. Tell me!"

"I should never have allowed my children to read English books."

"It wasn't the books. It wasn't the library. It was one of our own."

Mrs. Shnitzer's chin shook. "Maybe it's not true," she said. "It could be a growth. I've heard about things like that. They can do a surgery . . ."

"Is that what you want?" Surie asked. "It's too late for an abortion."

The woman reared back and struck at Surie with her handbag. "Shame on you!" she hissed. She hit Surie again.

"I'm pregnant," Surie said. "Please don't hit me. You could hurt my babies."

The woman dropped her handbag. She began to cry. "I told you so you know that I will keep your secret. As you will keep mine."

"It's not possible," Mrs. Shnitzer whispered. "You're lying. You're a great-grandmother. What kind of witch are you?"

Surie sat down heavily in the chair lift and pressed the button. She was exhausted. The chair began to rise, jerking on its tracks, groaning. The girl's family would respond out of fear, no matter what she said. "It wasn't her fault," she said in parting. "She's a child. That monster threatened to hurt her family if she said anything."

"What is a woman like you doing at a place that does *abortions?*" Mrs. Shnitzer called after her. "So many people respect you. If they only knew what a goyta you really are."

Surie lifted her head. She folded her hands over her belly. She did not look down. She had forgotten to ask Val to check the babies' heartbeats.

She wasn't ashamed of the work she did. It was good work and she was proud of it. She thought that if Lipa were to come home now, she would handle him differently. Better. Perhaps not in the eyes of her community but in her own eyes. And she would be a different mother for the twins too, more compassionate, kinder, less afraid.

As the chair rattled past Dead Onyu's apartment, the old woman came out to the stairs, and Surie wondered what she had heard of the conversation. Her mother-in-law's hearing, unlike Yidel's, was acute.

"Onyu, what will become of me?" she asked, but Dead Onyu only smiled at her as the chair turned the corner and continued upward.

"People are awful, but I couldn't love you more," she said.

The chair kept on rising and rising, all the way past Tzila Ruchel's apartment and up to her own.

That night, for the first time in months, Surie pushed their beds together and curled up with her face pressed against Yidel's chest. He blinked at her, his hands not knowing where to settle, hovering above her shoulders. "May I?" he asked, before drawing her closer. She told him a little bit about her day. She tried to describe how she felt without telling him too much, and Yidel, without asking any questions, held her.

"I'm not an abortionist and I'm not a witch," she said. "I'm just trying to do something good for the women of this community. Something that hasn't been done before."

"Remember," he said, "when you had your miscarriages? You always named the babies. You wanted to know where they were buried. You wanted to hold them for a while. Surie, you have never been one for living entirely within the community. You have often made decisions based on your heart. Nothing the rabbis or I could have said would have changed your mind. Small-enough things. And you know I don't live one hundred percent by the rule book either." His love of news programs on the radio. Singing in the shower. "We can live with such small deviations. They aren't hurting anyone."

She was sure that he knew she was pregnant.

"A little girl came into the clinic at the hospital while I was working today," she began, yearning for Yidel's wisdom and insight, yearning for truth. Without him, she was nothing. "She grew up in Williamsburg. One of us . . ."

FOURTEEN

The middle of May and the holiday of Shavios always brought the most beautiful weather, the soft winds, the cornflower-blue skies. Robins tugged worms from the soil. Cardinals called from the power lines. Ducks returned from wherever they went in the winter and sailed once again on the river. Surie found a black duck and ten ducklings in the paddling pool that had been left out all winter in the backyard. The mother duck sprang from the pool, but the little ducklings weren't strong enough to make it over the lip. After watching the duck get out and then return to the water several times, all of her ducklings frantically peeping and calling for her, Surie took a plank of wood and floated one end of it in the pool. The ducklings climbed onto it and were able to get out. They waddled to the side fence in their little red shoes and waited at the chain-link gate until Surie opened it.

Tzila Ruchel's children made paper roses and taped them to the windows of their apartment. Outside, a few real roses bloomed and the tree of heaven bloomed too and the streets filled with its pale green pollen. In the very early morning and late evening, rabbits emerged from under houses and nibbled on the long grass. Skunks climbed up from the banks of the river and pawed through the bags of garbage at the doorways. They snuffled at the fence and tried to dig underneath to get at the chickens in the backyard. Everyone would be coming to her house, so Surie got up early each morning before going to the clinic to make cheesecakes and cheese Danishes and blintzes and cheese dumplings, the special dairy foods for the holiday.

She made gingerbread men, and as she piped on their faces, she thought of what her babies would look like when they were born. Their tender pink skin, the rosy stork bites on the backs of their necks, the wisps of hair over the soft spot on the tops of their heads, their fingernails, so flimsy and small that they couldn't be cut with scissors but would have to be bitten off.

"You made gingerbread babies!" Miryam Chiena squeaked when she saw the biscuits with their pink bows and little blue yarmulkes.

There was a little less than two months until the babies would be born. Her skin was tight and hot and itchy. Embarrassingly, her belly button showed in the front of all of her dresses. It was hard to find a comfortable position in which to sleep for the pain in her hips and knees. But it seemed that ever since she'd met the little girl at the hospital, she'd been eager to see the faces of her own babies.

———

The night before Shavios, Surie was awakened not by the need to use the bathroom but by the sound of feet running

on the stairs and Tzila Ruchel calling her name. She grog-
gily threw on her old ponzhelo and slippers and came to
the door.

"Hurry, Mommy. Hurry!"

She ran down the stairs with Tzila Ruchel to Dead
Onyu's apartment. The living room was in disarray.
Dead Onyu had risen in the night and, disoriented, fallen
and hit her head. She lay on the couch, wrapped in a blanket. Her turban was covered in blood and her eyes were
closed. There were dark purple spots covering her arms
and part of her face. The sound of her breathing was very
loud. Dead Onyu had fallen before, once breaking a hip,
once a wrist. Surely those injuries had been more serious
than this?

"She's not waking up. Tatie came and checked her and
then he said we should call Hatzolah," Tzila Ruchel said.
And right then, there was the sound of a siren and more
footsteps running up the stairs. Yidel directed the men of
the volunteer ambulance service where to go. He'd been
waiting downstairs in his robe for them to arrive.

Surie picked up Dead Onyu's hand. It was very cold
and it lay limp in hers. "Onyu," she said, "don't go." But
it seemed to her that just at that moment, a tremor passed
through the hand and there was a strange gurgle and she
felt something rush past her and out of the door, passing
the paramedics as they came in. They dropped their kits
on the floor and pushed her aside.

"Give her room to breathe," one of them said, but then
he bent over the couch and listened to Dead Onyu's heart
and it was obvious from the way he withdrew quickly that
she had died. The Chassidic men who had trained to be

paramedics shouted to one another and pumped her heart and forced air into the old woman's lungs. They brought in the defibrillator and shocked her. They tried for twenty minutes, thirty, to bring her back to life, but they could not.

"What is going on?" cried Dead Opa, who could only hear all of the dreadful sounds but not see what was happening. "What is happening to Faige Bruche?" And Yidel held his hand and took him into the kitchen and made him sit down and drink some tea, and after some time, he began to sob. "No," came the voice of Dead Opa, breaking. "No! It was supposed to be me first."

When the Hatzolah men left, Surie went and sat on the floor next to the couch where her mother-in-law lay. She held her hand again and whispered apologies to her, sorry that she had not always wanted to come downstairs right when Onyu called, sorry not to have been a better daughter, sorry she had not seen her for a couple of days, sorry that she had not known the old woman was dying. She wished she had listened to Dead Onyu and told Yidel, so that they all could have quietly celebrated the good news together, instead of forcing her mother-in-law to keep secrets from her own family. She kissed Onyu's hand and covered her with a sheet, and then she and Tzila Ruchel laid her on the floor with her feet pointing toward the door and they lit beeswax candles all around her. Tzila Ruchel poured a glass of water on the floor and covered the mirrors with tea towels. Toward dawn, the oldest of Tzila Ruchel's children and the youngest of Surie's children came in and touched the sheet that covered Dead Onyu and then sat on the floor and began saying tehillim with their mother and their father and their grandmother and their grandfather and poor Dead Opa, who though he knew the psalms by heart could not bring himself to say any. "Onyu," Surie whispered, her hands folded over her stomach, "if one of these babies is a girl, I will give her your name."

Early, early, the women of the Chevra Kadisha arrived and they lifted Dead Onyu from the floor and carried her into her room and placed her on boards, and there they washed her gently and combed her hair and cleaned her nails and took off her rings and dried her and wrapped her in linen shrouds and placed her in a plain wooden box, and all the while they prayed, and Tzila Ruchel, outside, prayed, and Surie, lying on the couch, exhausted, whispered all the psalms that she knew for Faige Bruche, the daughter of Miryam Chiena, born in 1929; a girl who had avoided Nazi capture inside a cave near the Tisa; a young woman who had met her husband in a DP camp near Vienna in 1946; a mother who had borne sixteen children and raised them all to be devout Jews; a woman who had treated her like a daughter for nearly forty years and taught her how to be a good mother-in-law; a grandmother and great-grandmother who had adored her grandchildren and who had lit a candle for every single one of the close to one hundred of them each Friday night. Surie prayed that Dead Onyu's soul would fly directly to God. That her pure and holy soul would intercede with God and make sure that the birth of the twins was easy and that the babies were healthy and that Surie wouldn't die. She prayed that Dead Onyu's life, next time, would be perfect.

Everyone in the community shared in the death. Death was so common, such an ordinary part of life, that it was not hidden in the way that death is hidden in the outside world. The body was not pumped full of chemicals and made up with lipstick and rouge to look as if it were alive. Throughout the community women baked bread and cakes and cookies and roasted meat and chicken and grated potatoes and zucchinis and carrots for kigelach to feed all of the people who would come to mourn the passing of Dead Onyu. The young men, Surie's sons, went with their cousins to dig part of the grave themselves out of respect. The funeral had to be held as soon as possible in the morning because that evening at sunset Shavios would begin and the body could not be held over for three days. Tzila Ruchel and Surie called as many people as they could and asked each person to call several more, and by 10:00 a.m., despite the holiday, a crowd had formed outside the Rodney shil, the men closest to the building, the women, wearing scarves over their wigs, on the other side of the street. Did you hear that the house bucher of Rabbeini Shlita is a chusson with the daughter of Reb Shulem Modche Ashkenazy? The levaya is going to di alte chelka in Kiryas Joel. How many ir einiklach did she have? How many maidel babies? The voices of the Ruv and the Dayan floated out of the shil on loudspeakers. What a beautiful yiddishe shtib she built up. Her einiklach are all going in the way. A black van pulled up to the curb and the director of the Chevra Kadisha went into the shil with some men to carry the box downstairs, feetfirst. As the men were leaving, Dead Opa came and tried to stop them by standing in the doorway with his arms outstretched. "Don't take her yet," he said. "Please, please, don't take her yet." And he said "please" in English because for this and for many other difficult things, their family had no Yiddish words.

———

After the eulogies at the shil, Surie sat at home with her daughters and daughters-in-law. The neighbors had brought in low chairs and bagels and hard-boiled eggs. There was nothing to do. They were forbidden to prepare for the holiday that night. They couldn't read a book or chatter or eat, so they just sat in silence and waited for the men to return from the cemetery. Yidel and his brothers and all of the young men had gone out to the grave site in large black cars that belonged to a community service for just such occasions. They'd had a car long ago when the children were much smaller, a monstrous old station wagon, but now they didn't need a vehicle. Strangers had picked the family up after the eulogy at the synagogue and taken them out into the country. The cemetery was on a stony hill in Kiryas Joel, surrounded by an ugly concrete fence.

Dead Onyu's sons would carry the plain box up the hill. Directly behind the box, Yidel would lead Dead Opa up the hill. The old man had gone out wearing a thin black cotton robe. The belt would flap at his side, undone; underneath, his shirt was ripped, from the collar to the heart. Behind the family, all of the men would walk in a long line, single file because the space between the graves was so narrow. There would be no women at the cemetery despite the fact that Dead Onyu was much beloved by those who had worked with her in school and, later, in the bikur cholim.

A red hawk flew above the river, just beyond Surie's window, circling. When she went to the window to watch it, instead of the river, the sky, the hawk, she saw the gash in the soil where Dead Onyu would be buried. How deep it was, how dark! She stood at the window, her heart beating raggedly. Some of Dead Onyu's friends from the DP camp sat in the living room behind her, fingering coverless psalm books that were fat and soft from use. They murmured the words of the psalms from memory, without turning the pages, but all she heard was Dead Onyu's voice saying, "Tell him."

Dead Opa would speak at the cemetery and Yidel would speak and his younger brothers would speak and they would all say kaddish in ancient Aramaic for the woman who lay in the ground. Even the angels could not be jealous of the humans who had such holy words in their mouths, because angels only understood Hebrew.

And so Dead Onyu would be buried with the fresh air of the country and the blue sky of the day and the tears of her husband and her sons and grandsons falling into the dirt that they threw down on top of her. Her sons would take up shovels and strike them into the loose soil piled up next to the grave and they would fill the hole, quickly, quickly, for it was almost time for the holiday and they still had to drive all the way back to the city. Great slabs sealed the graves. Carved gray stones named those who were buried in the women's section of the House of the

Dead. Not a blade of grass grew there. Not a shrub or a flower. The wind would blow and the birds would sing. *Tell him. Tell him.* Outside Surie's window, the hawk circled and circled. After Surie had walked behind the black van down Rodney and watched it turn the corner at Bedford Avenue, she'd washed her hands in the middle of the street and flapped her wet fingers in the air and only then remembered that pregnant women were forbidden from attending a funeral.

By the time the men returned home, there were many people waiting inside, ready to comfort Yidel and his siblings. They would be able to mourn for only a couple of hours before the holiday arrived and then they must all pretend to be happy, for the joy of a holiday pushes away sadness. A meal of hard-boiled eggs and bread and lentil soup had been laid out on the table. Yidel mumbled a blessing, lifted an egg to his mouth and bit off a piece, and then laid it back on the plate. He chewed and chewed, sipped from a glass of water, swallowed.

Surie was not allowed to mourn, as she was not one of Dead Onyu's children. She could not rip her clothing. She could not sit on a low chair. Tzila Ruchel was not an official mourner either. They stood together in the kitchen, brushing at their faces. When Yidel stood up to get something from the bedroom, Surie went in after him.

"Yidel," she said, "I have to tell you something."

He looked right past her. His eyes were swollen almost shut. His skin was as white as paper.

"I'm pregnant."

He didn't respond. She searched his face for anger. There was none. But neither was there joy.

"With twins. We can name one of them after your mother."

He still didn't respond. She touched his arm and he shook her off. "Not now, Surie. The shiva," he said. "It's not appropriate." She looked at his face. She looked at his ears. He was not wearing his hearing aids.

"Yidel!" she screamed as he pivoted and made for the door.

He turned back to look at her, frowned, put his finger on his lips, and walked out to the main room.

Hands were reaching from below the ground to drag the twins from her womb. In the cemetery, the heavy stone over Surie's mother's grave slid off and an unrecognizable skeleton peeled back the soil as if it were a sheet and climbed from its earthen bed and walked toward her. She closed her eyes. She wished she had not gone to the funeral. She wished Yidel had been wearing his hearing aids. She wished she could go and put her head in Dead Onyu's lap. She was tired, so tired.

Back in the kitchen, she felt as if she were collapsing into herself. A particular powdery odor that reminded her of Dead Onyu floated on the air and made her feel ill. The machinery in the Navy Yard groaned and the boats in the river shrieked. Just outside the kitchen, her best friend from school, Breina Trabitsh, looked at her second-best friend, Yitel Moshkowitz, trying to figure out how to speak to Surie. Eventually, they whispered some brief words of comfort.

"I'm pregnant," she said to them.

They both blinked. "Have something to eat, Surie," Breina said, steering her toward the dining room and filling a plate.

Even though Dead Onyu wasn't a mournable relative, Leah'le Schwimmer and Chaya Feiga Weisz, Toltzie Hirsch and Bunia Posen, Frimet Goldstein and Eidel Hornstein, former classmates, all brought trays of food and pots of soup, kissed her, and said how sorry they were. "I'm pregnant," she said to each one.

"Don't worry," they said. "You'll feel better in the morning."

"One of your daughters can name a child after their great-grandmother."

"I was full of feeling when my mother-in-law died too."

One of her friends laughed and then put a hand over her mouth. "Surie," she said sternly, "this is no time for jokes."

It was very close to candlelighting time when the last woman backed away and then there was just Val left, standing in the doorway, her hands clenched together, an uncertain smile on her face.

"You're here," Surie said, coming toward her and putting a hand out to be shaken. Instead, Val pulled her closer and hugged her. "How did you know what happened?"

"I called your number when you didn't come in and one of your daughters answered the phone. I thought you had decided it was too much of a risk to work with me."

"I do not put myself on a risk when I come to the hospital," Surie said. "It is more of a risk for my grandchildren, but what can the community do to me? I'm an old lady." It wasn't really true. There were so many things the community could do to her. But she would not share them with an outsider.

She was inexplicably grateful that Val had come. Someone who believed her. Someone who knew that this old, old woman was, in fact, expecting twins. *Happily* expecting twins. And all day, from the first moment since she'd been called out of bed, she had felt a familiar dragging in her groin. She had gone to the bathroom several times to see if she was bleeding, but she wasn't. And yet. And yet. "I felt something today," she said. "Down here."

"I can check if you like."

Yidel, his brothers, and their sons were praying the mincha prayers in the living room with a group of men from the next-door building. Yidel's sisters were on their way to their own homes. Tzila Ruchel had taken Surie's boys downstairs to her house. Surie led Val back to the bedroom and locked the door.

There was nothing wrong. A wave of relief ran over Surie. She hadn't known she was holding her breath all these days, worried about the lack of movement. The midwife put a hand under her arm to help her sit up. "You're fine," Val repeated. "You're definitely getting ready to have these babies, though." Val laughed and so did Surie, but then they both abruptly broke off, remembering they were in a house of mourning. "You are probably just feeling strange because of everything. Drink more water so you don't get dehydrated. When you cry a lot it's easy to get dehydrated and it's been shown to exacerbate Braxton Hicks contractions."

They sat on the edge of the bed without talking. In the other room, the men chanted the prayers.

"When you said it might only be a risk for your grandchildren if you work for me, did you forget that you will have two new children soon? Isn't it risky for them?"

"No," Surie said. Then, ashamed because she had momentarily forgotten the twins: "Yes."

The chanting rose, louder and louder, and all of the men called out, "Amein." Surie mumbled "Amein" too.

"What could happen to them?"

How the secular world loved to dwell on the ways in which order was maintained within the community. Excommunication. Arson. Acid. The journalists couldn't get enough dirt. Young men sentenced to prison cut off their payos so that it would not be obvious that they were Chassidic before their photographs were splashed all over the newspapers. Even in their deepest shame, they stayed loyal to their people.

If someone outside her family found out that she was studying to be a midwife, when the time came to enroll her children for the new school year no places would be available in all of Williamsburg. Anywhere. Yidel's calligraphy would no longer be the most popular. No one would hire him or their sons to write a new Torah scroll. A stone would come through their front window. His beard could be forcibly cut off in the back of a moving van. Playdates would be canceled. The meat from the butcher would always be too fatty and the paper bag would tear through on the way home. The cookies would be broken and taste of bleach. The eggs would have blood spots. Marriage suggestions would dry up.

But worse than that, people might try to convince Yidel to divorce her. Though they'd both vowed never to even say the D-word, the community wouldn't allow a bad influence to remain. They'd insist he get rid of her. Her children would be told not to talk to their mother. Her grandchildren would never see her. If it went to the

secular courts, they would side with the powerful community rulers. There had been other cases in the community where women weren't following the rules. Their
hair hadn't been shaved off, or their tights were too see-
through, or their high heels made too much noise on the
sidewalk, or their dresses were too tight. She'd helped
drive such women out of the community. Once, it had
been because the woman had sewn a skirt out of men's
old silk ties and insisted on wearing it. More often than
not, the women changed their minds and followed the
rules. The woman with the skirt made of ties had not.
She'd been furious. That woman had done some stone
throwing of her own.

Surie rocked on the edge of the bed. Why had she
thought bringing that textbook home was worth the risk?
The job at the hospital? The clinic suddenly seemed empty,
a waste of her energy. Dangerous. She didn't trust herself
to speak. Within her, this deep dragging, a sharp, slicing
pain from her rib to her hip.

Yidel knocked at the door.

"Surie? I want to lie down. I'm very tired."

When Val unlocked the door, he looked at the midwife with surprise. He remembered her, of course, from
Purim and from earlier, from the births of all of their
children.

"She checked my heart. It's been fluttery all day,"
Surie said. He was wearing his hearing aids now. "She's
just leaving."

Val frowned at Surie. The midwife passed a hand over
her face. She pressed her fingers into the corners of her
lips. She put her giant hands on her hips.

"Tell him," Val said. *Tell him. Tell him.*

"Tell me what?" Yidel asked.

"About the pregnant girl," Surie interrupted. Now that the moment had come, she wanted to tell Yidel about the twins in private. It wasn't something to share with Val or anyone else. "I know I wasn't supposed to talk about her at all. Confidentiality. But I had to say something. It was killing me."

Val passed her hand over her face again. "Rabbi Eckstein, I'm sorry, but I'm going to have to ask you to keep what you heard about the Shnitzer girl a secret. Can you do that?"

Yidel looked from Val to Surie. Her face was bright red and she was glaring at Val and the midwife was furious too.

"Don't come in to the hospital tomorrow. Call me."

"Fantastic," Surie said flatly. She brought up a hoarse kind of laugh.

Val said goodbye and edged past Yidel.

He waited until after he heard Val's footsteps going down the stairs before saying, "Don't lock the door when you are in a room with her. That lady is weird. I don't trust her. I can't believe you agreed to work with her every day. And would you please, please stop that laughing." He rolled over on his side and looked at Surie. "You're not . . . you wouldn't . . . you two aren't . . . ?" He shivered. "This world . . . ," he said. "We need the Messiah."

Surie put her face down into her pillow and wept from frustration.

Yidel slipped out to sit with Dead Opa. After an hour, he came back to check on her. She was half-asleep,

murmuring. Did she need anything? She wasn't looking
so well. Her face was covered in sweat and the quilt, over
her chest, was trembling. How was her heart? He came
to her bedside and took her hand, feeling for her pulse,
though she made no response. He said, very softly, that
he would return soon and then he went away. Surie, in
her fitful sleep, knew he had visited, but had not fully
opened her eyes because she had been talking to Lipa.

For the last month, on the bus and walking over the
bridge and washing the dishes, she'd imagined herself sitting in the park listening to the chittering of the squir-
rels, a bright new double stroller and two clean babies in
front of her, Lipa once again at her side. In those dreams,
she'd been young and her back didn't hurt and she never
had aching legs. It was a measure of pride to her as a mother
that she had somehow dredged from deep within herself this trembling flame of happiness. She'd dreamed,
over and over, of telling Yidel and of his whoop of joy,
the way he'd swagger around the neighborhood telling his
friends that he, a man in his sixties, was to be a father. And
of twins.

But she'd also dreamed about the clinic, working there,
studying the textbook at lunchtime and taking the tests
for lay midwives, attending her first birth, delivering a
Chassidic woman and giving the instructions in Yiddish.

Now, she was trapped in a nightmare. Her darkest
fears, terrors that came upon her late at night, rose up and
papered the walls of her bedroom. Both babies had Down
syndrome. They lacked brains. They were fused together,
two heads on one body, alive but monstrous. She died in
labor. The babies died in labor. There was blood, so much

blood. Even after she told everyone that she was pregnant, no one believed her. People talked about her as if she were crazy. They left brochures for Bellevue in the vestibule.

Her children were furious at her. Medical skeletons danced in her closets, jeering at her ignorance. Val grew to twice her actual size and snarled with a mouthful of polished marble teeth that had been filed into points. Gravel dust coated every surface of her house. Women walked past her windows, crying for help, but she was trapped in her bedroom. Yidel believed she'd been unfaithful. He thought she'd sinned with the Satan. Her beloved husband cried himself to sleep every night and never touched her again.

FIFTEEN

She had once asked Dead Onyu if the customs were different in Romania and the old woman had frowned, remembering:

Before the holiday, my father took the goose to the shochet and the butcher took out his long knife and said the prayer and slit the goose's neck, and then my mother and I sat and plucked the feathers into a pillowcase, a new pillow for my dowry, and then we kashered the bird on wooden planks drilled full of holes, and we sprinkled it with handfuls of salt we'd gathered at the seaside, and then, when it was ready, we stripped all of the fat from the meat and boiled it down and the best treat of all was the gribbenes, the fried pieces of fat, after all of the liquid had come out of it, and we children would fight over them, and if you had one piece, you would get married in four years and if you had two, you'd get married in two years, but if you had five pieces, it meant you would get married that very year.

When the matchmaker strolled through the village without his umbrella, it meant he was going to talk with

Shifra Leah, the baker, but if he strolled through the village with his black umbrella, it meant he was going to speak about a match and all of the children would hide behind the little blue picket fences and watch to see where he was going. And afterward, if we heard laughter, we knew there would be a wedding. And if we heard crying there might be a wedding too but it would be a poor one and there wouldn't be any fat herring.

The Rebbetzin wore a crown made of silk and pearls and gold embroidery and all of the women made it for her. The silk came up the river on a barge and was sold at the market, and my mother was the one who bought it, many yards, because of the many pleats that would be sewn into the cloth, and my aunt bought the fine gold wire and my grandmother cut the pearls off her own pearl necklace and they asked me to draw the design for the embroidery because all day I drew flowers and ferns and swords and lions into the dirt. I was so proud to be chosen. I was ten.

Before Rosh Hashanah, my brothers went to the river and peeled strips of bark from the willow trees there, and then they wound them into the shape of shofars, and they ran around the village, blowing them and making crazy sounds from these little trumpahten and the fathers would chase them and try to grab them away, and it was the only time the boys could run from their fathers and not expect to get a smack on the bottom.

I was afraid, the first time I went to get my father from the synagogue on the late afternoon before Yom Kippur. My father knelt on the floor in his white kittel, his beard folded on the parquet, and my uncle beat his shoulders with a belt, not hard, you have to understand, just taps, but still.

The girls in our family were all married with the same dowry, two feather beds, two feather blankets, six feather pillows, a dozen heavy linen sheets, four lace curtains, a sofa, twenty envelopes full of seeds for the garden, ten good laying hens, and a bookshelf full of fine-printed Hebrew books. My father gave the groom a gold watch, and my mother sewed him his linen shrouds. But that was only for my sisters, because by the time I married in the DP camp, I had no parents, only one sister left of seven, no brothers, no cousins, no nieces, no nephews.

———

From now on, there would be no Dead Onyu by Surie's side, sitting next to her on the holidays, listening as she spoke of her children, advising her about her life. From her place at the women's table, Surie looked across at Yidel, sitting at the men's table in the next room. His mouth was flapping open and shut, but she could tell that he was not singing. The expression on his face shifted between a blurred sadness and no expression at all. This pushing away of mourning an impossibility. His ancient father, Dead Opa, sat next to him, his head in his hands. The sons, the sons-in-law, the grandsons, all swayed in unison. They were singing a song that their great-great-grandfather, Dead Opa's father, had composed. In the middle of the wordless song, the overhead lights went out and they were left sitting in candlelight.

"What happened to the timer?"

"Yoish! A two-day yontiff and no lights."

The timer, in the rush after the funeral, had remained set for a standard Shabbos. But on Shavios, the lights needed to remain on all night.

"It's not the worst thing."

The weak light calmed the children. They leaned together, trading secrets in whispers. Babies dozed on their mothers' laps. The singing grew softer, warmer, and the young girls rustled on the benches and cooed like roosting birds. The littlest decided to play a game of bahaltereich. Who will be it? Eins, tsvei, drai, lozer lokker-lai, okn bokn, beiner-shtokn, onk, bonk, shtonk. They hid in the dark corners, scaring themselves, getting caught with little yelps and cries. The bigger girls jumped rope but were told to put away the shtrik. The older girls dared one another to say tongue twisters. "Can you say fir por portzelayne farfurkes?" The food was carried in and out in huge tureens, the plates whisked off the tables and replaced with clean ones. Between courses, Surie's teenage boys washed the dishes and dried them, and as they worked, their voices rose and fell as if they were studying Gemara instead of rinsing plates. They were rehearsing the little speeches they had prepared for the long sleepless first night of the holiday. They twisted their payos between their fingers. A knife fell and landed with its point stuck in the floor. They looked at one another, said, "We have an enemy," and burst out laughing, then hushed themselves. To rejoice? To mourn?

Small boys fought and called one of their own a liggener and dragged the liar to arbitration by the fathers. The house filled with an undercover ripple, like mice nibbling the roots of periwinkle on a warm night. A subdued sound, given away only by the almost invisible rise and fall of the leaves as the mice moved from plant to plant, by the faintest gestures among the cousins. In the flickering light of the candles, Surie looked across at Yidel again, at his gray beard and his dark eyes, and—wanting to rip up the secret that divided them—knew with the blackest certainty that she would tell him about the twins the moment he came back from the all-night reading, early the next morning, just before dawn. She would stuff the hearing aids into his ears herself if she had to. She wanted nothing more than to erase this division between them. They had made this world together. She wanted all of him. Without barriers.

That night, her sons and grandsons came in and out, picking up sheet cakes and cartons of cigarettes and carrying them back to the shil where all the men stayed up, awake, waiting for the giving of the Torah, and Surie's daughters and daughters-in-law stayed behind for a while in the living room, telling stories of the Baal Shem Tov and not a few stories about their families and their friends, and there was hushed laughter though it was a house of mourning, for the joy of the holiday took precedence over the sadness.

Surie had carried the candelabra into the living room, and sometime close to midnight, the candles began to gutter and the room filled with the exquisite smell of extinguished beeswax. The children squealed and moved closer to their mothers.

"It's so dark, Mommy!"

The women, over a dozen of them, were tired, drifting in the dim lighting and the late hour. The smallest girls lay sprawled on blankets on the floor, asleep, sucking their thumbs. The schoolgirls tried to play kigelach in the light coming inside from the streetlamp, their tiny hands hitting the floor, scooping up the small metal cubes, and then catching the one main cube as it fell.

"I'm going to stay up until Tatie comes home," they said to one another, even as their eyelids drooped. And it was just like Pesach, when the littlest ones tried to stay awake for Eliyahu the prophet but couldn't and fell asleep in their chairs and under the table.

This was the beginning of summer, the most beautiful soft nights, when the air was full of the sound of tree frogs and stars could be seen above the Brooklyn Navy Yard in the deep blue sky. The children could feel the release of some of the bonds of the year. School would end soon and many would go up to the Catskills, to bungalows and to camp. And the mothers, too, felt this release, even Surie. She looked around at the children and was filled with a deep joy that soon two more children would join them. "Tzila Ruchel," she said, whispering in her daughter's ear, "you're going to have two new siblings."

Tzila Ruchel stood up and stretched her back. "That's nice, Mommy. I'm glad you've found someone for Mattis. Let me know when they are going to meet. I'll make some fancy cakes, bli neder. Hi ho, it's time to go downstairs," she said. "To bed. Miryam Chiena, will you take the girls?" This was a signal to the other women that it would be permissible to go home, to say that they had stayed up long enough on Shavios night.

"No, Tzila Ruchel, that's not what I meant," Surie said. She leaned on the arm of the chair and levered herself up. "Wait." She wasn't ready for the peaceful night to end, for if there was ever a time to tell her daughter, now, when they were both so mellow, was it. "I'll make coffee."

All except Tzila Ruchel trickled out and Surie was left in the kitchen with her third daughter. "Let's get the dishes put up," she said, and they finished washing the dishes the boys hadn't and wiped them dry and squeezed them back in the crowded cabinets. Then they took baked goods from the freezer and laid them out on the tables for the following morning. They worked quickly and in total silence. They were both tired. "There's some left," said Surie when the kitchen shone. She held out a pot of black coffee. "It wouldn't do to waste it." She sat down at the tiny kitchen table and, looking up at Tzila Ruchel, poured herself a large cup. Tzila Ruchel shook her head.

"The girls will be wondering where I am." She took off her damp housecoat and hung it on a nail above the window to the roof.

"I wasn't talking about Mattis," Surie said. "I'm pregnant. Can't you tell?"

"Don't be ridiculous! That's not possible!" Tzila Ruchel shook her head but then dropped her gaze and eyed Surie's stomach. "Oy." Tiny twitches moved across Tzila Ruchel's face. First her eyebrow, then her nostril, then her cheek, then her lip. "Are you sure it's not a tumor? Have you seen a doctor?"

Surie took a sip of the coffee. She pressed her shaking hands around the cup. "It's twins."

"Gevald! You can't be serious. What were you thinking?" Tzila Ruchel was halfway out of the room, her feet running though her body was stationary.

"Even my doctor thinks it's a miracle, but my daughter thinks I am revolting."

"Mommy . . ."

"You do."

"When?"

"In two months. A little less maybe."

"Gottenyu! We're ruined. Absolutely finished. As if Lipa wasn't enough! If you haven't married off Mattis by then, he'll be unmarriageable. And what was Tatie thinking . . . how could he . . . ? You're so—"

"Old," Surie said, right as her daughter said, "Obese."

They stared at each other. Surie felt a terrible pain in her stomach. She tried to smile. "I'm excited," she said. "They'll keep me young."

"Stop it!" Tzila Ruchel said. "Uch, it's so disgusting! I don't want to think about it anymore!" She backed away from Surie, who continued smiling. "I can't even look at your face." Would Yidel react this badly? The other married children? Surie's lips were so dry that they began to crack.

———

After drinking all of the coffee, though she knew she shouldn't, Surie cut a large wedge of chocolate cake and took a bite. She could never eat enough to satisfy the twins. On the way to her bedroom she saw, standing in the shadow in the corner under the leaking skylight, Onyu and Lipa. A drop of water fell onto the floor. Surie put out the hand that wasn't holding the plate and it passed through Lipa's chest. Dead Onyu opened her mouth and inside were three rows of shining metal teeth. There was

dirt on her lips, a fur of frost on her cheeks. She smiled at
Surie. "Not long now," she said.

Lipa lifted his hand and waved. He looked again like
her little boy, with his long curling payos and the suit she'd
sewn for him when he was twelve. He seemed to be getting shorter as she watched. The black wall behind him
shone brighter and brighter. He was a cartoon of himself,
a silvery outline. He was a few scratches in the paint. He
was just a faint odor. He was gone. "No!" she said. "Wait!"
A fist inside her guts clenched. She slapped the iron ladder. Bananas fell to the floor. Her ears rang. There was a
line of mold running from the top of the wall to the bottom. "Lipa!" she cried. "Come back!" She stamped on the
bananas. "Why are you always running away from me?"
she yelled. She kicked off her dirty slippers, trod the pulp,
and felt it ooze up into her stockings. Everywhere, the
scent of bruised fruit.

When she reached her room, it was in complete darkness. Usually she left a small light burning, but even this
had been affected by the timer. It seemed as if a dark mist
hung overhead, obscuring the map of Europe on the ceiling and the narrow windows. After putting on her nightgown, she propped herself up on pillows and angrily ate
the cake. Then she tried to find a comfortable way to lie
down, but each direction she turned felt bad, and her back
ached. She pushed a cushion between her legs and then
pulled it out again. The water in the cistern gurgled. In
the hallway, the skylight dripped. A pair of mosquitoes
whined. Something in the Brooklyn Navy Yard thumped
rhythmically. The apartment was empty and yet the floor
creaked, there came a sound like nails being pulled from
a board, and the wind made the pegs on the washing lines

up on the roof chatter. Her bed was first icy cold and then
much too hot, the pillow too firm and then utterly flat. It
was only after she had turned the pillow over for the ninth
or tenth time that she realized her belly was getting hard
at regular intervals, that the ache in her back might be the
beginning of an electric something that tingled and ran
around to the front. She sat up and fished for her watch,
but in the dark, she couldn't see the hands. It was still
yontiff. She couldn't turn on the light.

Had she drunk enough water? She'd had that coffee.
But coffee, she remembered, was a stimulant, perhaps not
the best choice. She stood up and walked into the kitchen
to pour herself a glass of water. Her belly was soft. Her
backache couldn't be the result of the low chairs for the
shiva because she hadn't sat in them. She made the blessing and sipped the water. She went back out into the
living room with the glass and looked at the seven-day
candle on the bureau that had been lit for the soul of her
mother-in-law. It was flickering in the slight breeze from
the window. To think that a life could be lost so easily.
Where did the soul go when it left the body? Of course,
it went to God, but where was that, exactly? And how
did it free itself? She opened the top drawer of the bureau, took out a partially used candle that she lit from the
yahrzeit licht, and then carried it carefully into her bedroom. She dripped some wax onto the plate and stuck the
candle to the porcelain. The room filled with shadows.
Flickering mercurial light shone in the windows and in
the mirrors. She looked at her watch. It was 3:27. Somehow, over an hour had passed since Tzila Ruchel left.
Yidel would be home after 5:00.

As she was putting her watch back onto the bedside

cabinet, her belly began to tighten and she bent over and moaned. It was not the lighter contractions that she'd been half aware of experiencing earlier in the evening. This one meant business. It gripped her around the waist and dug its fingers deeply into her spine and it did not let go. Surie broke out in a sweat. She twisted and sweated and gritted her teeth. It was an awkward position, bent over the cabinet, and after the contraction was over, she'd have to move. She swung her hips from side to side, her eyes on the watch face. A minute, a minute and a half. But that couldn't be right. Such long contractions happened late in the delivery, not at the beginning. "No," she growled, biting at her lips. "Not now. This is the wrong time. Not now."

SIXTEEN

That first contraction unnerved her. For many minutes afterward, all she heard was the dripping underneath the skylight. Below her own rotting floorboards, the rain had reached down into Tzila Ruchel's apartment. Her daughter's ceiling, at that corner, was stained and black, and when it rained heavily, in the spring and the autumn, drops fell from Tzila Ruchel's ceiling and made her floor as black as Surie's, despite the pots she placed under the drips. The damage even reached down to Dead Onyu's apartment. And to the basement.

After the second contraction, some men walked by outside, their footsteps echoing between the buildings as they made their way home from saying the tikkun for Shavios. But none of them sounded like Yidel, who walked with a particular heavy step and then a slight rasp of the other foot, not exactly a limp. It might have been some imbalance related to his deafness, because he hadn't limped as a younger man.

Just as the third contraction was loosening, she felt a twist below her ribs, some kind of deep interior movement, followed by something resembling a pop, and then the sensation of moisture between her legs. There was an unnatural silence; all of the sounds of the city momentarily stilled and then began to roar and buzz and whistle and whine and hum and tick and drip again.

———

Because of the holiday, she was not allowed to touch the phone to call the midwife until she was certain that labor was under way. The contractions were irregular. How would she know if it was false labor? Would she commit a sin by calling if the labor fizzled out? If Yidel had been home, he would have been sent to ask the rabbi if they might use the telephone on the holy day. He would have roused one of his buddies from the emergency medical crew. Instead, she told herself that when the contractions were five minutes apart, she would call the midwife herself. It was too far to walk to the synagogue, and anyway, no women would be there at four in the morning. Even if she somehow managed to get there, she wouldn't be heard over the voices of the thousands of men. She wanted to have Yidel nearby, but he didn't come and he didn't come, and eventually, she let the wanting go.

When Lipa first came home with his green glasses, Dead Onyu put out her hands and kissed his forehead and told him he was her favorite grandchild. The old woman could still see then.

It was raining harder. It drummed on the old roof and fell spattering on the floor beneath the skylight. There would be puddles in the cellar. What did the water carry down to the basement with it, first from her apartment, then from Tzila Ruchel's, then from Dead Onyu's?

What would all the grandmothers think when she passed by with new babies? No one would believe they were hers. The birth would be almost as miraculous as that of Sarah, wife of Avraham. She wasn't as old as the matriarch, but she was carrying twins!

Surie walked back and forth from her bed to the bathroom. Sometimes the contractions caught her in the hallway and she leaned against the wall and held in her voice so that Tzila Ruchel, downstairs, would not hear. And sometimes the pains came when she was in the bathroom and she pulled against the towel rail and crouched and her eyes squeezed shut, sweat rolling down her face. It seemed, within a very short amount of time, she no longer remembered what she had been thinking during a contraction. Now the crushing was all darkness and bright lights inside her eyelids, pulsing vermilion streaks and yellow explosions. She knocked over the glass of water on the bedside table and kicked the broken glass under her bed. "Mazal tov," she muttered. Each time she came back to her room, she forgot and again stood in the puddle and tracked it out into the hallway, where she stepped in the mashed bananas and tracked that back into her room. It was too late to roll down her stockings or find her abandoned slippers. It was too late to go downstairs for Tzila Ruchel, even had she wanted to, for she could manage only a few steps on the tips of her toes and those with difficulty. But was this real labor yet? She wasn't sure.

In between the contractions, she leaned against whatever was there, trembling.

———

She had forgotten to switch the laundry from the washer to the dryer. Yesterday. Or the day before yesterday? She hated the smell of mildew.

———

She had never asked her mother what her own birth had been like. Easy or hard? There was no one left to ask.

———

Mamme, Mamme!

———

Sometimes she fell asleep for a minute or two and woke up when an urgent tingle formed in her spine. She thought she should time the contractions, but she couldn't find her watch. She thought that it might be the moment to call the midwife and then forgot.

She sat on the toilet and felt some relief, but then, as her belly tightened, she rose up, away from the pain, and began to whimper. Years earlier Val had told her that when a contraction came, she should say, "Yes!" instead of crying, "No!" but now she cried, "No! No no no no!" Her denials fused together and came out as an ugly bellow.

She was not strong enough to endure labor.

Though middle-aged women came into the clinic for IVF treatment and it was technically possible to help them conceive, pregnancy for the old was a form of torture. No one would go through it if they knew what it would do to their body. It was hard enough to climb the stairs.

Her feet were swollen and numb. There was a high-pitched buzzing in her ears. Her knees felt as though

razors had been inserted between the bones. She wanted
to kill Yidel.

She leaned forward on the toilet and felt between her
legs. In the darkness, she could not tell whether what she
felt was blood or some other fluid, so she stood up and
edged over to the window and held her hand up against
the frosted glass. There was not enough light in the bathroom to see anything. Surely she was far enough along in
the labor that the regular laws of the holidays would not
apply? Could she switch on the bedside lamp? She would
have to wait for Yidel. Where was he? As usual, not
home. As usual, in the synagogue. Why was he never
home when she needed him? She could die, broken open
on the linoleum, and he would still be out with his buddies, singing songs, smoking, eating cake.

That wasn't fair. She knew it wasn't. He was a good
man. But at the next contraction, she screamed his name.
She was sure she had never been so angry. She bit down
on his name and shook it, grinding her teeth, biting
her lips.

Before the next contraction came, she began the movements necessary to kneel on the floor. She was desperate
to arch her back. She was halfway down when the contraction leapt upon her. She fought against the pain as if
it were a tiger. An urgent bellow of *no*s boiled out of
her throat. It was the loudest sound she had ever made. It
didn't stop. She roared and roared. Some new sensation
gripped her, utterly alien and yet deeply familiar, a sliding
and twisting, a burning heat that rose up from her legs
and accelerated through her spine. She held her breath and
began to push against this thing, and she roared again.

Balanced there, halfway between the toilet and the floor, one foot raised, she closed her eyes and bore down, blinded by a thousand brilliant lights bursting in her eyes. The only relief for such a fierce burning was pushing, so she pushed again. She'd call the midwife soon. Everything would be fine.

Outside the door of the bathroom, she heard her granddaughter Miryam Chiena yelling, "Bubbie? Bubbie? Are you all right?" The handle turned and the door shook in its frame. She lunged across the room and leaned against the door, keeping it closed with the full weight of her body, taking a deep breath and holding it throughout the next contraction, a weak one.

"I'm good," she croaked when she was released. "Miryam Chiena, darling, go downstairs."

"What is all the noise?"

"Something is stuck," Surie said, and she made an ugly wet sound with her mouth and her lips, something she'd done as a child and giggled about, to hint at the personal nature of the sticking. "Leave me alone, little lamb." She just had time to lean over and flush the toilet before she again had to close her eyes and hold her breath, willing Miryam Chiena downstairs and back into bed with her last moment of control.

"Good night, Bubbie. I'm glad you're all right. I'll tell Mommy you have a tummy upset."

The child's footsteps receded down the hallway. Surie's lips were bleeding from biting her mouth shut.

"Open your eyes and see your baby being born." That is what her midwife had told her. But it wasn't time for that yet. Surely not. Still, Surie got both feet underneath her and gripped the edge of the toilet seat, squatting, and she panted. She was still wearing her stockings. She should unbutton them from the garter belt.

It was happening too fast. It was wrong. It had never been like this.

Those thoughts were buried underneath the avalanche of the next contraction.

"No!" she cried, but then, shakily, she changed it to, "Yes!" A *yes* like a crowbar forcing a lock. She opened her eyes and knew something was wrong. She couldn't be ready for delivery. Surely this was just Braxton Hicks? She hadn't even called Val. The doctor had said a hundred times that she had to be in the hospital, supervised. It was too dangerous. How big were the twins? She'd been afraid to eat. At seven months, he'd said they probably weighed less than two pounds each, a fifth of the weight of her other children at the same age. It was her fault they were so small.

She did not see the infant's scalp with its creamy vernix and wet strands of hair. Neither did she see a little bottom, squeezed dark purple. There wasn't enough light. Instead, she felt a strange fluid-filled membrane bulging from her, something like a water balloon. Her heart fluttered. A watermelon had grown from a tiny seed tossed carelessly into her waiting field, and now it had rolled perilously downhill, faster and faster. And with the next push, the sac twisted, there was muffled flailing, a soft movement, and the thing slid out farther, and with another push, she caught it.

The sun must have been coming up, because there was a pale blue rectangle at the window. Perhaps it was five thirty? Her mother's clock had rung, but how many times? She didn't know. She was still filled with the unbearable urge to push.

They were born seconds apart, their cauls still intact. Their hair glittered and danced like falling snow inside iridescent, filmy globes that bulged as the babies moved. She laid them on her warm belly and watched as the early morning sun was refracted through their identical amniotic sacs, forming rainbows on the tiles beside her. She could see they were tired, and she was, too. They were swimming the longest distance now, and as their sacs collapsed, she heard a faint cry, a dying note played by a bow not perfectly aligned with the violin.

SEVENTEEN

Shortly after the delivery of the placentas, Yidel came home. At the sound of his footsteps on the stairs, she hauled herself upright and pulled her nightgown down to cover her legs. It was still possible, perhaps, that she could get away with saying nothing.

"Are you up?" Yidel said. "I stayed behind a little to help clean up."

He waited, as he always waited, outside the bathroom door, and he chattered on about what each man had said, and what the Rebbe had said, while she said nothing, crawling around quietly wiping the floor and the toilet and herself. The bathroom slowly filled with bright light from the south-facing window. The space reverted to being a bathroom. "Would you like some tea?" he asked. "I am not quite ready to go to sleep. Full of adrenaline, I think. And I have something for you."

He always brought her a little square of pound cake from shil. It would be dry and crumbling, wrapped in a piece of brown paper towel. He would put it in her hand and she would want, as always, to kiss his dear cheek.

She leaned against the door. How had she ever kept anything from him? And why? All those stupid reasons in her head. What about her heart? "Yes," she said. "I'm coming." She asked him to wait a moment, that she wasn't quite ready, and he said he would get water from the urn and make tea. He said he would be in the kitchen, and it was almost as if that part of him that understood silent language knew she wanted to speak to him about something specific. And why shouldn't he know? He was her husband. They had been married for forty years.

Outside, the sun rose and rose and the tiny scraps of white clouds fell apart and became absorbed by the blue, blue sky. In the tree of heaven outside the bathroom window, goldfinches chaffed one another and flew from branch to branch, swaying on the very finest twigs, their scant weight barely enough to bow the tips. On the fire escape, Dead Onyu's Swiss chard and romaine lettuce and radishes continued to grow in buckets, unaware that she was gone.

When Surie shuffled into the kitchen, Yidel stood up as he always did, from respect, and she bowed her head.

"Aha!" he said gleefully. "I see I'm not the only person with a present today! What do you have there?" he asked of the shopping bag she held in front of her. "Is it a pie?"

"Let's drink that tea," she said.

How many times had they sat and drunk tea in the early morning hours when the light was blue, and always Yidel had taken out the tattered *Tzeina U'Reina* and read one of the stories to her, and always he had said, "These stories are as good as the best food."

But this time, when he sat down, he didn't take out the old leather-bound book and he didn't rifle through the pages looking for a favorite story to tell. There was only the table between them with its laminated cover and the ironstone teapot and the crumbling square of cake and the two glasses. There was the little bowl of sugar cubes because they both still preferred to drink tea sucked through sugar held in the teeth rather than stirred into the liquid. There was the spotlessly clean kitchen, and Surie, bent over, her scarf falling sideways so that the small dark prickles of her shaven head showed at the neck. She looked and felt ill. Couldn't he see? And there was the plastic bag on the table. The terrible guilt of it.

Yidel pulled his chair round to her side and reached for her hand, but she pulled away. "You can't," she said. A bleeding woman may not touch her husband and he may not touch her.

"What's happened?" he asked, puzzled, two lines appearing between his brows. It had been years since she had bled.

"I tried to tell you," she said. "But you didn't have your hearing aids in." Was she really going to blame him? "It came on suddenly, and before I could call for help, it was over."

"Is it the cancer?" he whispered, because years earlier there had been that scare with cancer, but they had gotten through it. The cancer might always be his greatest fear.

"No, no," she said, and tears welled up in her eyes and she brushed them away angrily, because his voice was so tender and it would not be tender when he knew. She would force herself to tell the truth to him because unless she ripped down every lie between them, they would never be able to go back to the way they had been.

He looked her over carefully. Her scarf was covered in dark brown fingerprints. Small blood vessels had broken in her face and in her eyes. She was panting and shaking as if she had a terrible fever. There was blood under her fingernails. Though he was an EMT and had seen her like this many times, his brain was slow to connect the dots.

"Should I call an ambulance?" he said haltingly, after a moment.

"It's too late," she said. "It's over already. All I need is to lie down and go to sleep. I can take care of myself."

He stood as if he were going to help her rise, and then, puzzled and afraid, he said, "What's over?" and she gestured toward the plastic bag, but when he pulled the bag toward him and began to open it, she smacked his hand away.

"No," she said. "Don't look at them."

His head snapped up and he looked at her. "Them? What are you saying?"

"I'm naming them," she said. "Like I did before. And one of them, the boy, I am naming after Lipa. The other one, I think she was a girl, I'm naming her after Onyu."

His face crumpled. "What have you done, Surie?" His shoulders collapsed into his chest, but his cheeks flooded with color. "Was it with someone at the hospital?"

"You fool! You *know* me!" she said. "I would never be with someone besides you!"

"But why didn't you tell me?" he asked piteously, and

then he turned and—on the holiday—dialed the number for Hatzolah on their old rotary phone. He requested an ambulance be sent to their address. At the sound of the siren, the neighbors would gather around to hear what disaster had caused an ambulance to be called and they would whisper among themselves in hushed tones, guessing. But no one would know what had really happened. It was too late to stop the ambulance from coming, but that didn't mean she had to go downstairs with the paramedics, her scarf askew, the back of her housecoat bloody. She would refuse.

The moment he hung up the phone, he lunged toward the bag, snatched it from her, and looked inside. Then he clenched the top of the plastic shut and sat down and fat tears oozed from his eyes and fell into his beard.

"I don't want them buried in that cemetery. I want them to go somewhere nice. Where there are trees and maybe some flowers. Wind blowing over them. Water. There must be somewhere like that. Maybe they could be buried with Lipa in San Francisco."

"Oh Surie," he said. "Such a miracle came to us and I didn't even know. Why? Why didn't you trust me?"

She picked up the cake and put it down again. It fell apart. "I can't understand myself," she said.

After a long moment, he whispered, "Please don't leave me."

He was just like one of the children. Yidel poked at the cake, pushed the two pieces together. It broke into several new pieces, disintegrated, became merely a mass of yellow crumbs. He looked up at her, and when she still didn't say anything, an odd coughing sound came from his mouth and Surie, to her horror, realized he was sobbing.

"I'm not going anywhere." She poured him a glass of tea and pushed a sugar cube toward him. "I *should* have told you. I tried to. I just left it too late." But this was not the worst of it. Their little faces. The blood vessels luminous in their tiny ears. She gripped the edge of the table.

He whispered the blessing over tea—everything is created through Your word—and swallowed several times. He looked around the kitchen before saying, "I want our babies to be buried with my mother. If it's allowed. What do you think?"

"I'm going to tell the children what's happened," she said, her voice much too loud. "I told Tzila Ruchel last night. Before . . . this. And I'm going to say the whole story about Lipa too." The transparent strands of their hair falling like mist through her fingers, vanishing.

"What does this have to do with Lipa?"

"I'm going to tell them. You can't stop me. I'm sick to death of not talking about things. We're a family." Their mouths. The fragile bones of their jaws.

"No," he said. "Surie! That's not the right thing to do. I know you're not feeling like yourself. I'll get help. Maybe you can go to one of those kimpeturin houses? Would you like that? I think the Seagate one is closed, but there's that gorgeous house in Kiryas Joel."

"Are you crazy?" She was almost yelling. She who never yelled. "Me? I'm going to go to a recovery house full of young women and their newborn babies?" She clawed at her scarf, scratched her neck. "Sometimes you have no sense." She closed her eyes. She opened them. Still she saw their pursed lips, the peeling skin. Still she smelled them on her hands.

His head drooped. "It's true," he said. "If I were a better husband, the husband you deserve, I would have noticed that you were . . ." He waved his hand toward her belly. "What kind of a man . . . ?"

She didn't know what it was about him: the way he kept on glancing at the paper bag, the tears that hung like tiny jewels in his beard, his inability to say the word *pregnant*, the way he was always so *nice* even when she was very, very *not* nice. It made her long silence feel almost justified. And she did not want to be right. Their skin. Their eyes. Their toes, so small. She wanted, more than anything, to be wrong about the community, about Yidel, about them as a couple. She wanted to be wrong about herself too. And so she said, "I'm tired of the way everything is a secret."

She hadn't known Yidel was hovering at the edge of rage. On the outside, he'd looked the same as always. His shoulders still curved around his chest as if to protect his heart. His hands lay quietly on the table. The lines around his eyes and at the corners of his mouth made it seem that he might, at any moment, smile. But a dark shadow she had never seen before moved across his face, a dark purple, the blackening of the skin of an eggplant as it roasts over a fire just before it turns to ash.

"Are you joking?" he said. He stood up. His fingers curled tightly into the palms of his hands. "It's *you* who has been keeping secrets."

"Because I had to."

"You didn't have to. You *wanted* to. Am I the kind of

husband who has ever been upset with news of a pregnancy? Am I the kind of man you can't talk to?" He was
patting himself all over his chest, his big fat hands going
pfff pfff pfff. "Are you afraid of me? What aren't you telling me, Surie?"

She stood up and almost knocked into him by mistake,
and he raised his arm against her, as if to ward off a blow.
Perhaps he was just surprised.

Shlimazal, she thought. His shirt was untucked, he had
cake crumbs in his beard, watering, red-rimmed eyes, a
fusty unwashed smell drifted from his clothing. He was
the very picture of a charity collector, the kind of man
who begged on street corners for copper coins, avoiding meaningful contact with other people, staring at the
gutter. It was only through him that she knew his calligraphy was desirable. He'd told her at every chance.
Gloating.

He was fat too.

She was always having to make apologies for him.
"Oh, my husband doesn't really go out much. He's far too
busy." Yidel didn't like strangers, he socialized only among
family members and then on holidays. He didn't like
people's quirky little ways or variations in accents, when
he had so many quirky little ways and a strange accent
somewhere between Amish and dog. Yidel had a bad attitude toward life, a superior look.

It had really been Yidel who couldn't accept Lipa. That
much had been clear after the funeral. Had her son come
to her first, she would have learned to love him in that
state, that gay state of his. Yidel just said things, but he
didn't mean them. Forty years of marriage and here they

were. All those years of faithful commitment meaning-less, if he was going to accuse her of adultery. He really didn't know her at all. She gripped the edge of the window and lifted the sash. The birds weren't out yet, but there was the smell of the river, the rush of sound from the bridge. Maybe, after all this was over, she'd go down to the bus as she did every day: the overly warm seats, the rise up into the sky, the steel girders flashing by, the water far below, and then back down into the city, a different city entirely, though only twenty minutes away, the thermos of coffee warming her lap, the textbook with its photographs of the unseen and unimagined, her Post-it notes in bright pastels spilling from the pages. Sometimes she'd fall asleep on the ride. By nine, she'd be at the hospital, in the aqua-colored coat with her name embroidered in the front. She'd be pulling on her first set of nitrile gloves and checking the list of patients for the day. But where was Yidel in that dream? Where were Tzila Ruchel and Miryam Chiena and Dead Opa?

Surie leaned forward, peering out into the soft blue morning light. The sun made the white tiles of the kitchen glow, one by one. She readjusted her scarf. It used to be her favorite time of day, this moment when all of the children had left and the mothers vanished and the streets were empty and silent and only an occasional plastic bag tumbled across the asphalt. It was three floors down to the chickens in the yard and the concrete. *I want something different.* It seemed to her that she had been thinking this thought many times a day for many months.

"It's chilly," Yidel said. She hadn't noticed. A brilliant fire was burning inside her chest, eating her flesh from the inside out. "Could you shut that?"

"You can," she said, "if you care that much." But she took hold of the window and levered it closed. It had always stuck a little. It stuck now. Her irises, in the reflection, seemed orange.

"I've called the midwife," he said.

"Val."

"Who else? I think I hate her. But you could die. Couldn't you die? She said I should take you to the emergency room."

"I don't care," she said.

He studied her with his tired red eyes. She smiled.

"That's not funny."

"I mean it."

"The Hatzolah men will be here soon."

She sat down in the chair again. He sat down beside her. "Tea?" he asked, and he poured her another cup and pushed a cube of sugar across the table.

She missed Val, who was easy to talk to, a sort-of friend who had never known Lipa, someone with whom it had been briefly possible to be a mother with a dead gay son. How she stared and stared at the old-fashioned Bakelite telephone. But Val probably hadn't forgiven her for telling Yidel about the girl from the community. Telling other people's secrets, when all along she hadn't been able to tell her own! And for pretending to have told Yidel about the pregnancy when she hadn't. That too. Surie didn't think there'd be any going back to the hospital. Val thought secrets revealed something about strength of character, and for a while, Surie had felt the same. But now, she knew that they didn't. Secrets were the root of all weakness.

———

When the men from the ambulance service arrived, they talked about Surie as if she were not in the room with them, and she gazed off into space as if she were not there.

"Patient is fifty-seven." The senior EMT, one of Yidel's best friends, speaking into a walkie-talkie, tapped his finger on the table. "And she just gave birth, alone, on her bathroom floor, to twins. Obs wobbly. Call in a dirty birth and bring up a trolley."

"What difference does it make?" Surie said. "The babies are dead. My worst fear has already happened." She lined up the knot of her scarf on her spine, untied it, and then pulled the knot tight. An image: the babies' cords, wrapped around their necks. Had that really happened? Or was she conflating their deaths with Lipa's? She thought that something else, not strangulation, had afflicted the twins. Those sounds, the whining hisses, so similar to the breathing of asthmatic Mrs. Shnitzer. A cascade of unfamiliar words from the textbook: *fetal lung maturation, prophylactic corticosteroids, surfactant, stress.*

"You're looking better, I *think* you are, at least. Do you want more tea? A cookie before they take you to the hospital?" Yidel asked. Her eyes were still on the window. Every minute or so, a seagull flew past. Or a pigeon. Yidel blew his nose.

"I'm not going anywhere," she said. "Unless it's to my own bed."

"My mother died and now this."

She had, for the moment, forgotten about Dead Onyu.

———

"Don't say a word to anyone," Yidel said to the ambulance crew after Surie refused to go with them. "Not even your wives. This can't get out."

The emergency technicians waited half an hour for her to change her mind. Finally, they looked at their former chief, Yidel, shook their heads, and went away.

"I can make you some eggs. Or a sandwich? Maybe heat up some soup?"

"No," said Surie. "I'm not hungry." She was freezing cold. Her whole body shook. The attending on the crew had checked her blood pressure three times. *Dirty birth* is what he'd written into his notes. Oxygen offered. Obstreperous patient.

"All right," he said. "What's next, then?"

She wouldn't let Yidel near her. A half hour later she went into the bathroom and came out wearing a different nightgown. Staring at the tiles had taken a long time. She had waited for something to climb out of the grout. Her children had been there, and then they hadn't. Where had they gone? Her hands ached with emptiness.

"I'll check in on you in a bit," Yidel said. He put his EMT pack on his bed, opened it, and began laying out paper packages. He looked as raw as she felt.

"Stop it. I don't want you to be nice to me. You should send Tzila Ruchel."

She lay in bed, imagining telling the whole story of the pregnancy and the rushed birth to her mother. "Poor lamby," her mother would have said. She had lost her husband, Surie's father, when he was fifty. She would know what this feeling was like, the blank emptiness unfurling ahead of Surie. The fear of all those years of solitude. "Make it right," Surie's mother would have said. Anything not to live alone.

She should say something to Yidel when he came in the next time.

"Good plan," her mother said.

At eleven o'clock, Yidel came in backward, pushing open the door with his rear end, carrying a tray of tomato soup and bread and grape juice.

"How are you doing?" she asked, not looking in his direction now that he was in the room.

"I've had better days." He set down the tray and put the glass of juice on her bedside table. "Thanks for asking. For a while there, I didn't think you cared."

———

Soon, the head of the Chevra Kadisha would arrive to take the tiny bodies. It was the first morning of yontiff and the boys would get up and want breakfast and the grandchildren would come upstairs, hoping for a slice of Bubbie's cheesecake. Life wouldn't wait for her. That one moment, in the bedroom, when she had asked after him and he'd thanked her, that had felt better than almost anything that had happened to her in months.

All that running to the hospital. She'd just been running away from a series of conversations for which she couldn't find words. She thought she might actually loathe the smell of the antiseptic with which they washed the floors each night. And the odors of the foreign foods. That doctor, with his sharp, arrogant face! It had been all right, translating for the women, but it couldn't replace this, which was real, which mattered, which was hers.

————

Yidel made her eggs again for lunch. It was the only thing he knew how to make well. Those stupid chickens with their egg-laying songs—she'd been woken up by them, at the crack of dawn, for years, and why? She could have used earplugs. She could have taken the shochet out into the yard and asked him to kill every one of the birds. But the ridiculous creatures had made her happy. Their hopping. Their chirping and trilling. The way they flocked to her feet when she went outside and stared up into her face with adoration. The reliable way they gave her an egg each morning, a fresh egg that she could make into whatever she wanted. When had she stopped getting up at their call? When had she begun setting an alarm so she wouldn't miss the bus to Manhattan?

Yidel was sitting on his bed, watching her sleep.

"Hello," said Surie, opening her eyes. "Don't worry. I won't bite."

"You do sometimes."

"Yes," she said. "I do. It's a wonder you can put up with me."

The corners of his lips almost turned up. His eyes searched for hers, but she was pretending, again, to sleep. She could just see his face through her eyelashes.

"I don't want to have to cook food for this family for the rest of my life. For one thing, they'll all complain that I don't cook as well as you," Yidel said.

"That's the best you've got? Food is what should keep us together?" She was more than a little insulted. Sitting in his bed, he didn't remember their quiet conversations, their intimacies?

"I was joking. Surie, you know I was joking." Never had she heard his voice so subdued, so plaintive.

"Right."

"I'm not used to talking about . . ." He stood up, walked around the room, opened and shut the wardrobe door. Flashes of light raced across her bedspread. "Anything."

"Oh well, no need to change now." She could have kicked herself. She opened her eyes. "How do you feel? About your mother. Everything?"

"You know me."

She pulled the blankets up to her neck. "You should take a nap. I'm going to."

He took his pillow and his blanket and she heard his footsteps descending the stairs to Dead Opa's apartment. Her heart, also, seemed to be falling through the floors of the apartment building, falling and falling, like the rain that trickled in through the skylight. She didn't sleep. She looked around the room, at their wedding portrait on the wall above Yidel's bed, at the card Tzila Ruchel had made for him, tucked under the glass on the bedside cabinet, at his soft black leather slippers, one heel worn down more than the other. She looked and looked and thought of Yidel, the calligrapher, the father, the husband, the man. All those months of wondering what had happened to her. He must have been in hell.

"I can't believe he hasn't thrown you out." Tzila Ruchel was perched on her father's bed. Her scarf had been tied so tightly that her eyes had turned into slits. "I would have. I think I would have."

"Don't be a fool," Surie said. Her daughter could be so aggravating. "It's not like I kept a secret from him for forty years. It was just a few months. And it's not a sin according to the Torah."

"It was a pregnancy. Two pregnancies. That's hardly nothing."

Her holier-than-thou daughter was right, of course, and that made it all the more annoying. She wanted to complain about Tzila Ruchel to someone, but Dead Onyu was gone. And besides, Dead Onyu would have told her the same thing. When Mattis Lep Tup came in to say kiddush for her that night, the second night of the holiday, she asked him about his teachers.

"We don't really have teachers in zal, Mamme. We're supposed to be independent learners." At seventeen. Eighteen. She'd missed his birthday, running to the hospital.

"Did I know that?"

"Yup. We've all told you."

There it was again. While she'd been congratulating herself on being a good mother, the everyday stuff of her children's lives had been passing her by. Her chest felt tight and hot, though supposedly there was no breast tissue left to fill with milk. Her sons went to school in a dark old building she'd never been allowed to enter. Their entire lives, really, were a mystery to her. She was sure that Mattis had not come to her room voluntarily. "Would you tell me a funny story that happened in school? Something that made you laugh?"

He looked to the right and then to the left, as if there might be another Mattis sitting nearby. He was so much like his father. "I don't know. Maybe? Why do you want to hear one?"

She didn't remember being hard on him, but she must have been, that he feared punishment at his age. "I won't get you into trouble." She hadn't punished her children. It had been Yidel's job, though he hated it.

Mattis glanced at her and then looked away. He sat on his hands.

"Last week," he said. "Something happened last week . . ." She wasn't sure she'd ever heard him speak about anything with her, anything that didn't have a definite outcome. His voice changed as he told the story, dropped into a note that if she had to describe it, she would have called friendly. Is this what it had been like for Yidel and Lipa, walking by the side of the river?

"Are you going to be all right, Mamme?" Mattis stood next to her bed.

She looked up at him. When she was feeling better, she'd call the matchmaker. There was nothing wrong with him. He was lovely. "I lost a baby," she said. "Two babies actually, but I'm fine. I'll be fine. Don't worry."

"Tatie is very upset." Poor Lep Tup. His face was bright red. Unmarried, uneducated about birth, he'd been told she had a very bad stomachache. Nothing more.

"Your father gets upset easily. You know how he is." *Weak.* "Mooshy. Tzila Ruchel thinks he should throw me out of the house for keeping the pregnancy secret. She said she would, if she were him. Who on earth does she take after? Where does she get that goyishe attitude? Not your father for sure."

"The next time she needs you to babysit, she'll forget everything she said." He already had his hand on the mezuzah. He was backing away. A fine sheen of sweat covered his skin.

"True," Surie said. "I should tell her no if she asks, after those dreadful comments. But I won't. My grandchildren don't need to suffer."

———

The days were just beginning to lengthen toward the great long stretches of summer. The meal, in the dining room that she had decorated as a young bride in the sixties and never updated, went on and on. Chairs scraped back from the tables. People moved to and fro. Songs were sung. It was late before Yidel returned to the bedroom carrying a plate of cold food.

"Eat up," he said.

"I was waiting for my meal for a long time." He could have put his head around the door and seen her wide-awake, but he hadn't. She'd spent countless hours training him to be a good husband, and still he had no qualms about leaving a postpartum woman without food. The worst nurse in the hospital knew better than that.

"We thought you were sleeping."

She didn't like it when people made excuses. Do it right the first time. That was her motto. Then you won't need to make an excuse.

"Awake-dreaming only," she said.

"I wish I'd had the chance to dream about our twins."

She snorted. "I wish I'd had the chance to talk about Lipa. But everyone shut me down."

"Surie, you *told* me not to talk with you about Lipa. You said it was too upsetting . . ."

She remembered now. Shouting at him in the kitchen. Throwing something. Maybe it had just been a dish towel. Well, it *had* been too difficult. She'd been glad, at the time, not to hear Lipa's name, not to see his photographs in the albums. His small and shining face.

"I wanted you to notice. By yourself."

"All you had to do was ask." He stood close to her and bent down to speak quietly. His big brown eyes searched out hers. "Surie. It must have been hard, keeping that secret."

A thin wail rose from her, though she tried not to let it out.

"Yes," he said. "Yes. I know."

They sat like that, her crying almost soundlessly, him nodding, until the lights in the main rooms went out. Sitting in the park with a double stroller, two children kicking their legs in the sunlight. Their hands on her skirt, her back, her face, so many times in a day. The pleasure. The wish for some solitude. Their tiny fingers. Their pale blue skin. The regret. And then it was as dark as it had been the night before, an inky blackness, and she was so afraid.

"Can I get up?" she asked. "I don't want to be in here." The corners of the room bulged outward. Her nightgown seemed huge and coarse, a soggy sausage casing made of flannel. She'd made it herself with room to expand if need be but perhaps had gone overboard.

"Come on," he said, and he led the way out of the room, along the hallway with its stripe of mildew, and to the front window. She was an ocean liner to his tugboat. "I'll get you a chair," he said. "You don't have to stand."

"How do you know where I want to sit?" she asked. He sat on the lowest step of the folding step stool, which squeaked under his weight.

"It's your favorite place. How many times have I come home from shil, and you are standing here, watching the river." He looked up at her. She leaned forward and pointed out a nylon hammock floating in the water, to the bright green light on a warehouse on the other side of the channel.

"Is that where you go in your mind?" he asked. "When you don't want to be here in Williamsburg? With us?"

Stop it, she wanted to say. You think you know me, but you don't know alef.

Still, in the whole world, there was only one person who could have led her to that window.

Another man would be yelling, throwing things, stamping around the room, demanding answers. Is that what she wanted? He was almost . . . the word she was looking for was *impotent*. And yet was that the worst thing? He sat next to her, folding a sheet of newspaper into a boat, remembering it was a holiday when folding was not allowed, forgetting again. The boat had three sails. It had tiny flags fluttering in an invisible breeze. Any other woman would have been thrilled to get off so easily. Why did she hanker for a sign of brokenness in Yidel?

She and Yidel had always kept secrets, but all of them had been shared with each other. Their first kiss in the yichud room after they were married. How he'd closed his eyes and lightly pressed his face against her ear. The next time, he'd kept his eyes open. His lips had touched hers and it had been thrilling. Yes! That was something she'd never talked about with anyone and never would. All those times at night, well, that was something everyone kept secret. It was private, what happened inside the four walls of their bedroom. And if she was truthful with herself, she only wanted Yidel—not some other nebulous person with a whole new set of faults. All she wanted was for him to take her fingers between his and make that gesture he was so fond of, lifting her hand in the air as if she were a queen.

But what a fool he was! He couldn't even yell at his wife when she deserved it. He'd barely cried for the twins. He was afraid he'd be eating cat food instead of Surie's good gefilte fish. For goodness' sakes, in sixty years, he'd never even left home! Those people in the hospital, they'd laughed when she'd said that. "Mama's boy," they'd said, winking. "All kinds of special. I bet he's the sort of man who wants to nurse. Like a little baby."

Surie had been so afraid of bringing home damaged babies, children with some problem that would tie up her every waking moment for the last forty years of her life and who would mark the entire family with an indelible stain. Paradoxically, she was still furious with Yidel because he *hadn't* been worried about those things. Even though she hadn't told him she was pregnant. Anger was such a slick character. It couldn't be defeated with logic.

They would never divorce, but there would always be this thing between them now. Did every couple, married for a long time, have such awkward, lumpy tangles in their history? Did they think about it at night, or did they try to forget? Dead Onyu and Dead Opa had not seemed to have anything like it. Surie would have known. But perhaps not. Perhaps there was no way to know what really happened in the lives of other people.

But if she died? For a moment, she pictured Yidel sitting in the matchmaker's living room, meeting older women who were thinner than her, who wore fancy earrings and modern suits. Those women wore high heels and nice diamond necklaces and their hands were moisturized and they smelled faintly of roses. The matchmaker would describe Yidel as a catch. A holy Jew. A good father and grandfather. And he was all of those things. But if Yidel, God forbid, was the one to die first? What would the matchmaker say about her, Surie? At best, a distracted mother, forgetful, fat. Slovenly in her personal habits. At worst, a liar. A sneak. Seduced by the secular world. Behind her hand, the matchmaker might mouth the word *murderer*. Surie thought about the concrete pad in the chicken yard where the shochet slit the throats of her hens. It was right underneath her bedroom window, three floors down. That concrete could at least be a quick end if the complication between them proved unbearable.

EIGHTEEN

"We should go to a therapist," Yidel said sometime in the night when they both weren't sleeping. "That man who sees people in his apartment?"

She almost hated him then. Hadn't he heard her when she told him the story of the little pregnant child in the clinic? The Ecksteins had already sent one son to that man, the so-called therapist, and look where it had landed her boy. In the morgue. She didn't want to send her marriage to cold storage.

And she didn't need a therapist to tell her about her own life. She'd been lonely since California, since Lipa. It was as if, somehow, the reliable transistor radio that was her marriage had slipped off a frequency that played soothing classical music, and all she could hear was static. Same machine, different results. She hadn't even tried to put it back on the correct station. Instead, she'd twisted the dial and played the kind of music that she knew was forbidden. Anything to block out the awful silence.

"Go to sleep, Yidel," she said.

"I don't want to lose you over this."

"Nobody's losing anybody. Can't you just let it go already?"

"Besides the twins. We lost them."

"Besides the twins." And Lipa.

———

In the late afternoon of the second day of Shavios, after she thought everyone had left the house, she went downstairs, one step at a time, and out into the street. She was wearing an old housecoat and a turban, her house slippers. The stockings she'd found under the bed soiled with bloody fingerprints and crushed banana. The people she passed stared at her but did not say anything. So as not to have to see them, she crossed onto the houseless side of the street and continued walking. Hypocrites. It was difficult even to lift her feet, and she trembled, drained.

She walked slowly down Division to the river. It was the same as it always was. The line of gravel at the intersection of the road and the path. The sound of water. The smell of it. The call of the birds. The boats going to and fro, the tall, twisting mirrors that were the buildings of Manhattan, the purple-and-yellow clouds massing in the northwest like bruises. The slop and gurgle of the waves under the pier. Somewhere behind her, small boys playing tag. She leaned against the broken railing and watched the water unfurl like a flag, like a silken scarf. It moved so fast. It was never the same and always the same.

Yidel hurried out of the house, hopping and tying one boat-sized shoe. His weekday shoe, not his holiday ones, which slipped on. He looked both ways, up and down the street. He walked quickly toward her, breathing heavily.

"Where are you going?" he asked.

She looked at him. He looked a lot like a bulging, leaking chocolate cake in a plastic bag from a second-rate bakery, a babka. But his mother had just died. And the twins had too. "I'm already here," she said. "At the river."

The water was almost black at that time of day. It twisted around the pylons. The cranes in the Navy Yard cast long shadows across the water and over her face. She shook the loose railing back and forth. Red flakes fell into the water, floated for a few seconds, and then sank.

"My mother came to America on a ship that arrived right over there," he said, pointing. "And my father."

Hers had too.

"It's time for shil," she said. "Hadn't you better go?" If this were the last time she spoke to him, what would she say? And why did the slanting afternoon sun in his eyes make her think she could see right inside them?

He said something in response, but she wasn't paying attention.

"I wanted to be a good mother," she said. "I had a notebook from the time I was six, where I jotted down ideas, things I thought would make me . . . beloved."

"You are." His beautiful brown eyes looked tired.

"Lipa didn't come to me to tell me his troubles. He came to you. All of the children do."

"And that doesn't sit right with you? They only come to me because they love you too much to make you sad."

In the water, below her feet, was a long black plank. It was filled with deep gouges and shiny with oil. It was chained to a line of floating balls. A bell rang in the yard, and right afterward she heard the automatic end-of-class bell at her granddaughters' cheder, even though it was a holiday and all the children were at home. The boys behind her shouted gleefully. The littlest one had been tagged. From a window, a turbaned mother leaned out and called for the children, and they called back. Surie put her fingers in her ears. She did not want to hear their voices. She kicked a few pieces of gravel down onto the plank and it tipped and the gravel slid into the water. The colors of the oil slick swirled and changed and blended and came apart again.

"I wanted to get it right this time and look how I messed it up."

"What did you think would happen? Your not telling me about the twins makes it feel like you blame me for what happened to Lipa. Were you hoping to just go off somewhere by yourself?"

"No," she said. "Of course not. I don't think so. I don't know." What would she have said if he came to her one day, wanting to redo their life together from the beginning, finding fault with something they had both loved? Would she have stood calmly, as he was standing, one foot resting on the lowest rail, gazing out at the river?

She moved away, six or seven feet farther away from their home, and she didn't wait to see if he followed.

"So, are you saying this was my fault? Because I was the one who talked with Lipa?" he said, catching up to her again. "*Both* of us talk with our sons. They come to you for a kind of motherly love I can't give. They come to me for advice that you don't have. That's why there are two of us. So that between us, our children are able to get what they need."

She wanted to lie down, but she'd never been a far-shloffener, the kind of woman who slept in the daytime. She took several more steps without saying anything. Now she was up against the wooden fence of the lumber merchant. Spray-painted on the boards in twenty-inch blue letters, the word *peace*. The first few drops of rain spattered the front of her housecoat. Yidel's hand was next to hers on the railing. He was talking loudly. The way her heart carried on. It was difficult to breathe.

Two children ran down the cul-de-sac, stopped, and pointed at her.

"Goyta," cried the oldest like a seagull. Non-Jew, he called her. Is that what it had come to?

"Farvos hot zi nakete fis?" the younger asked the older.

"Get away from her," shouted Yidel, and he ran at them, his long black coat flapping, like a crow, like some dark angel. "Her feet aren't naked! She's a great-grandmother! And tired!" he said, and he stamped and shook his fist, and they scattered, screeching and laughing. She glanced down and saw that one of her stockings had come loose and crumpled around her ankle. A narrow sliver of bare skin showed below her hem. Her face flushed. She felt scorched. Quickly, she bent, pulled up the stocking, and fiddled with the clip through her clothing.

A group of women walking and talking together came to the end of the street and, seeing her, became quiet and walked back the way they had come.

"Really," he said. "Why do you think Lipa spoke with me instead of you? Do you honestly think he loved me more?" he asked.

Along the bottom of the massive pylons was a line of

bolts. Long strands of green weed hung from them and moved this way and that in the water.

"No," she said. "Maybe?" A chain swayed, clanking, in the rising wind.

"Surie."

"What kind of mother am I, that my own son was afraid to talk with me? I wish I could erase it all, every time I ever said something mean to him, every time I criticized his hairstyle or his clothes or his stupid"—she wiped her eyes—"glasses."

"You made all of his clothes. Every bite of food that went into his mouth. You taught him to read long before he went to school. And his soft heart? That came from you, Surie. Not from me."

"Remember how he liked to run his hand through the fur on your skins? You kept the softest ones out of the lime for months."

"He loved those challos with the shiny little noses you made specially for him."

"He used to stand behind you, watching, while you wrote. I don't think you ever knew, he was so quiet."

"The last thing he said to me? That he couldn't bear to cause you more pain. Those aren't the words of someone who is afraid of their mother."

Her Shabbos ponzhelo, light before, was completely dark from the rain. What was she doing standing outside in the twilight, her stockings filthy, her housecoat clinging to her body? The rain fell heavily. It filled the gutters and rushed down the hill. On either side of where she stood, the gutters ended but the water continued, arcing outward before falling into the river. She turned and looked at her husband.

"To become an adult, a child must hate the ones he loves the most," he said. "Lipa hated me too. He hated all of us sometimes. They all do. But they love us as well."

"Tzila Ruchel couldn't look at me today."

"You can hardly blame her."

"Nice."

The rain pooled inside Surie's collar. She shivered. A group of girls stood nearby, shivering under the trees, but then walked away fast, holding their hands over their heads, silent and intent on reaching shelter. She was looking down, wondering at the way raindrops created notes in the oil slick, a sorrowful soundless music, when she heard him speak.

"Come home," he said, holding out his hand.

She wiped the rain from her face, turned back. He had a beautiful hand, with long, clean fingers. No ink on them today. Yidel looked around to see if anyone in the street had noticed. There was no one left. He crooked his index finger, beckoning to her despite how irregular it was, despite the risk of community disapproval. To take his hand now, while she was bleeding, would be against every law they lived by. It was outrageous even if she wasn't bleeding, to hold hands in public. Licentious. She took a single step away from him, but oh! How his face fell! How the lines cut deeply at the corners of his mouth. Yidel, who had never done her any harm. Hesitantly, she took a step toward him.

"Thank you," he said. He sighed. "They are calling you Dead Onyu. The grandchildren. There has to be a cantankerous woman in the house, speaking her mind and avoiding convention. My mother groomed you for the position. Please come back."

They stood in the rain, in silence, staring down at the river. The water was olive green and foamy, brown and black and purple, full of leaves and sticks, syringes, Metro-Cards, and mushy ticket stubs.

"An old man like you can't manage the house by yourself."

He smiled. "I can try. I've got to find something to do in my retirement." She had made a fancy cake in the shape of a Torah and hidden it in the freezer for his birthday, which was only a few weeks away.

His hand still lingered in the air between them. "Come on," he said. "Tomorrow they'll be talking about it in the mikva: old Eckstein was holding his wife's hand in the street, for shame, when he thought no one was looking. At least I'll have something to confess on Yom Kippur."

"That won't be the worst thing, I'm betting," she said, tilting her head to the side, the better to look into his lovely brown eyes. Still, she didn't touch him.

"I gave Lipa the money to leave town," Yidel said. "He didn't steal it from your purse. I did. I thought I wanted to get him out of Williamsburg. I was ashamed of him. What kind of father is that? Ashamed of his own son." He shook his head. His payos, wet, sprinkled droplets of water that fell on her hands where they were held, clenched, in front of her empty belly. "But at the bus station, right as he was getting on the Greyhound, I ran after him. I put my arms around him and I never wanted to let go."

"I still have his glasses," she said, and pulled them out of her pocket.

"The things parents do . . ."

"Yes," she said, and she took his hand.

They turned and began to walk up their street. The rain fell and fell, washing the rubbish from between the cobblestones and behind the crevices, all of Williamsburg's abandoned things, rushing downhill and falling in a crescendo of sound into the river, where it was swept out into the vastness of the Atlantic Ocean.

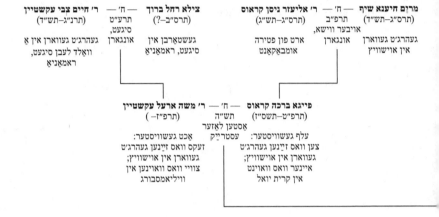

ר' חיים צבי עקשטיין
(תרנ"ג–תש"ד)

געהרג'ט געווארן אין א
וואלד לעבן סיגעט,
ראמאניא

ח' —
תרע"ט
סיגעט,
אונגארן

צילא רחל ברוך
(תרס"ב–?)

געשטארבן אין
סיגעט, ראמאניא

מרים חיענא שיף — ח' — ר' אליעזר ניסן קראוס
(תרס"ג–תש"ד)   תרפ"ב   (תרס"ג–תש"ג)
              אויבער ווישא,
געהרג'ט געווארן   אונגארן   ארט פון פטירה
אין אוישוויץ   אומבאקאקאנט

פייגא ברכה קראוס — ח' — ר' משה אראל עקשטיין
(תרפ"ט–תשס"ז)   תש"ה   (תרפ"ז–)
              אסטען לאזער

אכט געשוויסטער: עסטרייק   עלף געשוויסטער:
זעקס וואס זיינען געהרג'ט   צען וואס זיינען געהרג'ט
געווארן אין אוישוויץ;   געווארן אין אוישוויץ;
צוויי וואס וואוינען אין   איינער וואס וואוינט
ווילעאמסבורג   אין קרית יואל

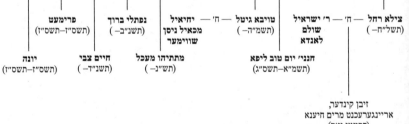

צילא רחל — ח' — ר' ישראל   טויבא גיטל — ח' — יחיאל   נפתלי ברוך   פרימעט
(תשל"ח–)   שולם   (תשמ"ה–)   מכאיל ניסן   (תשנ"ב–)   (תשס"ז–תשס"ז)
              לאנדא   שווימער

חנני' יום טוב ליפא   מתתיהו מעכל   חיים צבי   יונה
(תשמ"א–תשס"ג)   (תש"נ–)   (תשנ"ד–)   (תשס"ז–תשס"ז)

זיבן קינדער,
אריינגערעכנט מרים חיענא
(דרייצן יאר)

משפחס עקשטיין פון וויליאמסבורג, תר"נ–תשס"ז

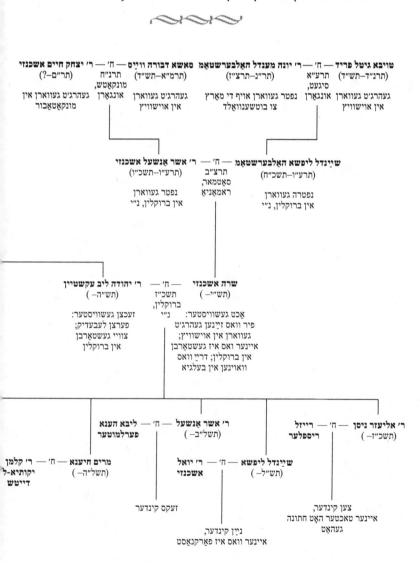

ר' יצחק חיים אשכנזי — ח' — **יונה וויים** — ח' — **סאשא דבורה וויים** — **יונה מענדל האלבערשטאם** — ח' — **ר' יונה מענדל האלבערשטאם** — ח' — **טויבא גיטל פריד**
(תר"ם–?) תרנ"ח (תש"א–תרמ"ב) (תר"נ–תרצ"ז) תרע"א (תרנ"ד–תש"ד)
מונקאטש, סיגעט,
גהרג'ט גווארן אין אונגארן גהרג'ט גווארן גהרג'ט גווארן נפטר גווארן אויף די מארץ אונגארן גהרג'ט גווארן אויף די מארץ
מונקאטבור אין אוישוויץ צו בוטשענוואלד אין אוישוויץ

ר' אשר אנשעל אשכנזי — ח' — **שיינדל ליפשא האלבערשטאם**
(תרע"ו–תשכ"ו) תרצ"ב (תרע"ח–תשכ"ח)
סאטמאר,
ראמאנ'א נפטרה גווארן
נפטר גווארן אין ברוקלין, נ"י
אין ברוקלין, נ"י

ר' יהודה ליב עקשטיין — ח' — **שרה אשכנזי**
(תש"ה–) תשכ"ז (תש"י–)
ברוקלין,
נ"י
זעקצן געשוויסטער: אכט געשוויסטער:
פערצן לעבעדיק; פיר וואס זיינען גהרג'ט
צוויי געשטארבן גווארן אין אוישוויץ;
אין ברוקלין איינער וואס איז געשטארבן
אין ברוקלין; דרייַ וואס
וואוינען אין בעלגיא

ליבא העענא פערלמוטער — ח' — **ר' אשר אנשעל** — **ר' אליעזר ניסן** — ח' — **רייזל ריספלער**
(תשל"ב–) (תשכ"ז–)

ר' קלמן יקותיא-ל דייטש — ח' — **מרים חיענא** — **ר' יואל אשכנזי** — ח' — **שיינדל ליפשא**
(תשל"ה–) (תשל"ד–)

צען קינדער,
זעקס קינדער איינער טאכטער האט חתונה
געהאט
ניין קינדער,
איינער וואס איז פארקנאסט

IN GRATEFUL ACKNOWLEDGMENT

Eagle-eyed, persistent, and generous agent and editors: Rebecca Caine, Emily Forland, Jenna Johnson (extra extra love), Georgia Richter, Fred Shafer, Sona Vogel, Lydia Zoells.

Beloved early readers: Leah, Shterna, Yuda, and Ariellah Goldbloom, Tova Benjamin, Lisa Burnstein, Bruce Aaron, Pam Marcucci, Shterna Friedman.

Kindhearted and supportive writing buddies: Ray Daniels, Riva Lehrer, Nami Munn, Audrey Niffenegger, Matthue Roth, Rolf Yngve.

Hilarious and fun fact-checkers: Chavie Laufer, Sheindy Weichman, Moishe Schwartz.

A NOTE ABOUT THE AUTHOR

Goldie Goldbloom's first novel, *The Paperbark Shoe*, won the AWP Prize and is an NEA Big Reads selection. She was awarded a National Endowment for the Arts Literature Fellowship, and has been the recipient of multiple grants and awards, including fellowships from Warren Wilson College, Northwestern University, the Brown Foundation, the City of Chicago, and the Elizabeth George Foundation. She is Chassidic and the mother of eight children.